HURT
MOUNTAIN

HURT MOUNTAIN

A NOVEL

ANGELA CROOK

LAKE UNION
PUBLISHING

Text copyright © 2024 by Angela Crook
All rights reserved.

No part of this book may be reproduced, or stored in a retrieval system, or transmitted in any form or by any means, electronic, mechanical, photocopying, recording, or otherwise, without express written permission of the publisher.

Published by Lake Union Publishing, Seattle

www.apub.com

Amazon, the Amazon logo, and Lake Union Publishing are trademarks of Amazon.com, Inc., or its affiliates.

ISBN-13: 9781662515804 (paperback)
ISBN-13: 9781662515798 (digital)

Cover design by Caroline Teagle Johnson
Cover image: © victor s. brigola / plainpicture; © Tashka / Getty

Printed in the United States of America

This book is dedicated to Mary Rynes, my Llama sister forever, and everyone else who took the time to read and correct my work and cheered me on during this fantastic journey.

Chapter 1

Brandon Hall was on what should have been a routine patrol around the property that surrounded the Raycom Corporation—along Highway 24, a lonely two-lane highway mostly used to bypass busy I-25 on the way into and out of Colorado. As far as Brandon was concerned, 2013 had been exciting enough. He had been looking forward to it ending on a whisper of pure boredom. But it seemed Mother Nature had her own plans. Thanks to a bizarre thunderstorm that had blown into the Springs around midnight, knocking down trees, raining golf ball–size hail, and even setting a hundred-year-old church on fire, several of his men had been called off, forcing him out of the comfort of his office and into the once-familiar security vehicle. Not that he minded.

After serving twenty years as a military policeman, most of his time spent right here in Colorado Springs on Peterson Air Force Base, he was admittedly having a bit of a struggle adjusting to the demands of his new duties. Ever since his promotion to head of security months before, he'd found himself more and more confined to the large cushy office, buried in paperwork, refereeing squabbles among his personnel, and sitting through endless meetings with company bigwigs and local law enforcement.

Some may have viewed the office and visibility as perks of the position, but more and more, he was wondering if he was a good fit. His fiancée, Lisa, joked that he was worried about the job making him soft, and maybe she was right, but as he stared into the strange dim morning, his nerves were as taut as they had been on his first solo patrol as a young airman.

A car was stopped on the side of the road. The headlights were on, and he could see at least one occupant, but he didn't detect any movement from inside. *Likely drunk or freaked out by the storm.* He pulled up behind the car and flipped on his emergency lights.

Yellow light reflected off the rear window as he reached for his radio to call the information in to dispatch. Instead of the efficient voice of Margie, the overnight dispatcher, he heard only static. With a sigh, he jammed the brim of his hat over his brow and pushed open his door, pulling on his rain slicker as he stepped into an early-morning downpour that drove into his body like fists.

The car appeared to be an older-model Honda Accord, but he couldn't be certain since the decal was missing. The right side of the vehicle was hanging off the side of the road. The right-rear tire was almost completely flat, and the left was bald. The license plates were missing, and it had more rust than its original red paint. Long scratch marks led away from a large dent in the trunk, making it appear that the car had barely escaped the talons of some great hungry beast.

As he approached the vehicle, he could hear loud rock music coming from inside. His hand found his gun on his hip, and he thought about Lisa and the tears in her eyes as she'd stood in the doorway that morning, convinced that the rare thunderstorm was a bad omen. He prayed she wouldn't be right.

At first he thought the window was open, but as he got closer, he saw the jagged remains of broken glass. A girl sat clinging to the steering wheel, her eyes almost swollen shut. Drool ran in a trickle from the side of her mouth, which continued to move, though he couldn't hear any words over the blaring music. Dried blood was caked under her nose and crusted her upper lip. Her hair was a mass of tangled knots. Her lips were cracked, and blood had seeped through slits where the skin had opened up.

Shock sent a surge of electricity through his body, dimming the sound of the music and making him forget the fierceness of the rain as she turned her head to face him.

"Miss, can you turn down the radio?" he said, raising his voice to be heard over the music. The girl continued to stare at him but didn't respond. He reached for his flashlight, never taking his eyes from the girl or his hand from the butt of his weapon.

"Miss, can you hear me?" he yelled into the howling wind.

The girl turned away from him, staring straight ahead at the empty road, her lips moving soundlessly. Brandon felt the hair rise on his arms as he stared at the blank face. A violent burst of lightning ripped open the dark morning sky, illuminating the interior and briefly revealing a large lump in the back.

A black man lay sprawled across the seat. His misshapen head was turned toward Brandon, but the only thing remaining of the man's face was a mess of blood and bits of white shards that he knew must have been bone.

Brandon snatched his pistol from his holster and pointed it at the girl.

"Take the keys out of the ignition and throw them out of the car and slowly exit the vehicle," he demanded. Still, she didn't move, except for her lips, which continued to move soundlessly to the music. The song—"Angel," an Aerosmith classic from his teen years—under other circumstances would have brought happy memories of his glory days. But now, more than anything else, he just wanted it to stop. He slid the gun back into his holster. Still clutching the flashlight in one hand, he slowly opened the car door, uncomfortably aware, for the first time, that he was alone.

"Miss, please turn down the radio!" Brandon shouted. When the girl still didn't move, he reached inside the car and took hold of her arm with his free hand, praying that she would offer no resistance. Once he got her out of the car, he was able to get a good look at her for the first time.

Carly. The name popped into his head without warning, and for an instant, he felt the familiar rush of guilt and pain, turning his stomach liquid. Clenching his teeth together so hard he felt a throb of pain in his jaw, he forced the memory away before it could form completely, and he turned his attention back to the girl.

She was small: he guessed around five feet, weighing at most ninety pounds. She was African American but not as dark as the man in the back seat. In fact, her skin wasn't much darker than Brandon's own.

She was wearing a nightgown, a white cotton slip-like thing that a little girl would wear, except it looked like something from another time. The front was soaked with blood, but it was impossible to tell whether it was hers or someone else's—maybe the dead man's. Her back left no such doubts. He felt his whole body go cold.

The thin gown had been ripped open, and he could see blood still seeping from open wounds that covered her from her shoulders to her buttocks. *A horsewhip?* That was his first thought, but he couldn't wrap his mind around such inhumane treatment of a child. The girl stumbled into him, and he looked down and saw that her bare feet were covered with what looked like burn marks.

"Jesus. What happened to you?" he asked.

In answer, the girl sagged against him, smearing his already-soaked raincoat with blood. As gently as he could, he lifted her into his arms and carried her to his car, where he laid her down in the back seat. She almost instantly lost consciousness.

He closed the door, reached into his pocket, and pulled out his cell phone. The icon showing he had only one bar seemed to mock him, telling him what he already knew: he wouldn't reach any help that way. Still, he dialed the numbers, praying for the sound of some bored 911 operator's voice in his ear.

Instead, he watched helplessly as the circle turned in a pointless loop, leaving him as he was—alone. He hated the idea of her suffering a single second longer, but there was one more thing he needed to do before he could get her the help she so desperately needed. Stuffing the useless phone into his pocket, he took a deep breath and made his way back to the car to confirm that the man was beyond help, at least any this world could give.

Chapter 2

She was hot, so hot. Was she sick? She heard muffled voices, but they sounded as if they were coming from a great distance, like someone trying to talk to her from underwater. Was she dead? She wanted to open her eyes, but they were so heavy. She began to panic as she realized that she was not able to move her arms or head. She lay still and concentrated on the voices that seemed to surround her until they became clear and she was able to understand what they were saying. They were talking about her.

There were two people: a woman and a man. The sound of the male voice filled her with terror—she knew that men brought pain—and she tried to move again. The woman's voice was kind but seemed sad.

"The medication's wearing off. She's going to need another dose," the woman said.

"Yes, Doctor, right away," he said.

"It's such a shame. Who would do something like this to a child?" the doctor said.

The scent of vanilla, like what they used on baking day, engulfed the girl as the doctor bent over her. She felt cool, gentle hands touch her face.

"Honey, can you hear me?" the doctor asked.

The girl wanted to let her know that she could, but her voice wouldn't work.

"We're going to take care of you," she said.

The girl thought she felt the doctor's fingers against her cheek for just a second, but she couldn't be sure. Darkness was rolling in like the fog on the mountains in the morning, and she welcomed it. The voices drifted farther and farther away, until there was nothing, and she was nothing.

Chapter 3

Dr. Olivia Blake stared down at the figure lying in the hospital bed. After performing an examination, the doctor knew she was a teenager or nearly so. She was so small. Who could have done such damage to this girl, and why? The media was already clamoring for a photo, something to splash across the evening news, to help find her family, they said. It would be impossible to tell what the girl looked like until the swelling went down. But Olivia guessed she was a beautiful child.

"What's your name, angel?" she asked, reaching out to touch the girl's hot cheek, not expecting—and not receiving—a reply.

The image of a child with a headful of copper-colored curls and hazel eyes shining bright with mischief appeared so clearly and suddenly in front of Olivia's eyes that she stumbled back. In the time it took her to blink, the picture was gone, as if it had never been there. But it had. The proof was in the pain that ripped through Olivia, leaving her feeling as if someone had taken a scalpel and cut her wide open, without the benefit of anesthesia.

She was losing control. It was this little girl, she thought, wiping away the sweat that had appeared on her brow. Silly of her to think that she had healed, that she could ever heal from the loss of her own daughter. Her Carly. It didn't seem to matter how much time passed;

asleep or awake, her mind never stopped torturing her with the question of what had become of her child.

Best to pass the case on to someone else. She knew it was the right thing to do, but even as she thought it, she knew she wouldn't. With a final glance at the girl's too-still figure, she turned and left the room to face the lobby full of police, reporters, and everyone else clamoring to find out about the girl.

"Dr. Blake, a word."

Olivia didn't want, or need, to turn around to recognize the hospital chief of staff's executive assistant calling her name. Instead of slowing down, she bowed her head, as if engrossed in the chart she was carrying, and quickened her pace. She managed to put two more feet of distance between them before he galloped up beside her, gasping for breath.

"Dr. Blake, didn't you hear me?"

"Obviously not, David. What can I help you with? I'm on my way to speak with the police and the media."

"Don't you think Dr. Iso should be the one to decide who would make the best spokesperson for the hospital?"

"Let me guess—you feel that person would be *you*."

"Well, I know that this case must be very sensitive for you. I mean, I wouldn't want this tragic incident to stir up bad memories."

"Don't go too far, David," Olivia said, nearly knocking the man down as she pushed past him, every nerve in her body as alive as if she had been struck by lightning.

As vicious as she knew David Pierce could be, his willingness to use the pain of the loss of her child to diminish her and elevate himself had taken her off guard, leaving her feeling exposed and angry. How many others were thinking the same thing? Were they right? An image of a beautiful laughing child flitted across her mind, and she squeezed her eyes shut against sudden tears.

✳

Brandon leaned against the vending machine and watched as Olivia stalked into the waiting room. He'd been worried when he saw her name listed as the doctor on call when they'd brought the girl in. The storm on her face confirmed his biggest fears.

It had been four years since they'd shared their own nightmare. Two years since their marriage had taken its last whimpering breath. People had it all wrong when they said time healed all wounds. As far as he could tell, it hadn't done anything but resign him to the fact that life did go on, whether you wanted it to or not. He and Olivia had continued to live—or rather exist—making the best of their new reality, he with Lisa, and she with work.

Now, here was this girl, and that haunted look he knew so well was back in Olivia's eyes. Willing himself to stay calm, he slammed his mind shut on the past and watched as Olivia faced the hungry crowd.

Her eyes scanned the room quickly as she entered. The space, normally a private lounge for the families of seriously ill patients, had been transformed into a pressroom flooded with cameras, lights, and microphones and was much louder than the hospital normally allowed on an ICU ward. The twenty or so chairs that had been set up facing the podium were filled, and reporters stood against the walls. A row of empty chairs sat behind the podium. As Olivia stepped up to the microphone, the room grew silent.

"Good evening. I am Dr. Olivia Blake," she said.

Brandon looked over the heads of the reporters, gathered like so many crows on a wire, as she recited a short statement. All it had taken was one nosy reporter with a police scanner. As soon as the 911 call had gone out, they'd descended like a pack of wild dogs, refusing to leave, scavenging for any piece of information. How many of those same reporters had been in this room four years before, when he and Olivia had stood behind a makeshift podium clinging to each other, begging for the life of their child?

"Dr. Iso, the hospital chief of staff, will be the point of contact for all questions concerning the as-yet-unidentified female patient with critical injuries brought in this morning. He will be joining us shortly to take your questions," she said.

"Dr. Blake," a reporter who looked fresh out of high school shouted from the front row, "is she awake?"

Before she could answer, the room was filled with voices shouting questions from every direction.

"Do the police have any suspects?"

"What were her injuries?"

"Can you verify the number of victims found at the scene?"

Brandon moved from the rear of the room around the throng of reporters and toward Olivia. She hadn't seen him yet, and he had hoped that she wouldn't have to, but the look of quiet defeat in her eyes as she tried to control the mob of reporters was more than he could stand.

Olivia raised her head and looked in his direction just as the door swung open.

Dr. Iso, Commander Redwood, and David Pierce entered the room. Dr. Iso acknowledged the reporters with a nod and a brief wave, but as he approached Olivia, there was a scowl on his face. Commander Redwood stared emotionlessly into the crowd, planting himself in a chair beside the podium, waiting his turn to speak, while David nipped at Dr. Iso's heels like a puppy starved for attention.

Brandon couldn't hear any of the conversation, but the raised color in Olivia's cheeks as she turned and walked to her seat told him that she wasn't happy with whatever was being said.

"Someone's getting knocked down a peg or two," a woman said in a low voice.

"Do you know who that woman is?" a masculine voice asked.

"Isn't she the doctor in charge of the girl's case?"

Brandon had started to move toward the door, intending to leave behind the gossip that he knew would soon follow, when the room fell silent. David Pierce approached the podium. His bulbous eyes and thick neck made Brandon think of a toad. Olivia sat perched on the edge of her chair, staring down at her hands clasped in a tight knot, resting in her lap.

"Good evening," he said, pausing to look around the room. "Thank you for your patience. As most of you already know, I am David Pierce, executive assistant for the hospital's chief of staff, Dr. Iso. I will serve as your point of contact for all future media inquiries.

"Behind me, we have Dr. Iso; Commander Redwood of the Colorado Highway Patrol, who will be heading up the investigation; and Dr. Blake, who's been overseeing the care for the young girl who was found on Highway 24 this morning. From here on out, we'll refer to her as Jane Doe, until she can be identified.

"I'll read a short statement regarding the status of the investigation. Then we'll take a few questions," David said, taking a moment to gaze around the room as reporters snapped pictures, the smile twitching at the corner of his lips ruining his attempt at feigning concern.

"'Jane Doe is a twelve-to-fourteen-year-old African American female. She is five feet tall and weighs eighty pounds. She has light skin and curly, reddish-brown hair. She was found in a red older-model Honda on Highway 24 during a routine patrol by security personnel for Raycom Corp. Photos of the car have been distributed to each of you, and we ask that you share them with the public. The girl is currently being cared for in our pediatric intensive care unit. If anyone has any information pertaining to the identity of this child, or recognizes the vehicle, they should contact the Colorado Springs Police Department or the Colorado Highway Patrol.' Thank you."

Before David had finished speaking, reporters were on their feet, waving their hands in the air as the room exploded with questions.

"Settle down and take your seats, everyone. We'll get through as many questions as we can," he said, pointing to a small blonde woman.

"Gretchen Fields, *Colorado Springs Gazette*," she said. "Thank you, Mr. Pierce. My question is for Dr. Blake."

"Dr. Blake, if you would," David said, turning his back to the crowded room, but not before Brandon saw the flash of anger cross his face as Olivia stepped back up to the podium, looking as if she were headed to the gallows.

"Dr. Blake, have you spoken with Jane Doe?" the reporter asked.

"No, she has not regained consciousness at this time," Olivia said.

Thirty minutes of fruitless questions followed as Olivia, Dr. Iso, and Commander Redwood each found creative ways to say "I don't know," until David Pierce finally raised his hand, signaling the end of the news conference.

As Olivia turned her back on the room of frustrated reporters, one man stood up and made his way through the throng of people to the front.

"Dr. Blake, one more question, please," he said, silencing the room. "I'm sorry to revisit such a difficult time for you, but I'm sure we'd all like to know how you've found working on this case, having endured such tragedy in your own life?"

Brandon felt sick to his stomach as Olivia turned and came face-to-face with Sheldon Myers, reporter for the Colorado Springs Fox News affiliate, Channel 21. The devastation of losing a child was a hell Brandon wouldn't wish on anyone, but he and Olivia had survived it, beaten, bruised, gutted even, but still clinging to each other.

Four years ago, Sheldon Myers had been the new face in town, having fled New York after being involved in a scandal in which he had published false information about the mother of a missing child.

Whether it was carelessness or malice depended on who you asked. After the distraught mother, who was later cleared, killed herself, Sheldon had dropped everything and moved to Colorado Springs to lick his wounds and rebuild his career.

Unfortunately for Brandon and Olivia, their tragedy had collided with his ambition, leaving them wide open to every one of his manipulations. He had taken full advantage, first painting them as tragic victims, and then, when it suited him, turning on them, to cast them as the suspects in their own child's disappearance.

He had dragged them into the public eye—accusing, demonizing, and judging them, over and over again—until they could find no comfort in each other, or anyone else. It was more than they could bear. In the end, the constant barrage of suspicion from the public, and their own guilt at not having protected their child, had driven the final nails into the coffin of their marriage.

※

Olivia froze. Midstep, halfway to freedom, she froze. Silly of her not to have anticipated his presence. He was the lead reporter, had been ever since his "hard-hitting" reporting of Carly's disappearance. Of course he would be here. A part of her had known, but she'd simply refused to acknowledge it. She still dreamed of that voice sometimes. Every time, she would wake up drenched in sweat and tears. She hated him. He was worse than a vulture. At least a vulture waited until its prey died before it picked their bones clean, but not him. Sheldon Myers liked to be up close and personal when the life faded from a victim's eyes.

"Dr. Hall?"

That, too, was intentional, the use of that name he knew was no longer hers. She wished she had the strength to shrug it off, but she didn't. The blow landed right in the center of her gut, as intended.

She could hear the whispers gathering now as she stood rooted to the spot. She didn't want to, but she had no choice. She turned to face him. He smiled at her, and every memory that she had locked away for these past four years burst free, washing over her in a giant wave.

Carly, with the red-gold curls, hazel eyes, and a smile that rivaled the summer sun. Celebrating her first birthday, playing in the park, holding her hand on her first day of school, laughing with her friends. Her picture on the missing person flyers that had littered Colorado Springs for months. Taken. Missing. Stolen. Kidnapped.

She was going to faint. She could feel it happening, the pins-and-needles sensation crawling up from her toes, around her legs, snatching the air from her lungs, as it spread through her chest, until her head felt like it was filled with cotton, blotting out all the sound from the room.

Olivia grabbed the podium in front of her; faintly she heard yelps of surprise, seemingly coming from a distance. He reached her just as her knees buckled, wrapping his arm around her waist, holding her upright as she raised her eyes to his.

Brandon. She closed her eyes against what she feared must be a hallucination, but the solid wall of his chest, where her head rested, and his arm around her waist did not disappear as the room was bathed in harsh light from every camera.

"Be brave, Livvy," he whispered.

It had been almost like a mantra back then, and just as they had countless times before, those three words seemed to give her the strength to stand tall.

She felt his arm around her for just a moment before it slid away as she raised her head to look into the crowd.

"Please excuse me; it's been a long day. To answer your question, Mr. Myers, how I feel does not affect my care of this or any other patient and is inappropriate to address in this forum. Thank you," she said, turning away from the reporters.

As she stepped back from the podium, Brandon reached out toward her, his hand stuttering in the air for the barest of seconds, as if it didn't quite know where to land, before coming to rest on her elbow instead of around her waist, where it had once lived.

Chapter 4

Brandon followed Olivia down the sterile hallway, neither of them speaking as she led him to one of the crash rooms that doctors sometimes used for sleep on their breaks between long shifts. When Olivia was a resident, Brandon would often visit her in some of these same rooms, where they would cuddle together on the narrow beds for a stolen hour or two. Sometimes this would be their only time to spend together for days on end.

"This brings back memories," Brandon said.

"Yeah," she said, feeling like a teenager on a first date. She couldn't help it. He still looked like he could be an actor in one of those big-budget action movies, with his tall lean frame, thick reddish-blond hair, and blue eyes.

"How are you?" he asked.

"I'm good," she said. "How's Lisa?"

If she could shrivel up in a ball and roll away, she would have in that moment. She could have said anything else, like, "Thanks for saving me from making an ass of myself on national TV." But nope, not her. She had gone right for the petty jugular, and there was nothing to do about it now. To try to fix it would only make things worse for both of them, she knew, as she watched a burst of color spread across his cheeks, shaving twenty years off his face, making him look like a naughty little boy. She used to love to make him blush, back then. Now it just made her feel sad—and a bit lonely, too, if she was being honest.

"She's fine," he said, his eyes not quite meeting hers.

"What are you doing here?" Olivia asked, moving from where they both stood frozen by the door to sit on the bed.

"I was the one who found her. I was first on the scene," he said, sitting down beside her.

"Oh God," she said, twisting her body so she could see his face.

For a moment he didn't speak. He just stared down at his hands. Olivia fought the urge to reach out and stroke his hair.

"I thought of her," he said softly.

"Don't," Olivia said, rising from the bed.

Before she could escape, Brandon reached out and grabbed her arm, pulling her back down beside him.

"I heard her voice and I saw her face, and for a moment it was all happening all over again, and then I thought of you. I wanted . . ."

As she looked into his eyes, she saw the raw pain she remembered from that moment when they had finally understood that their daughter's disappearance wasn't a simple misunderstanding. She hadn't just wandered out of the front yard or gone to visit a friend's house without permission. She was gone. Taken by God only knew what monster, for God only knew what purpose.

"Brandon, please don't. I can't," Olivia said, yanking her arm away from his light grasp, leaving him sitting on the bed as she fled the room, refusing to allow her mind to take her back. "I can't," she whispered, moving through the hall at a near run. When she stopped, she wasn't surprised to find herself standing outside the unknown girl's room.

Taking a few deep breaths to steady her nerves and her trembling hands, Olivia pushed open the door, happy to see that, for the moment, the room was empty, except for the tiny still body lying on the bed.

Instead of reviewing the chart hanging from the bed or checking her vitals, Olivia sank into the vacant chair provided for loved ones to keep vigil. She stroked the girl's hand. It could be days before she regained consciousness, and even then, with the extent of her injuries and the trauma she had suffered, it was impossible to predict her recovery.

"What do you think? Do you think she'll remember anything when she wakes up?"

The voice startled Olivia, and she turned to find Sheldon Myers standing behind her, looking down at the girl.

"How did you get in here?" Olivia asked as she jumped to her feet and reached for the call button.

"Wait, Dr. Blake, I can help." He grabbed her hand to stop her from pushing the button.

"Don't you touch me," she said.

"I'm sorry, but please listen before you have me thrown out. Don't let your bitterness hurt this girl."

"How did you get in here?" she asked again, trying to keep her voice steady.

"A good reporter has his sources," he said, his voice oozing the fake charm that she had once fallen for.

"Well, when I find out who your so-called source is, it will cost them their job. I don't believe I'll have to look too far."

"That's neither here nor there to me or this poor child. I'm just here to help. As you know, the more attention brought to her situation, the more help she'll receive."

"*Help?* Is that what you call what you do, Mr. Myers? How do you intend to help this *poor child*, as you call her?"

"By telling her story. Somebody out there knows who she is. Don't you want her to find her family, Dr. Blake?" he asked, raising his eyebrows.

"You bastard," Olivia said softly. "What about when her story doesn't suit you any longer—what then?" She clenched her fists at her sides. "How long before you turn on her, call her a killer, smear her name, and accuse her of unspeakable acts in front of the whole world? How long, Mr. Myers?"

"Olivia."

The voice seemed to be coming from a great distance, and she could taste the salt from the tears that streaked down her cheeks and pooled at the corners of her lips. She never saw him walk across the room, but she felt Brandon's arms around her, guiding her away from the reporter to a chair, where she sat, trying to stop her body from trembling.

She felt shame burn through her as she noticed Dr. Erik Walters, the hospital's chief of neurology, standing in the doorway, scowling at Sheldon.

"Mr. Myers, you are trespassing; please leave. Brandon will show you out," Dr. Walters said.

The reporter threw up his hands in mock surrender, but the smirk never left his face. "I hope you feel better, Dr. Blake. Everyone's not out to get you," he said as Brandon grabbed him by the arm, nearly dragging him from the room.

"It's a good thing we got here when we did; otherwise we may have had another patient on our hands," Dr. Walters said. "I was quite sure you were going to slug the bastard—not that he didn't deserve it."

"I'm sorry, Erik. I don't know what happened. He was here, and the next thing I knew . . ."

"You don't have to explain anything to me. I just hope Brandon doesn't hurt him," Erik said, walking across the room, reaching out, and giving her arm a gentle squeeze. "He really isn't worth it. How did he get in here, anyway?"

"I don't know, but I have my suspicions," Olivia said, turning away and walking back to the bed, where the girl lay oblivious to the drama surrounding her as she continued to sleep.

"Maybe you should call it a night. You look exhausted."

"I'm fine. I'm going to stay a little while. I want to review her tests before I go."

"Any change?" he asked.

"No, not yet."

"A damn shame. You know the FBI is involved now, don't you?" Erik moved across the room to join her at the girl's bedside.

"That's good. Maybe they can find her family," Olivia said.

"DNA should be back soon. Hopefully that will provide some answers."

"Let's hope." Olivia watched as Erik picked up the girl's chart, studying his face for any sign that he might see something she had missed. But his features remained impassive as he flipped through the pages before returning the chart to the end of the bed.

"Don't stay too long. There's nothing more to be done today."

"I know, Erik. But why do you think she hasn't woken up?"

"I don't know. Maybe her brain is just protecting her for a while. I believe, as her body starts to heal, she'll wake up."

"What if she killed that guy in the car?"

"We're doctors, not judges or God. Our job is to do our best to heal her body. But I'll tell you, when I look at her, I just don't see a killer, do you?"

"No, I don't," she said.

"It looks like she tried to save him to me. I just don't see how this child could have killed a grown man. Did you see his injuries?"

"I heard about them," she said.

"Well, they were as bad as you heard, and then some," Dr. Walters said. "I suggest we don't jump to conclusions. Let's just take things one step at a time, okay? She's going to be fine. Look who's back." He patted Olivia on the shoulder as he turned to leave, then paused at the door to shake Brandon's hand.

"You didn't hurt him, did you?" Olivia asked with a weak laugh as Brandon stepped into the room.

"I plead the Fifth," Brandon responded, his own smile looking more like a grimace.

"Thank you, Brandon, for everything you did today."

"You don't have to thank me. I'll always be here for you," he said, his smile traveling from his lips to his eyes. "I spoke to the police.

There'll be a guard outside the door from now on. No more unwanted guests."

"That's great," she said, hoping that he believed the smile she'd plastered on her lips. In all the madness of the day, she'd let herself fall back into the comfort of their old relationship, where he was the protector and she allowed herself to feel safe. But he wasn't her protector. Not anymore.

Just then the phone attached to his hip rang. Olivia recognized the wedding march ringtone and knew it would be Lisa, his fiancée. Brandon raised his finger, signaling her to wait as he lowered his voice and stepped away from her to answer the call. *No cell phones in the hospital.* She wanted to scream it out loud, and maybe snatch his phone from his hand and throw it against the wall, but instead, she choked down the newly awakened green-eyed beast and turned her attention back to the girl.

"I don't need him anyway," she whispered, trying to ignore how close she was to tears as she grasped the girl's limp hand. Pain turned to shock as the small hand closed around hers for just an instant, squeezing her hand in the briefest of hugs, before the fingers slid open and fell back onto the bed.

Chapter 5

She lay perfectly still in the semidark, listening to the strange sounds all around her. Her eyes felt dry and swollen, and as hard as she tried, she couldn't force them open wider than the smallest slit, so everything looked as if she were peeking through a crack. She was alone, lying on the softest bed she could ever remember feeling.

Every few seconds she heard beeps coming from somewhere behind her head. She tried to turn toward the sound but found she was unable to move. Her head felt disconnected from the rest of her body. Her arms and legs lay beside her like dead things, and it was hot, too hot.

Where was she? And where was Jacob? As if she had called him, his face appeared behind her closed eyes. The image was so clear she felt she could reach out and pull him to her. The smile that she loved was on his face, but something was wrong. It was his eyes; they were so distant and cold, almost as if he were . . .

"He's dead," a voice whispered. "They're all dead. You killed them."

"No," she said, forcing the word from her stiff lips.

Closing her eyes, she gave in to the darkness, retreating to the safety of nothingness.

Chapter 6

Olivia sat on the couch alone in her dark living room, staring into the empty fireplace. The only light came from the moon shining in, surrounding her in her own spotlight. It was cold, and she hugged herself for warmth. Though the switch for the fireplace was mere feet away, she felt too drained to make even that small effort. Instead, she lay down on the sofa, wrapping herself in the too-little throw she normally used to cover her feet, and she closed her eyes, hoping for sleep.

The wind had died down from the freak storm of the morning, but it still had enough strength to push the branches of the old tree that leaned against the house up against the window. It sounded like something scratching to get in. As she hovered on the edge of sleep, she thought of the dead man and the girl.

And then, as it seemed to do so often ever since the girl, her mind tumbled back to Carly. When she'd first gone missing, Olivia had tortured herself nonstop, her mind providing her with an endless menu of horrors her child was enduring.

Had she been targeted by a child molester who had managed to go undetected in their quiet, boring suburban neighborhood? Had she wandered away and gotten hurt, dying alone and afraid? Could she have been snatched by a wild animal?

Eventually, Olivia had convinced herself that she had been taken by some poor childless woman who must have become fixated on her. She told herself that her child was alive and well, being raised by a loving family. It was the only story her mind could accept. If she allowed herself to believe any differently, the pain of it would have driven her insane.

"You're alive. You're safe. You are loved," she murmured, pulling the cover tight around herself as she repeated the once-constant mantra.

※

The shriek of the doorbell shocked Olivia awake. For a moment she lay frozen in place, her heart slamming against her ribs, a scream lodged in her throat as her eyes scanned the room, her brain trying to make sense of the sudden disturbance. The bell rang again, and Olivia took a deep breath, her legs still trembling as she stumbled up from the couch and across the room to the door. *Note to self: Get a new doorbell. One with a soft ding-dong instead of a death screech.*

When she reached the door, she looked through the window and saw her friend Arlene Spencer standing on the doorstep, her five-foot frame drowned in camouflage, her bright-blonde hair scraped back into a severe ponytail, heavy-looking military-style boots on her feet.

Olivia opened the door, grinning, as Arlene stepped inside. "Well, hello there, GI Jane."

"What? You don't like?" Arlene asked.

"On you, it's adorable." Olivia reached out to give Arlene a quick hug.

"Adorable my ass," Arlene said, turning around to gesture at several news vans that had gathered at the end of her driveway. "I see you have company."

"I should have expected this," Olivia said, hating the queasy feeling in her gut as she thought back to the last time her house had been under siege by the media.

"Do you want me to take care of it?" Arlene asked.

"No, it'll only antagonize them. Like throwing raw meat to a pack of wild dogs. Come in, before they storm the house," Olivia said, taking a step back to let Arlene in.

"What are you going to do?"

"Nothing. Maybe if we ignore them, they'll go away on their own."

"And maybe I'll sprout wings and fly."

"Will you fly me away from all of this?"

"Of course, my friend."

"Thank you so much for coming to check on me, Arlene."

"You know it. Now, what do you have to eat in here?" she asked, stepping past Olivia to head toward the kitchen.

"Whatever you find," Olivia said. She followed Arlene and then took a seat on a stool at the center island while her friend busied herself with foraging in the refrigerator.

"You working that Jane Doe case?" Arlene asked, holding cold cuts and cheese in one hand and a loaf of bread in the other as she walked toward the island, leaving the refrigerator door wide open.

"For now. If David Pierce has his way, I won't be much longer. Want me to get that?" Olivia asked, nodding toward the open refrigerator door as Arlene spread the food on the island.

"You got any mayo?"

"Sure. Is there anything else I can get you?" She slid off the stool and walked over to the fridge, grateful for the tornado that was Arlene bustling through the kitchen, seeming to create warmth where none had existed before.

"No, that'll do for now. Oh, wait, grab the pickles before you sit down."

"Okay," Olivia said.

"What's David up to?" Arlene asked, handing Olivia a ham and cheese sandwich before beginning to make one for herself, stopping every now and then to pop a piece of ham into her mouth or take a bite of the pickle she'd speared with a fork.

"He thinks I'm taking too much attention from him, so I'm sure it won't be too long before he's whispering into Dr. Iso's ear."

"Stay out of his way as much as you can. I've heard rumors. Do you have anything to drink?" Arlene said, jumping off her stool to go root around in the refrigerator before Olivia had a chance to answer.

"I will, trust me. Hey, grab me one too," Olivia said, smiling as Arlene turned around with two cans of grape soda before the words were fully out of her mouth.

"Catch," Arlene said, pretending to drop her arm back to toss Olivia the cold can.

"You wouldn't," Olivia said with a grin as Arlene sauntered back to her seat, popping the top on the can and taking a deep swig before climbing onto her stool again.

"You know this crap is terrible for you, right?" Arlene said.

"Yeah, so is everything," Olivia said, swallowing back a hiccup as cold bubbles slid down her throat.

"So, what happened to this kid? I heard she killed a man. Is that true?"

"No. I mean, I don't know. There's no way to know yet. Brandon said . . ."

As soon as she said his name, she could have bitten off her own tongue. As much as she loved Arlene, she wasn't ready to face a barrage of questions about her ex-husband.

"Brandon?"

"Yes, Brandon. He was the one who found them."

"Oh. Did you get a chance to talk to him? Does he still look like Chris Hemsworth?"

"A little. And yes, he does. He was concerned about how I was handling the situation."

"I'm sure you told him that everything was fine, and that, as the strongest person in the world, you didn't need any help. Right?"

"It is and I don't," Olivia said, staring down at her hands.

"I don't get you. The man reaches out to you, and you slam the door in his face."

"I didn't. I just told him the truth. I'm fine."

"Sure, and I'm in love with Brad Pitt."

"Don't lie, Arlene, you know you are," Olivia said.

"Were. Schoolgirl crush," she said. "But that Angelina Jolie, for a nickel I'd—"

"Shut up," Olivia said, enjoying the surprise of a laugh as she pushed away the empty plate. She got up and put her arms around Arlene, kissing the top of her head. "Thank you for that."

"For what?" Arlene asked.

"For being you."

"My pleasure," she said, twisting around on the stool to return the hug. "You know, you should call Brandon and tell him about the reporter situation. I know he'd be glad to help."

"No. I'm not his problem any longer."

"Girl, stop. You know damn well Brandon would not consider helping you a problem."

"Maybe not, but I can't go running to Brandon every time I have an issue. The man is about to be married, so can we please drop it?"

"Fine, superwoman. If you're really okay, I'm going to go. I'm on call at first light."

"I'm fine. See you at first light."

"All right. But, Olivia, seriously, let Brandon in. He loves you."

"No, he cares about me, but he loves Lisa now."

"Please, he's only with her so he doesn't have to think about you. Besides, I heard that—"

"Goodbye," Olivia said, pushing her gently out the door and onto the porch.

"Fine, good night. But before I go, why don't you come out here so I can plant a big fat juicy one on you? It'll give old Ms. Helen a heart attack," she said, raising her hand and waving at the window of the house across the street, both of them giggling like schoolgirls pulling a prank as the curtain snapped closed.

"Good night, Arlene," Olivia said, leaning forward to kiss her friend lightly on the cheek.

"Sleep well, Livvy," Arlene said, running down the porch stairs. "Oh, and turn on the heat. It's freezing in there."

Chapter 7

Olivia stood in front of the third-floor hospital room window staring into the dreary day. It had been ten days since the girl had been brought into the hospital. The open wounds covering her body had started to heal, the swelling that hid her delicate features had subsided, and still she lay like a sleeping princess in a fairy tale.

Her brain had been scanned countless times, and specialists had offered their opinions, but still she slept, her small chest rising and falling steadily with each breath. No one knew why she didn't wake. As the fat raindrops splattered against the window, Olivia slid back in time, her hands fluttering up to her chest to cover her heart as the memory formed.

Olivia had come into the living room to get Carly for lunch and found her lying on the floor, still as stone, her beautiful red-blonde curls surrounding her head like a halo, her lips red, her skin chalk white. Olivia had stood in the doorway paralyzed with fear, staring at the unmoving child. When Carly leaped from the floor, shrieking with glee, "Mommy, I'm Snow White," Olivia marched her to the bathroom on shaking legs and scrubbed the red lipstick and powder off her face, covering her freshly scrubbed cheeks with kisses while tickling her soft belly until she squealed for mercy.

Though she had tried to dismiss the uneasy feeling in her stomach, the image of her daughter, lying still and pale as the dead, had worried her mind through the rest of the day and into her dreams that night.

Turning her back on the window, Olivia walked over and sat in the visitors' chair. One of the volunteers had brought a rocking chair into the room like the ones they normally kept in the maternity wards. Olivia thought she might have brought it especially for her. By now, everyone was whispering about how much time Olivia spent with the girl.

She knew she was giving David more ammunition to have Dr. Iso remove her from the case, but she couldn't have stopped, even if Dr. Iso himself had ordered it. She was drawn to the girl. She didn't even bother trying to rationalize her behavior as professional curiosity anymore.

Forcing a bright smile onto her face, as if the girl would know any differently, Olivia took her hand in hers.

"Good afternoon, angel," she said. "Another rainy one. I think it's rained just about every day since you came here. It's like even the heavens are sad for you. You must have a family out there waiting for you somewhere, a mom, a dad, maybe sisters and brothers. You couldn't have just fallen from space." The more they'd tried to find out who the girl was, the more it seemed she had done just that.

For all the media attention and her picture being splashed nonstop across the news nationwide, no one had come forward to identify her. Law enforcement had been equally frustrated by the dead man found in the car with the girl. The only thing that was clear was that the man was actually a teenage boy.

An autopsy of the body had shown that the boy had endured an inhuman amount of abuse in his short life. He had rope burns around his wrists, ankles, and neck. Scars that could have been made by a horse-whip covered his entire body, leaving trails of scar tissue and welts that had healed and reopened time and again. The letters *FH* were branded into the left side of his chest in small print, like the kind used by cattle farmers to mark livestock. Olivia was grateful the autopsy had also made it clear that there was no possible way the girl could have killed the boy. She simply wasn't physically capable.

"I wonder about your mother. Does she suffer silently, always wondering where you are, imagining the unspeakable horrors you may be enduring? Maybe she drinks herself to sleep, separating herself from her family and friends, hating God while praying for a miracle. How long has she been waiting for any inkling of hope?"

Olivia felt her mind sliding back to the past, to Carly. Instead of fighting against the memories, this time she let them come, sucking in her breath as the pain sliced through her, unchecked.

"I used to have my own angel once. Her name was Carly," she said, softly squeezing the girl's hand. "She was beautiful, just like you. She was so happy, so well loved." Olivia smiled, unaware of the tears that slid down her face.

"One day she was there and then she was gone, taken from us. I didn't even know she was my reason for being alive. Not until she was gone. I think about her every day, and after all this time, I can't stop wondering . . . I would give anything, my life, just to know . . ."

Olivia bit down on her lip to stop the scream of hysteria she felt rushing up from the back of her throat. Her whole body was shaking, and she realized that she was squeezing the girl's hand too hard. She opened her fingers, releasing her. Hysteria quickly turned into shock as the girl's hand clung to her fingers. In amazement, she looked at the girl's face and, for the first time, found clear brown eyes staring back at her.

"Sweet Jesus," Olivia gasped, leaning so close to the girl's face an onlooker would have easily believed they had caught the doctor kissing the unconscious girl.

"Angel, can you hear me?" Olivia asked, whispering as if she were afraid of scaring the girl back into oblivion.

The girl didn't speak, but she clung to Olivia's hand as her eyes moved slowly across Olivia's face.

"It's okay, you're safe," Olivia said softly.

Soon the equipment connected to the girl's every sense would sound the alarm. Nurses who had grown complacent monitoring the girl's never-changing vital signs would suddenly come alive. The room would be flooded with doctors, nurses, probably police officers, and maybe even the press, if David had his way.

Already she could hear footsteps hurrying down the hall, approaching the room.

"I'll be right here," she said, pressing the girl's limp hand to her lips before lowering it gently back onto the bed and turning to face the door just as a pretty red-haired nurse rushed into the room. She barely acknowledged Olivia as she swept toward the bed, where the girl lay, unmoving, her eyes fixed on Olivia's face.

"Sweetie, can you hear me?" the nurse asked as she bent over the bed and lifted the girl's limp arm. "Did she say anything, Dr. Blake? Her heart rate is off the charts—see how high her blood pressure jumped? What happened?"

Before Olivia had a chance to answer, Dr. Iso entered the room, followed closely by David.

Chapter 8

The girl lay perfectly still. It was quiet. The sounds of hogs calling, chickens screeching, and the ever-present buzzing of bloodthirsty mosquitoes that had once made up her world had been wiped away, replaced by the whispers that seemed to surround her.

She tried to reach for the distant voices, curious about what they were saying, but each time she failed, drifting back into the darkness before she could understand the meaning of the words.

I'm dead. I'm dead and set free.

Mother, she thought, willing herself to reach toward the sound.

She felt herself sinking back into the safety of the cloud of nothingness but focused on moving her fingers. Soft hands stroked her face. Words faded in and out, seeming to float around her head, as distant as stars. The girl struggled to understand, but the fog would not be denied. She was so tired.

CARLY!

The name shattered the encroaching darkness. Pain, instant and fierce, screamed from her hand, shocking her brain from its protective tomb. Sounds that had escaped her so many times started to take shape; her sluggish brain recognized soft sobs, and her eyes sprang open.

Carly. The name rocketed around inside the girl's head, clearing away the clouds for a moment. She opened her mouth and tried to force the name from her rusty throat, but no words would come.

The girl's eyes crawled around the dim room, taking in the rain splashing against the window, the gray walls, and the machines that seemed to cover every inch of space, before landing on the woman's face.

She wasn't old like the crone the Family called when someone needed healing. She had soft, warm eyes, the same color as the tea Mother used to make when someone was sick. She'd pulled her hair up into a ponytail, but reddish-blonde curls had escaped and lay against her cheeks and around her neck. The freckles that dotted her nose made her look like a little girl. *Like Carly.* Though that wasn't her only name. The girl with the sunshine curls had been called Sarah, at least by Father, but never Carly. She refused to accept the name Father said the Lord had provided and suffered the punishment for it. But when they were alone, she had been Sunny to the girl because she brought the light.

"Angel, can you hear me?" the woman asked.

The girl wanted to answer, but her mouth felt as if it were full of dust.

She watched the doctor reach out toward something she couldn't see. As the woman leaned over her, tears fell from her eyes and landed on the girl's face. She wished she could reach up and touch her fingers to the wetness she felt on her cheeks.

Carly. As soon as she thought it, Sunny's face appeared in her mind; the image was so clear she raised her hand to try to touch it. As if in answer, the room seemed to fill with the tingle of Sunny's giggle, and then she was falling back into the welcoming darkness. *Where's Jacob, Sunny?* she thought as she slid back into the nothingness.

Chapter 9

As Dr. Iso and David entered the room, David barely spared Olivia a glance before walking over to where the girl lay motionless, her breathing even and deep. The only sound from the bed came from the equipment that measured the girl's life one beep at a time.

"Dr. Iso, David," Olivia said.

"Dr. Blake," Dr. Iso said, bobbing his head in her direction. David grunted, waving off her greeting as if even this slight pleasantry were too much.

Asshole, Olivia thought, imagining herself smacking the smugness right off his face as Dr. Iso lifted the girl's chart from the end of the bed.

"Dr. Blake, could you bring us up to speed on the patient's condition?" David said. "There will be a news conference in a couple of hours. The entire country is anxious for an update on the poor girl."

Turning her back to David, Olivia stepped between him and Dr. Iso.

"Dr. Iso, I think a news conference might be a little premature. After all, there's very little to tell. Wouldn't it serve the hospital better to wait until we know what this new development means?"

"Dr. Blake, this is the first time the child has regained consciousness since she was brought in," Dr. Iso said. "Don't you think that's newsworthy? What if she can tell us who she is, where she came from, or even how she got to be here?"

Before she could answer, David pushed past her to stand beside Dr. Iso. "You're quite right, Dr. Iso. It's very important that we keep the public abreast of the situation. Maybe now that she's communicating, she can help us find her family."

"David, she's not communicating. She opened her eyes one time. She didn't say anything."

"Don't you think she must speak soon?" Dr. Iso asked.

"I don't know. I hope so. I only know that I don't think it's the right time for a press conference."

"No matter," Dr. Iso said, placing the chart back into the drawer at the foot of the bed. "We'll give the press an update, but maybe Dr. Blake's right. Too much exposure right now may not serve the hospital well."

"Yes, sir. Will you still take questions?" David asked.

"No, why don't you handle it this time? I have a meeting with a group of eager cardiology residents," he said, the frown disappearing from his brow as he walked from the room, leaving David and Olivia facing each other as if they were preparing to fight a duel.

"Dr. Blake, you've made your feelings quite clear, so frankly I don't see any need for you to stay either."

"Are you asking me to leave? Because I didn't realize you had that kind of authority."

"You are free to stay or go." He took a step closer to the girl's bed, watching her sleep as he smoothed the blanket that covered her tiny body. Then he turned his glare back on Olivia. "I was only thinking of you and your disdain for the media."

"How thoughtful of you, but I think I'll stay." She wanted him to move away from the girl. It felt like a violation somehow, him standing over her like that. The look on his face didn't help.

"Pride goeth before the fall," he said, the words so low she thought she might have misunderstood him.

"What did you say?" Olivia asked, taking a step toward him.

"Sheldon," David said, his shoulder banging into her arm as he pushed past where she stood.

"David, I got here as soon as I could."

Sheldon Myers stood in the doorway, his usual clichéd tweed sport jacket with leather patched elbows replaced by a crisp white button-down shirt tucked into a pair of pressed jeans. The wind had tangled the white hair he normally brushed into a dignified cap, wiping at least ten years from his overtanned face. His lips curved into what he must have thought would pass as a smile as he stepped into the room, his hand outstretched.

"You've gone too far," Olivia said, ignoring Sheldon's hand as she faced David.

"Dr. Blake. Are you okay? You look quite ill."

"Dr. Iso was clear—press is not allowed into the patient's room," she said, taking a step toward David.

"I heard Dr. Iso just fine. Sheldon is a friend. He's not here in his official capacity. He's just here to pick me up for lunch. Sheldon, sorry for the hysterics, but it's been an exciting day, and I'm afraid Dr. Blake is a little high-strung."

"Oh, that's perfectly fine. Dr. Blake and I are old friends, too, aren't we?"

Olivia turned her back on David and Sheldon and pushed the call button hanging from the girl's bed. "This is Dr. Blake; please send security to Room 369," she said.

"How dare you, you . . ."

"Watch it, David—the next words you say might cost you your job, if this stunt doesn't. Mr. Myers, I suggest you leave this room right now before you're the next headline on that program you insist on calling news."

"Dr. Blake, this is entirely unnecessary. David, I'll call you later," he said as he turned to leave, coming face-to-face with Brandon. "Mr. Hall, what a surprise. Wish I could stay and chat, but obviously this is not a good time," he said as Brandon stepped aside to allow him to leave.

"Well, you must be feeling pretty satisfied with yourself," David said. "Tell me, Dr. Blake, what do you hope to accomplish by trying to hide this girl from the world? Why do you think you know better

41

than anyone else what's best for her? Are you enjoying pretending to be the doting mother so much that you'd deny her a chance to find her family and return home, where she belongs? Whatever you might think, Sheldon can help—"

"David, stop. I don't want to do this anymore. I'm tired. Aren't you tired?"

Olivia wasn't just tired; she was dead-on-her-feet exhausted. It was like someone had stuck a pin in her, and all the adrenaline that had kept her going had run out of her. She wished she could fall into Brandon's arms and have him hold her. If she could put her head on his chest for just a moment, she felt like everything would be all right.

"You want the press conference? Fine, do the press conference. It's yours. You better hurry—it'll start shortly. I can't stand the idea of being in the same room with you for one more second."

"Fine," he said, then turned to walk from the room and squeezed past Brandon, who stood in the doorway, refusing to move for him to walk by.

"Are you okay?" Brandon asked once David was gone.

"I am now. What are you doing here?"

"I was just passing through and thought I'd stop by to see how things were going."

"'Just passing through.' What, did you have a burning desire for hospital cafeteria coffee?" Olivia said, recognizing the sheepish grin that always appeared whenever Brandon attempted to tell a lie.

"Are you insinuating that I'm not being entirely truthful?" he asked, walking across the room until he stood close enough to Olivia that she could have leaned into him by taking half a step forward.

The playful banter that had sprung up so easily between them disappeared, and Olivia felt as if they were standing together in a ball of electricity. Neither of them spoke as he reached out to caress her face. *He's going to kiss me.* It was wrong, she knew, but she couldn't stop it, wouldn't even if she could. She felt her body leaning toward him.

"Sunny."

The word, like the shock of ice water on heated skin, snatched her back to reality. Whirling away from Brandon, she rushed to the girl's bedside.

She lay staring up at the ceiling, her brown eyes clouded with confusion.

"Sunny," she said again, the word no more than a breath of air.

"She's awake," Brandon said, standing behind Olivia and looking down on the girl. At the sound of his voice, the girl's eyes widened, and she tried to raise her hands as if to protect herself.

"Angel, I'm here," Olivia said, reaching for the girl's hands. The girl's eyes stayed on Brandon. A whine like that of a hurt animal came from her throat, sending goose bumps marching up Olivia's flesh. "Brandon, I think you should leave, please . . ."

"How long has she been awake, Olivia?"

"She just opened her eyes a bit ago. I'll meet you in the cafeteria—just let me calm her down."

She didn't turn around as Brandon left the room. Instead, she sat on the bed next to the girl and stroked her hand until the keening sound stopped and she drifted back to sleep.

Chapter 10

Brandon stood outside the girl's room, trying to regain control of his thoughts. She was awake, and not a moment too soon. He had almost kissed Olivia. Damn it, what was wrong with him? It was this girl. This whole situation had started to mess with his mind. He and Olivia were over.

It had taken two years for Carly's loss to destroy their marriage, but after all the tears, the hope, the despair, and the disappointment, there had been nothing left for them to hold on to except the pain. If they had been stronger, maybe they could have found strength in each other, but instead, Olivia had found her solace in the bottom of a vodka bottle, and he had turned tail and run all the way to Manhattan, Kansas.

The first few months in Manhattan had been fueled by his anger. He'd spent his days working odd jobs and his nights drinking, looking for any excuse to start a fight, until he found Lisa. The thought of her twisted his stomach into a knot.

"Brandon, fancy meeting you here."

Brandon looked up to see Arlene standing in front of him, her trademark crooked smile on her lips.

"Arlene, wow, I didn't hear you come up."

"Yeah, some supercop you are. I could have smoked you without you even noticing. Liv told me you were around. How you been?"

"Well, I'm not a cop anymore, which you well know, but I'm good. How about yourself? You're looking good. How's Melinda—she still putting up with you?"

"She's wonderful. Twelve years and counting. She can't live without me. How long have you been back in the Springs?"

"About six months. Watch out," Brandon said, reaching out to take Arlene by the elbow as two children raced down the narrow hallway in their wheelchairs, bringing a smile to Arlene's and Brandon's faces.

"Ahh, to be a kid again," Arlene said.

"Should we stop them?" Brandon asked.

"Maybe, but I won't," Arlene said. "So, I see you already talked to Olivia." A sly smile curled her lips as Brandon stood in front of her, fidgeting like a guilty little boy.

"I know what's going on in that twisted brain of yours, and you need to stop."

"I'm sure I don't know what you mean. I'm just happy to see you back. You're looking good, too, and I'm sure I'm not the only one who's noticed."

"You never change. Always trying to stir the pot," Brandon said, reminding himself that he wasn't in high school as he fought back the urge to ask what Olivia had said about him.

"I'm hurt. Can't a girl express pleasure at seeing an old friend without any ulterior motives?"

"Not this girl," he said, lifting her up off the floor as he bent down to scoop her into a hug. "It's part of your charm, though."

"One of many," she said, kissing him soundly on the cheek.

"You're going to make me blush," he said, lowering her to the floor.

"Seriously, it's great to see you. You should have come around sooner."

"I know, I just didn't want to stir up any old . . . Well, some things are better left alone."

"Some things are and some things aren't," Arlene said. "Sometimes you can't avoid fate."

"Now you sound like my fiancée."

"Maybe you should listen to her," Arlene said, wagging her finger like a schoolteacher. "So, how is our girl doing?"

"She's beautiful," he said, his face flushing as the words tumbled out of his mouth.

"Yes, yes, she is," Arlene said, patting him gently on his warm cheek.

"Arlene, it's been great to see you, but I think I should go."

"Arlene, hey," Olivia said as she stepped into the hall between them. "What's going on?" she asked. "Oh, never mind, I don't even want to know. Arlene, whatever you've been up to, stop it, and Brandon, you know not to pay her any mind."

"What? I didn't do anything, did I, Brandon?"

"Who, you? Never," Brandon said, draping his arm across Arlene's shoulders.

"No? Then why do you both look like I caught you trying to steal change from the church collection plate? Guilty as hell," Olivia said.

Even though she was trying her best to look stern, Brandon could see her fighting back the smile from her lips, but her eyes just couldn't hold the lie.

"Girl, you're paranoid with a capital *P*. Nothing to see here, but I do have things to do, so I'll call you later. Bye, Brandon, great to see you," Arlene said, squeezing Olivia's hand as she walked away, leaving a trail of laughter behind her.

"That woman is something else," Brandon said, shaking his head.

"She is special," Olivia agreed.

"I should be going too," he said.

"You want to grab a cup of coffee?" Olivia asked.

"I better not; I need to get home. I'm late already. Lisa wants to—"

"It's okay. I have a ton of work to do. You know me, always stalling. It was great to see you," she said, turning and hurrying away.

"You too," he said to her disappearing back.

Brandon turned to face the girl's room. Hesitating for just a moment, he entered, being careful as he crossed the floor to keep quiet. He hadn't seen her since the night he'd pulled her from the car, barely alive.

When he looked down into her face, all the air seemed to rush from his body in a giant whoosh, and he had to reach out and grab hold of the bed's railing to stop himself from falling.

The swelling in her face had gone down, revealing a beautiful child. A child who could easily have been their Carly, if Carly had gotten the chance to grow up. Yes, there were differences. She was darker than Carly, but not by much. Her nose and forehead were a bit too wide, the shape of her eyes wasn't quite right, but he understood Olivia's obsession now.

"Carly," he whispered.

Someone had taken the time to brush her hair into a shining pony-tail held together with a pink satin bow, Carly's bow. The sight of it, wound around the girl's reddish-brown curls, brought tears to his eyes as he reached out to touch it.

"Oh, Olivia, what are you doing?" he asked the silent room before turning away.

As he walked from the room, he tried to push away the disquiet in his heart. He had been right from the start; she wasn't okay. Seeing that pink bow erased any doubts he had.

Four years and it felt like they were still trapped, would forever be trapped. Why now, and why this girl, when everything had finally started to feel like it could be normal? He stood in the hallway outside the girl's room, paralyzed with indecision.

He wanted to find Olivia. More than anything, he wanted to be with her right then. He wanted to talk to her about Carly, to hold her long enough for that haunted look to fade from her eyes, but he knew that if he did, he would never let her go again.

He thought of Lisa then and started to walk, moving through the halls as fast as he could without running, ignoring the concerned looks of the few people he rushed past in his desperate need to put as much distance between himself and Olivia as he could.

When he reached the exit, the doors slid open and he stepped outside. He stood there surrounded by the light spilling from the emergency room, sucking in great gulps of the frigid night air. While he waited for his blood to calm and his heart to slow in his chest, he had a feeling he was not alone.

He stared across the parking lot into a dense fold of trees and imagined someone was staring back at him from the darkness, waiting for him to make a move. He was so convinced for a moment that he took a few steps forward before he stopped, feeling foolish for allowing his emotions to get the better of him.

Slowly now, he turned away and walked through the parking lot to his truck, noticing for the first time the thin sheet of ice that covered the windshield and everything else.

As he drove home, his thoughts drifted to Lisa and Kansas. He would have died there, if not for her. If he was being honest, that had been his intention all along; he had just decided to take the scenic route.

Lisa had been the barmaid at the Dozens, a dive that was within throwing distance of the motel he stayed in after his arrival in Kansas. With his wages as a day laborer, he'd made just enough to pay the weekly rent and buy enough food to keep him alive. Anything left over he spent on beer and the pool table that took up most of the space in the bar.

It was rare he didn't end the night bloodied and bruised from a fight. He supposed that at some point he would have been successful in his suicide mission, if not for Big Russ Appleton, owner of not only the bar but the motel where he lived, and also Lisa's father. He always seemed to stop the fight right at the moment before it turned from a situation requiring a couple of bandages to a visit to the emergency room. Afterward, Lisa would help Brandon struggle back to his room, where he would wake up in the morning, alone, every part of his body throbbing with pain.

One morning he had awakened to find Lisa sitting in the worn chair beside his bed, staring out the window into the too-bright sun. A Styrofoam container filled with breakfast and a pot of hot black coffee sat on the table, waiting for him to open his eyes.

When she saw that he was awake, she quietly made him a plate and poured him a cup of coffee before speaking. "Brandon, you are no longer welcome in the Dozens," she said.

Shocked, he tried to remember the night before, but nothing would come. He reached for the place on his head that throbbed with pain and was surprised to feel a large cut on his scalp.

"My father convinced Mr. McHenry not to press charges with assurances to all the customers you would not be allowed to return."

Mr. McHenry was a quiet man who rarely involved himself in anyone else's business. Brandon couldn't believe the man could have been the cause of his injury.

"He hit you over the head with a glass, after you went after his son," she said, her voice devoid of any emotion.

Mr. McHenry's son Joe had suffered pervasive developmental delays, due to a brain injury at birth that limited his speech to two- or three-word sentences. He had never been able to learn to read, but that didn't stop him from loving stories, which the bar's regulars took turns telling him, each trying to earn one of his great belly laughs. He could never remember the words to a song, but he still loved music. When people first met him, they were often stunned to hear him call out the name of the artist singing a song he liked, whether it was a current pop hit or down-home blues. And he never forgot a face, no matter how much time had passed.

Big Russ had given Joe a job picking up around the bar and the motel. Every evening when he was done with work, he would sit at the bar and wait for his father to pick him up. They would eat dinner together, and Mr. McHenry would have a beer or two while Joe regaled the bar with stories from his day. It was a rare person who walked away without feeling at least a little happier after spending a few minutes with Joe.

He especially liked Brandon. Every time he saw him, he took great pride in presenting Brandon with some trinket that he'd found while he worked. The idea that he had attacked Joe made Brandon sick to his stomach. He was afraid to ask for the details of what had happened, but Lisa told him anyway.

"He brought you a ribbon and told you to give it to your daughter. You became upset and refused to accept the gift. Joe didn't understand and kept trying to get you to take it. You lost control and went after him. Poor Joe was hysterical. I think you would have actually hit him. Obviously, Mr. McHenry did, too, so he picked up the glass and hit you over the head."

As Lisa recounted the story of his behavior, shame washed over him. He asked if Joe was all right and promised to apologize. Later, much later, he had, but their relationship was never quite right again. Joe had never given him anything else. Instead of the smile that lit his face for everyone else, when he saw Brandon, he became nervous, ducking his head and hurrying away.

Brandon never went back to the Dozens, and that shame had never left him—neither had Lisa. From that day on, she came to his room every morning and presented him with breakfast. In the evenings they would walk together. One morning when she showed up, her arms were full of papers she had printed from the internet. He didn't need to read them to know what they said.

After he'd choked down a cup of coffee, he told her everything about Carly, Olivia, and the life he had lost. She held him while he cried, and afterward, he lay in her arms. It felt like the most natural thing in the world when they made love.

She moved into the room with him that same morning, and he started to rebuild his life: First he started therapy, initially at Lisa's insistence, but once he realized talking out his pain with a nonjudgmental stranger really did help, he went willingly, if not eagerly. Next he reached out to an old air force buddy for a job recommendation, happily signing on as a midlevel security specialist for Raycom Corp. Soon after, they moved from the cramped room to an apartment, and he asked her to marry him. She said no. He asked her several times after that first proposal, but the answer was always the same.

A year ago, she'd come to him and said it was time for him to return home. He'd refused to consider the idea, but she persisted. Once he accepted that she would never give up, he agreed, but only if she agreed to become his wife. Three months later, with a promotion under his belt, he had transferred back to Colorado Springs.

Since his return, he had gone out of his way to avoid Olivia. Then this girl. Now it felt like it was starting all over again.

"God help me," he said as he sat outside their little house that somehow refused to feel like a home, no matter how much time Lisa spent painting and decorating, looking at the dim light shining through the kitchen window.

She would have left the stove light on for him; she always did whenever he was late getting home. He imagined there would be a plate waiting for him in the microwave. The thought of it made him feel like an asshole. After everything she had done for him, he owed her so much more than mooning over his ex-wife.

Of course he had feelings for Olivia; he always would. So much had been left unresolved, but it was over. For better or worse, their story had come to an end, and he was with Lisa now.

As he reached for the key to turn off the truck, his cell phone vibrated against his hip. He reached to answer it, surprised to see that the number was from the highway patrol's office.

"Hello," he said, catching the call before it could roll into voice mail.

"Brandon, it's Amy," the voice said, sounding more like a young girl than the head of the Colorado Highway Patrol's forensics lab.

"Hey, Amy, what's up?" he said. They had been friends since the moment he'd stepped off the bus onto Lackland Air Force Base in San Antonio, the greenest of air force trainees, more than twenty years ago. He from Colorado Springs, with his laid-back calm, and she from Yonkers, New York, all frenetic energy and a desire to conquer everything. At first glance, it may have looked like an odd pairing. But after their first conversation, they clicked like twins separated at birth and had become inseparable. He smiled as he imagined her now, pacing around in front of a bank of computers, impatient for him to pick up the phone.

"Remember the vehicle identification number you asked me to research?"

"Yeah, I didn't expect to hear back from you so soon. I know it was a long shot," he said, glancing at his watch.

"You know I love this stuff, especially when it turns up something this cool."

"You found something?"

"You'll have to see it to believe it. When can you stop by?" she asked.

"How long are you going to be there? I just pulled up in front of my house, and I'm sure Lisa would appreciate it if I at least checked in. I haven't exactly been the perfect fiancé lately."

"No worries. I'll be here all night, if this baby allows, so take your time."

"Great. Thanks, Amy. See you soon."

"Awesome. You won't be disappointed."

Brandon's mind was already a thousand miles away as he turned his key in the lock. As soon as the door was open, the fragrance of lemon and orange from the tea Lisa loved filled his nose and brought a smile to his lips. He knew he would find her curled up in bed, her nose buried in one of her favorite mysteries, waiting for him to get home, as had become her habit ever since their return to Colorado Springs. He thought about taking a detour to the bathroom to shower off some of the stress of the day and give himself time to reset before joining her in their bed, but suddenly all he wanted was to see her face and find comfort in her arms, even for a little while.

"Hey there, pretty lady," he said, leaning against the doorframe of their bedroom. Just as he expected, she was propped up in the bed, a scarf of many colors wrapped around her head, wearing one of his plain white T-shirt as a nightshirt, a huge steaming mug of tea sitting on the nightstand beside her.

At the sound of his voice, she raised her head to look at him. The smile he loved so much filled her eyes before finding its way to her lips.

"Hey, yourself. I wasn't sure I was going to see you tonight. I heard the girl woke up."

"Yeah, it's been a day. I had to come see you for my sanity's sake."

"Well. Come on over here, and I'll share my tea with you," she said, throwing the thick comforter aside and beckoning him to join her.

"To be honest, I wouldn't mind something a bit stronger. I had to force myself not to stop at every dive bar I passed to get here. But I knew if I stopped and had that first drink, I'd never stop. It's this girl. I can't stop thinking about what she went through—what she's still going through. I see her suffering, and I see my Carly, and my heart breaks all over again. I wanted that drink so bad, Lisa. I needed something to just wipe my brain clean, just for a little while. Then I remembered I had something stronger than any drink here with you."

"Love," Lisa said, then closed her book and put it down beside her.

"Yes," Brandon said.

"Good, because I have plenty of that for you."

"I know. Same here," Brandon said, ignoring the surge of guilt that came along with the picture of Olivia that popped into his mind.

"How's Olivia holding up?" Lisa asked. And not for the first time, Brandon wondered if she could read his mind.

"She's fine."

"I can't imagine that's true. This must bring up a lot of painful memories for you both. Make sure you're there for her. She doesn't need to be alone right now."

"She's not alone. Trust me: Arlene will make sure of that."

"I'm sure Arlene will do her best to be there for Olivia, but there's no one who can understand what she's going through better than you."

"I hear you," Brandon said, walking into the room and sinking onto the bed.

"Maybe a quick nap?" Lisa asked.

"Yeah, but just for a little while. I have to go back out to see Amy."

"You sure it can't wait?"

"It could, but I'd just wonder about it all night."

"Yes, I know. Once a cop, always a cop, I suppose. But before you go, how would you like to hear about the doughnut shop murders happening in a small town in Middleville, Ohio?"

"I would love it," he said, settling into the bed to listen to Lisa's retelling of the book she was currently reading, laughing along with her as she added her own spin to the story that he was sure the author would never have approved of—"for dramatic effect," she said.

He hadn't meant to, but somehow, he must have drifted off to sleep. Lisa let him sleep for about an hour before kissing him awake. After making him a cup of strong, hot coffee, she walked him to the door.

"I know it's hard for you to see, but know you are right where you belong. This poor child needs you. Olivia needs you, and you need them too." She took him in her arms and pressed her lips against his before pushing him gently out the door.

Chapter 11

The girl stared up at the unfamiliar ceiling. She was alone. The room was dim, but outside, the hallways were flooded with harsh white light. The sound of murmuring voices drifted into the room from the open door. Occasionally, she would hear the ding-dong of a bell, followed by a mechanical-sounding voice.

If she turned her head, she could see the moon surrounded by distant stars outlined against the black night sky. They were the same stars she had wished on from the mean dirt yard outside the shack she had called home, but somehow, they seemed to shine brighter now.

She believed she was in a hospital. Once, when she was little, she had gotten so sick that even the old healer woman had thought she was surely on her way to meet her maker. It was the only time she had ever heard her mother talk back to Father, begging him to take her to one. Father had refused, and Mother had paid for her disobedience and lack of faith with a lashing as the Family was called to bear witness. It was Jacob who had explained what a hospital was; it was a safe place filled with healers.

She couldn't remember how she had come to be here, but she was alone, at least for now, and that felt like freedom. The only other time she had ever been alone was before Carly, when Father and his chosen members of the Family went gathering. Then she'd been locked in the Teaching Room, praying for their return at the same time she prayed for them to never come back.

She wondered where Father was now. Had he already called the Family? Had her sins already been judged? Jacob. An image of Jacob, stumbling toward her, covered in blood, flashed into her head. The clearness of it almost made her scream. She raised her hands to her face and was surprised to find they were clean.

"Run . . . hide." She recognized Sunny's voice, stretched tight with fear. Though she knew she must have been imagining it, she searched the room for her lost sister. As if she'd unlocked a door, a flood of memories rushed at her, making her dizzy as faces and voices collided, bringing back everything in one horrific instant. They were all gone now. Sunny, Jacob, Mother.

With a whimper she closed her eyes. *Where is the doctor?* she wondered. It seemed that every time she opened her eyes, the doctor was sitting in the rocking chair, staring down at her almost hungrily, or staring out the window, her face so sad it made the girl sad too.

Sometimes she would lie silently with her eyes shut so the woman wouldn't know she was awake. She didn't always understand what she was talking about or why she called her by a name that wasn't hers, but it was a name she knew well anyway. Carly.

Chapter 12

Olivia walked from the cafeteria, where she had slunk after the rebuff from Brandon, grateful that by some miracle she was able to escape the notice of the reporters who had set up camp at a table in the corner of the room. Her body was still hot from embarrassment. Had she seen pity in his eyes when he refused her offer? She could swear she had. With a groan, she took a quick sip of lukewarm coffee as appetizing as dishwater. From now on she would avoid Brandon at all costs. Obviously, his presence was robbing her of her sanity.

"It was just coffee," she murmured. Except it wasn't, and he had known it too.

She was tired, and as soon as she dropped by to tell the girl good night, she would retreat to the comfort of home, where she could hide her shame under her blankets. She was looking down to dig in her pocket for her phone, intending to call Arlene to see if she wanted to hang out, when she slammed into what felt like a wall.

Surprised, she looked up to find herself standing in front of a huge man, his skin the color of newly poured tar, his eyes as flat and cold as dried mud. Her breath caught in her throat as she looked into his face, and she felt her heart race.

A long, jagged cut on the left side of his face ran from the corner of his eye all the way to his chin. *Half an inch more and he would have been blinded,* she thought. His lips curved upward as he looked down, but instead of making him look friendlier, that lifeless smile made his face that much more awful. Olivia felt a chill run through her body.

"Sorry," Olivia said as she stumbled backward, her eyes never moving from his face.

With a grunt, he started to walk away.

He looks like the boogeyman, she thought.

"Sir, is there something I can help you find? It looks like you have a pretty bad cut; are you looking for the emergency room?"

She thought she saw a flash of anger pass through his eyes, but it was gone so quickly she wondered if she had imagined it.

He stood not moving, looking down at her, his hand in his pocket.

He has a gun, she thought.

Finally, he took his hand from his pocket and nodded.

"Emergency room," he said.

Relieved, she gave him directions and watched him walk away. Aware of the trembling in her body, she walked quickly to see the girl, trying to convince herself that everything was fine and that she was freaking out for nothing.

The girl was not asleep, as she had expected. Instead, she was sitting up in bed, clutching a pillow to her chest, staring at the door.

"He's here, he's here, he's coming for me," she whispered over and over, rocking back and forth in the bed.

"Angel, sweet angel, what's wrong? Who's coming for you?" Olivia asked, rushing to the girl and then wrapping her in her arms, trying to calm her down.

"He's coming for me," the girl whispered, pushing away from Olivia.

"Angel, no one can hurt you here; you're safe."

The girl stopped rocking and turned to face Olivia. "He's coming for me, for Delilah," she said.

"Delilah . . . Is that your name, Delilah?" Olivia asked.

"I am Delilah," the girl said, repeating the name as carefully as if she had studied it for a long time.

"Oh, angel, you remembered your name," Olivia said, throwing her arms around the girl, stunned at the words falling from her lips.

At first she remained as cold and stiff as a slab of marble in Olivia's arms, but slowly she began to soften, until finally her head rested on Olivia's breast. As Olivia held her close, she could see Delilah's lips moving. Olivia turned her head and lowered her ear so close to Delilah's mouth that she could feel her breath against her cheek, and she realized that Delilah was praying. Olivia held her there, wrapped in her arms, rocking her back and forth until Delilah's breath deepened and she had fallen asleep. As gently as she could, she lowered her back onto the bed.

"Sleep, angel," she whispered.

A noise like the sound of a grunt startled Olivia, and she whirled around toward where the noise had come from. The doorway was empty, but she couldn't shake the feeling that someone had been standing there only moments ago.

Probably David slinking around and collecting nonsense to report back to Dr. Iso, she thought.

"Good night, Delilah," she said, bending down to kiss Delilah on her forehead.

Outside the door, Olivia stood looking up and down the hallway. Nothing seemed out of the ordinary, but still she couldn't ignore the sense of unease that had settled over her mind like a fog.

From where she stood, she could see Officer Hernandez, one of the police officers moonlighting as a security guard whom the hospital had hired to keep watch over Delilah to stop overzealous reporters from sneaking into her room since her awakening. He was leaning against the nurses' station, flirting with Peggy, the young, generously endowed, redheaded nurse whom every man in the hospital seemed enchanted with. Celia, the head nurse, had turned her back to the flirting couple. Officer Hernandez stood up straight as Olivia approached, trying, but mostly failing, to wipe the sappy grin from his face.

"Dr. Hall—I'm sorry—Dr. Blake," he said, stumbling over his words, which let Olivia know that she had been the subject of conversation.

"Officer Hernandez," she said, ignoring the slip, even though hearing Brandon's name linked to hers gave her an unexpected thrill.

"Ma'am, is there something I can do for you?"

"I'm on my way out. The patient is kind of anxious tonight. I think seeing that you're on duty and keeping watch would help her feel more comfortable. If you don't mind, could you take up your post outside her door?"

"Yes, ma'am, I was just taking a quick break, making sure everything was okay with the nurses."

"Sure he was," Celia said without looking up from the book she was reading.

Olivia bit back a smile as color flooded Peggy's cheeks.

"Keep up the good work, Officer," Olivia said.

"Yes, ma'am. Do you want me to escort you to your car? You really shouldn't be walking out alone this time of night."

"I'll be fine," she said, but no sooner were the words out of her mouth than a picture of the man she had run into earlier leaped into her mind. Shaking her head to clear the image, she turned and walked away.

Chapter 13

For Brandon, walking into a squad room always felt like coming home, despite the years that had passed since his days as military police. Ignoring the buzz of energy that beckoned to him from inside the squad room, Brandon rushed onto a waiting elevator that carried him to the research department, which occupied the entire second floor. Normally at this time of night, the room would be empty save for the skittering feet of a few brave mice that rightfully took over after lights-out.

Tonight, Amy sat at her desk, her ash-blonde hair pulled back into a ponytail except for her schoolgirl bangs, which fell carelessly across her brow. Her desk was littered with open files and notebooks covered in her illegible scrawl. She didn't look up when Brandon walked into the room. Brandon knew that could only mean she had found something extraordinary.

He stood there, not wanting to surprise or interrupt her, waiting for her to notice his presence. As if she had heard his thought, she slowly raised her head, staring toward him but not seeing him, her eyes distant, her mind still stuck in the world she had been busy researching.

"Hello . . . Amy?" he called softly, easing her back into reality.

She blinked rapidly.

"Brandon," she squealed, rushing from behind her desk to throw her arms around him. "What the bejesus took you so long? I've been waiting for hours."

"Not true—it's only been maybe an hour, no more than an hour and a half, since I got your call."

"Try three."

"You're right. I'm sorry. I lost track of time."

"I guess I'll forgive you, this time. You won't believe what I found." She grabbed his hand and pulled him back to the desk.

"What is it?" he asked, looking down at the computer screen, at a shiny new car that vaguely resembled the one he had pulled the girl from.

"It's a 1988 Honda Accord, owned by Allison Moore."

"Who is Allison Moore?" he asked.

"Oh, you are so going to want to throw me down and make wild love to me for this, but try to restrain yourself. You know how jealous Mark can be. I'll settle for a kiss," she said, tapping her cheek with a finger.

"Amy, please, I can't stand it. Just tell me."

"Okay. Well, first of all, it wasn't easy. After all, I only had a twenty-five-year-old VIN to work with, but I persevered, and finally, with a little help from some friends at the DMV, I hit the jackpot. In 1988, Allison Moore was a fifteen-year-old ninth grader at Martin Luther King Jr. High School in Shaker Heights, a small suburb of Cleveland, Ohio. She was an A student and well liked by her teachers and peers, so says the report.

"As a reward for her good behavior, her parents bought her this car as an early sweet sixteen present. She wasn't supposed to drive the car alone, since she only had her learner's permit, but her mom let her drive the car by herself to her job at a fast-food restaurant, less than five miles away. The parents swore it was the first time. It was also the last time they saw their daughter. She and the car fell off the edge of the earth, until now."

Brandon sank into a chair, staring stupidly at Amy, struggling to find the words for all the questions flooding his brain. "You're right. Mark be damned, I do want to make wild love to you," he said, reaching for her.

"Maybe later," she said, swatting his hands playfully.

"Oh, Amy, you've outdone yourself . . . but how? How did a car from a twenty-five-year-old missing child case end up clear across the country in Colorado? What does it mean? Did the girl run away on her own, maybe with a boyfriend? Was she carjacked? Was she kidnapped and brought to Colorado? I have to talk to her parents."

"Not unless you know one of them ghost whisperers, you won't," Amy said.

"They're both dead?"

"Both of them."

"Damn. What happened?"

"Of course, it's sheer tragedy too. The mom never forgave herself. She developed a serious drug and alcohol problem. She got arrested a handful of times for possession. The police were pretty lenient. They all knew what the family had been through. The father did everything he could. He even had her committed for a while, but it didn't matter. Allison was their only child. On the fifth anniversary of Allison's disappearance, the mom hung herself. The father died of a massive heart attack the next year, though I suppose he was dead a long time before that."

"God, that might be the worst story I've ever heard," Brandon said, his mind spinning so fast he couldn't finish one thought before his mind raced down another trail.

"What are you thinking?"

"I don't know . . . I can't . . . I gotta go. I need to talk to the girl."

"What girl? You're freaking me out a little bit."

"The girl in the hospital. What if she knows something about Allison Moore?"

"How could she? Allison's been missing for twenty-five years. Unless . . . wait, do you think she's still alive?"

"Amy, I swear I don't know anything right now."

"Fine, but before you go sprinting off into know-nothing land, I got this for you. It's the old file, at least what's left of it. I made you a copy." She handed him a folder.

"You're amazing."

"I know it. I'll take my kiss now. And keep this between us, please. I know it's an old case, but technically it's still open, and since you're a civilian now, I really shouldn't let you walk out of here with it."

"How about a kiss now and dinner later, with Mark's permission, of course."

"Mark will be fine," she said with a grin. "You know I don't turn down free food. After all, I'm eating for two." She patted her round belly.

With a quick kiss to her cheek, he grabbed the folder and rushed out of the office, his brain spinning like an out-of-control top.

He had to call Olivia, he thought, dialing half the number before it hit him like a punch to the gut. Olivia wasn't the one he called anymore. After hanging up the phone, he walked into the squad room to get his bearings before heading back to the hospital. He glanced down at his watch. With a sigh he realized it was too late to see the girl tonight. It would have to wait until tomorrow. He should go home to Lisa, but he couldn't, not when his mind was so filled with thoughts of Olivia. He hadn't done anything wrong, at least not yet, but it still felt like cheating. So instead, he sank down into the chair in front of his friend and former partner Smitty's desk.

"Brandon, man, what are you doing here? Rowdy teenagers hopping the fence to shoot at prairie dogs again?" his friend asked.

"I was in the area and thought I'd swing by to check in on Amy. Is the LT in?"

"Hell no. You're the only fool who used to work all night. What's up?"

"You heard about the case with the little girl out on Highway 24?"

"Yeah, I heard. Perkins and Scott are running lead on that. And after you made Perkins look like a rookie on that academy murder right out the gate, I would keep well away. That man is like an elephant. He doesn't forget nothing. Especially being shown up by a security guard."

Perkins had been assigned to be Brandon's mentor right out of the police academy. Their first and only case together had involved the murder of the girlfriend of a young Air Force Academy cadet. Perkins had been convinced that the cadet had killed her in a jealous rage. After talking with the girl's friends and family, Brandon had disagreed.

After a little digging, Brandon had discovered that the cadet had been having a fling with another woman, and that woman had turned out to be the killer. Perkins had never forgiven Brandon for showing him up, no matter how many times Brandon tried to dismiss it as a lucky break.

"That's head of security to the likes of you," Brandon said, smiling, although he knew Smitty was right. Perkins was a good enough cop, but he was definitely a relic left over from the old guard. And petty enough to never forget a slight, real or imagined. "You're right, but I was first on the scene, so I just wanted to follow up on some details for my report. The LT asked me to drop off a copy when I was done."

"He just wants to talk to you about joining the force. You know you want to. Hell, everybody knows you want to. Why don't you stop playing hard to get and come on back home?"

"I don't know. Maybe because I get paid ten times more than you, and no one is shooting at me?"

"And yet, here you are. Hell, I think you're here more than I am."

"Well, you should show up for work more," Brandon said.

"Maybe. I'll give that some careful thought, but right now, I have to get home, before my dinner gets cold. You good?" Smitty let the smile slide from his face for a moment as he waited for Brandon to answer.

"Yeah, man, I'm just trying to work out a few things in my head."

"Well, for what it's worth—and knowing you, that ain't much—maybe you should start by taking your ass home and talking to your woman."

"I hear you," Brandon said, making no move to get up from the chair.

"Yeah, right. Like my mama always said, 'A hard head makes a soft ass.' Make sure you turn off the lights on your way out," Smitty said as he stood and walked away, laughing.

Who was he kidding? Smitty was right. It was time to go home. Allison Moore had been missing for two and a half decades; one more day wasn't going to change anything for anyone.

Chapter 14

Delilah sat up in the bed, her eyes wide open, staring at the open door. She wanted to run, but there was nowhere to go. Father was coming for her. She could feel his presence vibrating through her body. If she closed her eyes, she could clearly see his face, grim with determination, biding his time until he could slip past the nurses and the guard outside her door and whisk her away.

By the time anyone noticed she was gone, he would have carried her back to the farm, or maybe not. Maybe he would wrap his hands around her neck and squeeze until she was as free as Mother and Jacob and all the others.

No, not now, now that Sunny was gone, and Mother too. She was the last. No matter how furious he might be, his need for her was too great. She would be Mother now.

A shudder racked her body at the thought, and her resolve to remain quiet weakened. As she reached for the call button, an image formed in her mind of Jacob, his skull caved in, blood spewing from the hole in his head as he stumbled toward her. Instead of pushing the button that would summon the pretty red-haired nurse, she balled her hands into fists and waited.

A breeze, as soft as a kiss against her cold skin, pushed away the dark cloud of fear, replacing it with a long-forgotten memory. She and Sunny held hands as they ran through a field of dandelions, creating their own blizzard. She wasn't alone.

Chapter 15

Olivia sat on the couch in the empty living room, staring blindly at the TV. A pretty blonde reporter smiled into the camera as she prattled on about the weather or whatever. Olivia couldn't have said what if her life depended on it. Ever since she'd walked into the house and kicked off her shoes, she'd been as antsy as a child waiting for Christmas morning—except the nervous feeling crawling around in her belly wasn't at all pleasant. She'd made herself a cup of hot chocolate, thinking it would help her relax, but it sat untouched on the end table.

Delilah. It was always Delilah. She knew that the nursing staff were doing everything they could to make her more comfortable, including sneaking her special treats (which she refused to eat), hair bows, and funny socks, left folded neatly and tucked away in her beside drawer. Some of the nurses had even brought in books, magazines, and pen and paper, using their lunch or other breaks to try to communicate with her. But no sooner did they leave the room than the pen and paper would disappear.

When housekeeping changed her bed, they found the books and writing material crammed under the mattress, the magazines ripped to shreds and rolled into small, tight balls stuffed inside a spare pillow. Olivia knew because they reported everything concerning Delilah back to her, as if she were Delilah's own mother.

Brandon was right; she was too involved. She should step back, assign someone else to the case. She wouldn't even have to give a reason. Everyone would understand. Before the idea could gain any traction, though, she shook it off. Delilah needed her. Or did she need Delilah?

Something wasn't right. She could feel it, and before the thought was fully formed, she reached for the phone, then slammed it back down when she realized that she'd started to call Brandon. It was late, almost midnight. What would be a good excuse for calling an engaged man at this hour? She couldn't think of one.

After jumping off the couch, she paced back and forth, gnawing at the tip of her fingernail. What was wrong with her? She sank back down onto the couch, leaned forward, and bent over until her head rested on her knees. She closed her eyes and breathed deeply until she felt her nerves settle and she was able to listen to her heart.

Something was wrong—of that, she was sure. She didn't know if it was Brandon or Delilah, but she knew where she needed to be. After taking a moment to slide her feet into her shoes, she grabbed her purse and coat and rushed across the room and out the door, back into the night.

As soon as she was in the car, she dialed Brandon's number. It was wrong, she knew, but he would want her to call him, she told herself, her nerves tightening at the sound of his phone ringing in her earpiece. When she finally heard his voice, she released a deep breath, feeling some of her anxiety drain away.

"Brandon, thank God," she said.

"Olivia," he said, his voice sounding anxious through the phone. "Are you okay?"

"I'm fine. I just feel like something isn't right," she said, choosing not to lie.

"You caught me on my way home, but I really do need to talk to you. Maybe I could stop by?" he said, and she could hear the hesitation in his voice.

The idea of being alone with Brandon made Olivia's whole body flush. She nearly choked as she tried to spit out an answer through her suddenly dry throat.

"Well, actually, I'm not at home . . ."

"Oh, sorry, of course. I should have thought . . ."

"No . . . no . . . I mean . . . I'm on my way to the hospital. Can you meet me there?"

"Why? I thought you were off for the night."

"I am. I mean, I was, but I need to check on some patients."

"You mean *a* patient."

"Her too," Olivia said, hating the defensiveness she heard in her voice.

"Olivia . . ."

"Brandon, I don't want, or need, a lecture. If you want to talk to me tonight, you can meet me at the hospital."

"Could you meet me at the ER entrance? We can go in together. I'll feel better knowing you're not wandering around alone in an empty parking lot at this time of night."

"Okay, I'll see you there in about fifteen minutes."

"All right, Doc," he said.

She was smiling as she hung up the phone and drove, too fast, toward the hospital.

Chapter 16

As Olivia pulled up to the door of the ER, she was not surprised to find Brandon already waiting. When he saw her, he turned to wave to someone inside, and a young man in scrubs stepped outside.

"Marcus will take care of your car," Brandon said, pointing at the smiling young man.

"Thank you, Marcus," Olivia said, handing over her keys as she stepped out of the car to follow Brandon into the hospital.

"Marcus?" she asked.

"He's an orderly. Seemed pretty impressed by you," Brandon said.

"Hmm, I don't think I've ever met him, but thanks."

"I figured by the time you got here, you'd be on the verge of a nervous breakdown; God forbid you should waste time parking," he said with a grin.

"That obvious, huh? Well, I'm sorry, but I have this awful feeling. I'll just check on her, and once I know that everything's fine, I'll go home."

"You could have called," he said.

As they stepped off the elevator and into the pediatric unit, Olivia knew that something was wrong. Someone had dimmed the fluorescent lights, giving the hall an old horror movie feel. The nurses' station was deserted, and she saw no sign of Officer Hernandez.

"Damn it," Brandon whispered under his breath.

"Why do I feel like I was just dropped into one of those horrible teenage slasher flicks?" She resisted the urge to grab Brandon's hand as they rushed down the dimly lit hall.

"Where is everybody?" Brandon asked. Olivia knew he was nervous by how close his hand hovered over the pistol on his hip.

"It's pretty quiet here overnight," she said. "Betty's shift ended at midnight, so Peggy would be the only nurse assigned to stay at the desk on this ward. The rest of the staff would be spread out."

"Then where in the hell is Peggy?" Brandon asked. "And why are the lights so low?"

"I don't know where Peggy is, but sometimes the graveyard shift will turn the lights down to make it easier for the kids to sleep. They have a harder time than adults."

"Still . . . ," Brandon said, his eyes sweeping the hall.

"I know, something feels off," she said, relieved at having said the words out loud.

"Yeah."

As they neared the unattended nurses' station, an alarm started to beep. Olivia hurried around the desk to see which room the alarm was coming from and was not surprised to see that it was for Delilah. The clanging of the alarm had scared some of the other children awake, and the quiet hallway was filled with the confusion of frightened children's screams, as well as the shrieking alarm.

Olivia was so focused on reaching Delilah that she didn't see Peggy running out of a patient room. Peggy tried to pull back, but it was too late. Olivia heard a sickening crack rip through the air as their heads smacked together, and then everything went dark.

❋

As Brandon raced to where Olivia had fallen, nurses alerted by the shrieking alarm and the crying children rushed into the ward to see what was going on. As he lifted Olivia's head onto his arm, she opened her eyes and stared blankly around the hallway. A small gray-haired nurse crouched beside him on the floor, speaking softly to Olivia as she took her vital signs. A knot was already forming in the center of her forehead, seemingly doubling in size as he watched.

"Should she have an X-ray, or a CAT scan, or something?" Brandon asked.

"That's not necessary," Olivia said, trying to get to her feet.

"Hold on now, Dr. Blake, just take it easy for a minute," the nurse said, pressing her hand down onto Olivia's shoulder to keep her from trying to stand.

"Tina, I'm fine. Please go check on Peggy," Olivia said.

"Well, you know my name, that's a good start, but I think this young man might be right. You should probably go on down and get yourself checked out. Tina is taking care of Peggy. She's going to have a heck of a fat lip, and a lot of explaining to do, but she'll be fine," the nurse said.

"It's just a bump. I promise you, I'm fine."

Brandon could see by the nurse's face that she wasn't completely convinced, but one look into Olivia's eyes, and he knew they were fighting a losing battle. The nurse must have known it too.

"Well, she's going to have one hell of a headache," the nurse said. "You should get her home, but keep an eye on her tonight. You're going to want to watch out for vomiting, blurry vision, and any complaints of dizziness."

"What about that?" he asked, pointing at the knot that had started to look almost like a horn growing out of Olivia's forehead.

"It's fine, Brandon, honestly," Olivia said.

"Ice and Excedrin should do the trick, but it may take a few days for the swelling to go down," the nurse said.

"Okay," Brandon said as the nurse stood.

"I better go check on her," the nurse said, pointing to where Peggy still sat on the floor, sobbing hysterically, while Tina tried to wipe away the blood trickling from her nose.

"Idiots," Brandon mumbled, turning his attention back to Olivia, who was already trying to get up. "Hold on—let me help you," he said, putting his hands under Olivia's arm to help her stand.

✳

As Brandon lifted her back to her feet, Olivia felt the hallway dip and twirl out of focus. She closed her eyes and waited for everything to stop spinning. When she opened her eyes, she thought she saw a form drift from Delilah's room and glide down the hall, away from the commotion. Olivia closed her eyes and took a deep breath. When she opened them again, the hall outside Delilah's room was empty.

"It was just my imagination," she whispered, but the chill that raced down her spine told the truth.

With Brandon's help, she walked on wobbly legs to Delilah's room.

Delilah was standing. Her small body, outlined by the light of the moon streaming in from the window, seemed to sway from side to side as if caught in a breeze. Her hospital gown hung open, revealing the cruel scars crisscrossing her back. Although the wounds had healed quite a bit, Olivia still had to force air past the lump in her throat and the tears from her eyes every time she saw them.

Leaving Brandon in the doorway, Olivia walked across the floor to where Delilah stood in the middle of the room. "Delilah," she called, softly reaching out to place her hand on her shoulder. When the girl remained motionless, Olivia gently turned her around so she could look in her face.

"Delilah, what happened?" she asked, forcing her voice to remain calm.

Blood dripped from Delilah's hand, where the IV had been, and landed on her bare feet. The bandages that had protected her wounds had been ripped off and cast aside.

"Hurt," Delilah said.

"Oh, honey, I know you're hurt, but who did this to you? Can you tell me?" Olivia knelt down until she was face-to-face with Delilah.

"Hurt," Delilah repeated, her voice barely above a whisper.

"Never mind," Olivia said, gently guiding Delilah back toward the bed. As Olivia reached out to straighten the disheveled bed, she was surprised to find it wet with urine. In all the time Delilah had been a patient at the hospital, she had never had an accident.

"Is everything okay?" Brandon asked from his post at the doorway.

"Yes, but I need an orderly in here to change the bed. Can you go grab someone for me? The last thing I want to do is set off another alarm."

Brandon hesitated, his eyes swinging between her and Delilah. Olivia could see the struggle playing on his face, and her body tensed. Finally, he nodded and turned away, leaving her alone with Delilah.

"Come sit right here, sweetie," Olivia said, leading Delilah to the rocking chair. "I'm going to get you cleaned up and fix your IV and your bandages."

As Olivia filled a pan with warm water, her mind was racing. Had Delilah simply had a nightmare? Olivia thought about the form she'd seen leaving the room and wondered. Had it been a trick of the light? She wasn't sure. But the one thing she did know was that whatever had terrified Delilah was very real.

When she returned with the sponge bath prepared, she found Delilah sitting in the chair, staring at the open door. Olivia knelt until she was at eye level with Delilah.

"Delilah," she called, but the girl's eyes did not waver. "Delilah, no one will hurt you here, I promise."

Slowly Delilah's eyes moved from the door and came to rest on Olivia's face.

"Hurt," she said as tears began to slide down her cheeks.

"Hurt," Olivia whispered, taking Delilah gently into her arms as the silent tears turned into sobs.

Chapter 17

Olivia and Brandon sat across from each other in the cafeteria, coffee and bagels in front of them, almost untouched. The sun would be rising soon, and they were both exhausted yet too keyed up for sleep.

"Some night," Olivia said.

"Never a dull moment with you, is it?" Brandon said with a smile.

"Miss Excitement, that's me."

"Well, Miss Excitement, I had something that I wanted to talk to you about, but I really think I should take you home. We can talk later, after you get some rest."

"No, I'm fine. Whatever it is, spit it out," she said, feeling her insides tighten. After the horror of this night, she didn't know how she was going to listen to any more bad news; perhaps he wanted to talk about his upcoming wedding, or worse, maybe Lisa was pregnant. The thought made her queasy.

"Are you okay? You look green," Brandon said, reaching over to touch her hand.

"I'm good, honest. I'll be fine. Go ahead," she said, not wanting to delay the inevitable a second longer.

"Your hands are like ice," Brandon said, the frown of concern on his face breaking her heart.

"I'm fine," she said, forcing a smile to her lips.

"Okay, well, I've been doing some research on the car that Delilah was found in. I don't know what it means, but I wanted to see what you thought."

Olivia stared dumbly at Brandon, fighting the urge to throw her arms around his neck and kiss him until he was hers again. How many times during their marriage, when he was a military police officer, had they had this same conversation? Even though it was against policy to discuss his work with her, he'd always said that she was his other half and that he couldn't be expected to make a decision with only half a brain.

And so they'd sit at the kitchen table or cuddle on the couch, going through each part of whatever case he was working on until it became clearer for him. Oftentimes these sessions would end with fierce love-making, where it truly seemed they were part of the same brain.

※

Brandon concentrated on organizing the file on the small table between them, careful to avoid raising his eyes to Olivia's, too afraid of what he would find there. As much as he longed to take her into his arms and march back into their former lives together, he couldn't.

After a long silence, he took a deep breath and raised his head, plastering a smile as stiff as dried cement onto his lips.

"Okay, ready?" he asked, not waiting for an answer as he launched into the explanation of what Amy had found. When he was done, there was silence as Olivia flipped through the file, stopping to read and running her fingers across the surface of the pages as if trying to feel her way to an answer. Finally, she raised her eyes to his, and the pain that scarred her face made his heart lurch in his chest.

"What does it mean?" she asked, her finger tapping a picture of the long-missing car, brand new, the red glinting in the sun in the picture.

"I'm not quite sure," Brandon said with a shrug. "All I know is Allison Moore disappeared from the Cleveland area in 1988 after her parents gave her this car. The same car that Delilah and the boy were found in."

"You think she could still be alive?" Olivia asked.

"It's possible. Remember Mike Russo? He worked with me on Peterson."

"How could I forget? How many nights did you guys spend passed out on the floor after a few too many?" Olivia said, her mouth lifting slightly.

"Well, when he got out of the service, he went back to Cleveland. He's a detective with the police department there now. I called him and asked him to look into this case for me. Of course, he wouldn't have been around during this time, but his father, grandfather, and all of his uncles are police officers, so I'm sure if there's anything we don't know about this case, he'll find it."

"It seems that finding Allison is the key to finding out who Delilah is," Olivia said.

"Maybe so, but right now, finding my bed is all that I can manage."

"I second that," Olivia said, rising out of the chair as Brandon cleared the table.

"Come on, then; I'll drop you off."

"No, I'll be fine. I'm tired, but I'm so keyed up I need a few moments to calm myself down before I try to sleep, or you know me—I'll just end up pacing the floor."

"I insist. I'll put on some Jonathan Butler to help you relax," he said. "I'll even promise not to sing along to your favorite parts."

"Oh, the lies," Olivia said as he tried to hide the smile hovering on his lips.

"I'm hurt. Where's the trust?" he said, his smile growing.

"It would be a little easier to trust you if you weren't literally crossing your fingers in front of me," Olivia said, her own smile growing to match his.

"Well, my friend, it's either me or I can order you a ride, but there's no way I'm going to let you drive after the night you've had. I couldn't live with myself if something happened to you."

✳

My friend. The words hit Olivia like a dive into a cold pool of water on a hot day, drowning out the tiny flame that had begun to grow in the pit of her belly. He was her friend now. That's all he could ever be. Silly of her to think for even a second that it could be anything more. Hoping he didn't notice the effect his words had on her, Olivia yawned, covering her face with her hands just long enough to blink away the pain she knew he would be able to see in her eyes.

"Fine. If it'll make you feel better, I'll order a ride. You should get on home too. I'm sure your fiancée is wondering where you are. And I wouldn't mind some time alone to think about all of this."

"All right. I'll see you later," he said, dipping down to touch his lips lightly against her cheek. "Sleep well."

"Sleep well," she said, raising her hand to where his lips had touched.

✳

Brandon sat in the idling truck in the driveway of the small white house, willing himself to leave the car and face Lisa. He stared at the kitchen window, hoping for, or dreading, the sight of her moving around behind the curtain. By now she would be awake, sipping a mug of her own special brew while she listened to her birds sing softly from their perch.

He glanced up but saw no trace of telltale smoke drifting from the chimney. When the air turned crisp, as it was this morning, signaling the arrival of winter, Lisa loved to start the day by building a fire in the old-fashioned fireplace that dominated the living room. It wasn't strange at all for him to wake to find her curled in her favorite rocking chair, staring blissfully into the fire as if it were speaking to her.

He loved her, more than he had once imagined he ever could. The thought of hurting her tied his stomach into knots, but he would anyway. He didn't know what, if anything, would happen with him and Olivia, but he couldn't deny how he felt. How he had always felt. He had no choice but to tell Lisa the truth; to lie to her would be unbearable. Closing his eyes, he begged forgiveness from the heavens before exiting the truck.

Brandon opened the door and stepped inside, and his eyes locked onto the velvet box sitting on the counter, holding a small white envelope in place.

From where he stood, he could see the graceful swirl of Lisa's handwriting. There would be no confrontation, at least not now. Lisa was gone. His hand was steady as he picked up the envelope, but he couldn't bring himself to open it. He knew it was cowardly of him, but he couldn't face the pain of knowing he had hurt her after all she had done for him.

Instead, he picked up the small box and lowered it, along with the envelope, into the nearest drawer as gently as if it were a bomb waiting to explode before dragging himself to bed, drifting into sleep before his eyes were fully closed.

Chapter 18

Olivia sat at the table in the hospital cafeteria, with the biggest cup of coffee she could find sitting in front of her. Pain radiated from the knot in the center of her forehead, worse than any hangover she'd experienced during her past romance with the bottle.

It had gone down some, but not enough to stop the stares of everyone who passed by. Worse, David had been waiting for her as soon as she entered the hospital to tell her that Dr. Iso wanted to see her in his office, immediately. There was no need to guess why. The question was, How much damage had David already caused?

Her eyes felt like they were full of sand that she couldn't dislodge, no matter how much she rubbed at them. So, when she saw the woman gliding toward her, she closed her eyes and opened them again, slowly this time, adding a few blinks for good measure. She was the most beautiful woman Olivia had ever seen—at least in real life.

Olivia knew she was staring, but she was powerless to stop. She wasn't alone, though. Every set of eyes in the cafeteria seemed to follow the woman's every step. When the woman stopped in front of her table, beaming down at Olivia as if she'd found a long-lost relative, she nearly choked on her coffee.

"Dr. Blake," she said. Her voice seemed to warm Olivia from the inside out, and she realized she was grinning up at the woman, but she couldn't say why.

"Yes," Olivia said, wishing she had at least taken the time to smear on a bit of lipstick, not that it would have mattered. She was so mesmerized by the richness of her voice and the perfection of her onyx skin that she hadn't heard a word the woman said. "God, I don't know what's wrong with me. I didn't mean to stare—must be this bump on my head."

But the woman just smiled. "May I join you?"

"Of course. How can I help you?" Olivia said as the woman pulled out the chair across from her and took a seat.

"I'm Lisa," the woman said, reaching her hand across the table for Olivia to shake.

For a moment, Olivia sat there gaping at the woman, her hands lying on the table like two dead fish, refusing to reach up and grasp her slender fingers.

"Oh, sorry. I mean, damn, I didn't mean . . . ," Olivia said, nearly jumping out of her seat to grab the woman's hand before she could fully pull it away, squeezing too hard as she pumped it up and down. "I'm a mess today. It was a terrible night, and I didn't get much sleep."

Olivia felt the heat rush into her face as she tried her best not to squirm under Lisa's gaze, even as she wondered if her eyelashes had had a little help. How was it fair that one woman should have that skin, those perfect almond-shaped eyes, and those eyelashes?

"I'm sorry about keeping Brandon out so late. Things got a little out of control."

"No need. I know as well as you that once Brandon has his hooks in something, there's no stopping him. This little girl needs him right now, as do you," Lisa said so calmly that Olivia wasn't sure if she'd heard her right, or if she'd added the last few words herself.

"I'm sorry?" Olivia said.

"I'm being too blunt. It's a terrible habit, but one I find I can't—or maybe don't want—to break. Also, I'm afraid I'm pressed for time. I want to get on the road before it's too late. There's a storm coming, and I'd like to be safe in my nice warm bed before it lands."

Olivia struggled to make some kind of sense of the words she was hearing. "I'm sorry," she said again. "You said you're leaving? Brandon didn't say anything."

"I said *I'm* leaving. Brandon is already where he belongs."

"I don't understand," Olivia said. "Brandon loves you."

"We both know that's not true. Well, at least not fully. Brandon does love me, out of gratitude and friendship. I was there when he needed me. Now he's found his way back to you, and that's as it should be. My part in his journey has come to an end. I wanted to meet you, because I don't want you to allow Brandon to waste another second on misplaced guilt."

"But I can't. If you leave, he's going to feel terrible. He wants to marry you."

"Olivia, please, let's not waste time with half-truths. Be honest, with yourself if not me. What do you want more than anything else?"

"My family back." The words came out in a rush of air, leaving her stunned, breathless, and embarrassed.

She raised her eyes to Lisa's, half expecting to see a storm, but the woman just looked back at her, her face as cool and still as a lake on a hot summer's day, those warm brown eyes seeming to see right into her heart.

"Now we have the truth," she said, that slow smile spreading across her face as she nodded. "Life is short. You know this more than most. Don't waste time or any more of your happiness on guilt or regrets. Go to him. Love him."

"Wait, I need—"

"You have everything you need," Lisa said, her hand covering, then squeezing, Olivia's for just a moment before she rose from her seat and walked away, likely oblivious to the trail of awestruck stares that followed her until she disappeared through the door.

Olivia was sitting and staring down into the bitter, cold coffee, wondering if she'd imagined the whole encounter, when an announcement summoning her to Dr. Iso's office came over the loudspeaker. A few of the hospital staff who knew her, and whom she was sure had heard the story about last night, turned to look at her. She wondered what they would do if she stood up and asked them what they were looking at, but instead, she grabbed the coffee and dumped it in the trash, her mind still buzzing from the encounter with Lisa as she hurried from the cafeteria. *No sense making a bad situation worse,* she thought.

Chapter 19

Olivia sat in Dr. Iso's office, staring at the top of his balding head, her foot tapping incessantly against the floor as he peered through his glasses down at the report from last night's incident. For the hundredth time she shifted in her seat, unable to get comfortable in the silence of the room.

She wished she'd gotten more sleep, but she'd spent the little time she had before it was time to report for her shift alternating between tossing and turning, pacing, and trying to talk herself out of either returning to the hospital or calling Brandon. At some point, sheer exhaustion had won out, and she'd drifted into a light, unsatisfying doze, where her brain continued to churn, turning her thoughts into confused, senseless dreams that she could barely remember. Add to that the meeting with Lisa, which she still couldn't quite process, and she was as close to losing it as she had ever been.

"So, quite a mess last night," Dr. Iso said, finally raising his head and training his dark eyes on her.

Funny, she had never thought of him as birdlike, but now all she could think of was a crow, a cold, unblinking, wide-eyed crow, staring back at her like she was the first wormy catch of the morning. *God, I'm losing it,* she thought, trying to focus on his words like the responsible, intelligent doctor she was instead of the lunatic she felt like.

"Yes, it was," she said. "Quite a mess. Very traumatic for our patient, I'm afraid."

Dr. Iso didn't respond immediately, and Olivia started to wonder if there was something he was expecting from her.

Finally, he shook his head and closed the folder he'd been studying.

"Yes, I'm sure it was. How is she today?" he asked.

"I'm not sure. I didn't have a chance to check on her before coming to see you," she said, and even she could hear the accusation in her tone.

"Hmm, yes, well, it couldn't be helped. What do you think our next steps should be with this patient?"

There was no inflection in his voice, and his face remained blank when he asked the question, but Olivia could tell that he'd already decided; her answer was simply a test. So she took her time, breathing in deeply to calm herself before she spoke.

"Sir, last night's incident was unfortunate but was in no way her fault. She is recovering at the rate one would expect from someone so young who's experienced such severe trauma. It may take a little more attention from us all, but this is why we're here."

Dr. Iso leaned forward, drumming his long, perfectly manicured fingers against the folder in front of him, his eyes boring through her like lasers. "There is a note in the file that the child may have been hallucinating and may have tried to harm herself. Is this true?"

"No . . . well, it's impossible to know. She was distraught and obviously terrified. I wouldn't say she was hallucinating—more like a bad dream, or even a night terror—but I saw no sign that she was a danger to herself, or anyone else for that matter."

"Then can you tell me what happened to her bandages and IV?" Dr. Iso asked, not taking his eyes off Olivia's face as she fought to find the right words to protect Delilah. When none came, she sank back into her chair and shook her head.

"Dr. Blake?" Dr. Iso said.

"I don't know," Olivia said.

"According to the report, the child was alone when she was found, bleeding and insisting that someone was coming for her?"

"Yes, but again, I believe that was because she was confused."

"Is that really your professional opinion, Dr. Blake?"

"Dr. Iso, do you mind if I ask who wrote this report?"

"Why does that matter?" he asked, the frown creasing his brow, the first real sign of annoyance he had shown. She knew that bringing up David right then was probably not the best idea, but she felt that making him understand David's ulterior motives where Delilah was concerned was possibly the only way to keep the girl safe.

"It doesn't matter, but I don't believe David is being objective when it comes to this girl, so maybe he's not the most reliable source."

"What about you, Dr. Blake? Can you say that your treatment of her has been the most appropriate?"

"Sir, I—"

"No, let me finish," he said, raising his hand to stop her from speaking further. "The whole hospital's talking—no, the whole *city* is talking, thanks to these infernal leaks to the news—about your treatment of the girl. Is it true that you've spent nights in her room? No, don't answer that. Listen, Dr. Blake, I understand that you may feel a special connection to this girl. We've all had those patients, but that's what they are: patients. They're not ours. They're here for us to put them back together again and send them on their way."

"Where? Where are we going to send this child? She doesn't have anybody," Olivia said, fighting back tears that she knew would only prove David's point to Dr. Iso.

"That's none of my concern, nor the hospital's, or yours either. Our job is done, and it's time for this child to go on, whether it's to children's services or an inpatient mental health facility, whatever she needs. We've done our part."

"And if I disagree?" Olivia asked, continuing to fight, even though she knew the battle was lost.

"Olivia, don't do this to yourself. I'm not doing this to hurt you— quite the opposite, in fact. You have to let her go, for both of your sakes."

"When?" Olivia asked.

"Dr. Walters will be taking over the case from here on out. We've reviewed her chart, and he agreed that she should be ready for release within the week."

"Am I no longer able to see her, then?" Olivia asked.

"Dr. Blake, you're exhausted mentally and physically—anyone can see that. I think it's best that you take some time off and get yourself together."

"Is that an order?"

"Does it have to be?" Dr. Iso asked.

"No, sir," she said, pushing herself up from the chair and then forcing her feet to take the few steps to the door, even though she wasn't sure if her legs were strong enough to hold her upright.

"Dr. Blake," Dr. Iso said as she grasped the doorknob.

"Yes?" she said, her heart leaping with hope as she turned to face him.

"I'm sorry. I hope to see you back soon," he said, the steel in his eyes leaving no room for argument despite the gentleness of his tone.

She didn't bother to try to speak, just nodded as she opened the door and stepped into the hallway, then closed it behind her. She stood there under the harsh fluorescent light, her eyes closed and her head bowed, her back pressed against the door, her legs trembling so hard she didn't dare try to reach the bench only a few feet away.

The thought of Delilah living with strangers, no matter how well meaning, filled Olivia with an irrational panic. She told herself it was because of Delilah's fragility, which she supposed was partly true.

Though her physical wounds had healed, she still wouldn't communicate with anyone other than Olivia, and even then, she either refused or was unable to provide any information about her life before that early morning on Highway 24. She'd been interviewed by the best psychiatrist in Colorado and even a doctor visiting from New York who specialized in posttraumatic stress disorder, all to no avail.

"Dr. Blake?" The voice was like a hard slap across the face. Her head snapped up to see Sheldon Myers looking back at her. She must have looked as crazed as she felt, because he took a step back, surprise knocking the smugness from his face.

"Not now, Mr. Myers. For your own sake," she said, pushing herself away from the door.

"Olivia," he said as she turned her back to him and started to walk away. "I'm sorry," he called, stopping her in her tracks.

"What did you say?" she asked, rage making her feel light-headed as she spun around to face him.

"Look, I know you feel like you have a special connection to that girl, but everyone's saying you've gone too far."

"And what concern is that of yours, Sheldon?"

She didn't realize that she'd moved toward him, but she saw the alarm on his face as he backed away from her.

"You're right—maybe it shouldn't be my concern, but we all know what you've been through. And I know you feel like I may not have been fair in my telling of your story. Maybe you're right. I'd like a chance to make that up to you, if I could."

"How stupid do you think I am, Sheldon? You don't care about me or anyone else. You're just a nasty little snake slithering around here trying to make everyone else as miserable as you," she said, her anger now replaced by the hatred that flowed between them unchecked.

"I may be a snake, as you say, but that doesn't change the fact that this girl is *not* your dead daughter, as you well know," he said, the words slamming into her with the force of a closed fist, knocking away all conscious thought.

From a distance she could hear Dr. Iso's voice, but she couldn't make out what he was saying. She heard Sheldon scream, his voice pitched high with fear, as she stomped toward him, her hand raised, wanting nothing more than to inflict on him at least a tiny bit of the pain that he had dealt out for so long. Then she turned to see Dr. Iso standing in the doorway of his office, his face a picture of shock. And, finally, the tears came, rolling down her cheeks in streams as if they would never stop. She let her arm fall back to her side before turning and walking away.

Chapter 20

Olivia sat on her couch, hugging her legs to her chest. For the moment at least, the sobs had stopped, leaving silent tears to gather on her knees before trickling down her bare legs. How could she have allowed Sheldon to push her so far?

She closed her eyes against the image that sprang to her mind of standing in the middle of the floor, shaking like one of those tiny dogs that never seemed to be able to stay warm, words flowing from her mouth that were better suited for a drunken Saturday-night bar fight than the middle of a hospital, while Sheldon stared at her in horror. There was no doubt in her mind that she could have hit him, but by some miracle, she had found the self-control necessary to stay her hand long enough for him to scurry away to safety, like the cockroach he was.

A brisk knock on the door startled her. She didn't expect anybody and was certainly not in the mood to see anyone. She was sure word had spread that she'd had a breakdown. Maybe she had.

Dr. Iso had walked her to her car and told her that she wasn't allowed to come to the hospital, for any reason, for a week. After the week was over, he would reassess to see if any further action was needed. He hadn't said it, but she didn't need him to; he thought she had completely lost it.

The knock repeated, but this time she heard the scratching of a key in the door. "Fuck," she said, scrubbing the tears from her eyes. If anybody were to ask who she least wanted to see in this moment, her mother, Minnie Blake, would be number one on her list. Olivia leaped from the couch and ran into the bathroom, slamming the door closed just in time to hear her mother's shrill voice as she entered the house.

"Liiiivvy . . . dear, where are you? Why wouldn't you answer the door? I had to use my spare key," she said.

Olivia turned on the cold water in the sink as she looked in the mirror at her red eyes. God, the interrogation she would have to endure if her mother saw her face this way.

"Olivia, are you all right?" her mother called from outside the locked bathroom door.

"Yes, Mother, I just have a bit of a cold. I'll be right out."

"Fine, dear. I'll make you some soup after I unpack, if you have any food in this house," her mother called.

"Damn," Olivia said to her reflection, feeling the tears start to gather in her eyes again at the thought of being stuck with her mother.

They had been close once, back before Olivia had learned to think for herself and form her own opinions and beliefs. Then her mother had taken pride in showing her off to her friends, going so far as to dress them in matching outfits. There was nothing she'd loved more than when people would call Olivia her Mini-Me.

Olivia still remembered snowy winter days spent baking cookies with her mother, followed by hours of snuggling on the couch, watching cartoons or movies, where the beautiful princess was saved from some evil by the handsome prince, and they always lived happily ever after. Those had been the good old days.

It was high school when it had all started to fall apart. Suddenly, every choice Olivia made was wrong. Her friends, the books she loved, her music, her clothes—all unacceptable in her mother's eyes. But in the end, it was Olivia's rejection of her mother's religious beliefs that had destroyed any hope of them ever finding their way back to any semblance of the relationship they'd once shared. Still, sometimes she found herself wishing for her mother, whom she loved and who loved her so fiercely, to return, no matter how useless that wish seemed.

Olivia shook her head at the pitiful picture reflected back from the mirror as she listened to her mother's footsteps marching up the stairs, the sound of her suitcase thumping behind her as she went. With a final swipe at her puffy eyes, she turned and opened the door. As she climbed the stairs, she could hear her mother singing to herself. Despite everything, she felt a smile tug at the corners of her lips, until she poked her head into the guest room and saw the size of the suitcase leaning against the foot of the bed. Her mother was not planning on leaving anytime soon.

"God damn it," Olivia said.

"Olivia, don't you dare take the Lord's name in vain," her mother said, making Olivia feel like a child as she fell under her disapproving gaze.

"Sorry, Mom, I didn't mean anything."

"Olivia, have you been drinking?"

"No, Mother, I haven't been drinking," she said, irritation wiping away the momentary pleasure she'd felt at having her mother there.

"Well, don't act like it's not a valid question. I saw the news. It's awful about that child. Was that Brandon standing by your side?"

"Yes, Mom, it was Brandon."

"He looked wan. I don't know why you won't take him back. It's obvious he still loves you, and you know you'll never find anyone better."

"Mom, Brandon has a fiancée. You know that," she said. She'd rather relive the horror of that scene with Sheldon a million more times in slo-mo than tell her mother about Lisa's decision to leave. The mere thought of that conversation put every one of her teeth on edge.

"He's only with her because he can't have you. He'll never marry her—mark my words."

She could still hear her mother's voice squawking complaints about Lisa, but her mind had drifted back to Brandon. It had been so long since she'd thought about their marriage. It didn't matter. Contrary to what her mother or Lisa thought, Brandon was not hers. She had given up all rights to him when she shut him out, choosing to turn to her good friend vodka instead of sharing her pain with the only other person who could have understood how she felt.

"Olivia, are you listening to me?" her mother said.

"Yes, Mother, I heard you."

"Fine. I know you won't listen to me, but you know I'm right."

"Yes, Mother, you're absolutely right. I'm sorry, God," Olivia said, unable to keep the sarcasm from her voice.

"God don't like ugly, Olivia."

"Mom, honestly, I am sorry, but I'm having a really bad day. Why are you here?"

"I didn't know I needed a reason to see my child, but if you don't want me here, I can leave," she said, turning on her heel and walking out of the room before stomping down the stairs.

"You forgot your suitcase," Olivia mumbled, sinking onto the bed.

Instead of following her mother, Olivia returned to her bed and burrowed under the covers, the sound of pots and pans ringing through her head like cymbals until she finally, mercifully drifted away into sleep.

The familiar smell of her mom's chicken soup teased Olivia's nose. A night-light plugged into the wall created a small circle of dim light near the foot of the bed. For a moment Olivia was a little girl, safe and warm. As memories of the day crept into her consciousness, she closed her eyes, burrowing back down into the soft covers, determined to reject reality for a few moments longer.

There was a soft knock. Olivia heard the door creak as her mother eased it open. Brandon had promised to fix the hinge for years, but somehow life had always seemed to get in the way. After rolling onto her side, Olivia was reaching to turn on the lamp just as her mother stepped into the room holding a tray with a steaming bowl of soup, a glass of cold ginger ale, and a row of saltine crackers. She set the tray on the nightstand and leaned down to touch Olivia's forehead before sitting beside her on the bed.

"When you were eight years old, you had the most god-awful flu," her mom said. "You couldn't get out of bed for a week. I know you don't remember your grandmother very well, but she was a hard woman. I don't know why, exactly, but we could never find a way to get along. But the Lord blessed me with Helen. She was more a mother to me than the woman who birthed me.

"Back then we didn't drag a child to the doctor for every hiccup, so I went to Helen. She showed me how to make you chicken soup. She made you a tea, her mother's own remedy from the sap of the pine trees growing out back of the house. It was the only thing you could keep down for any amount of time. When your fever finally broke, I cried like a baby. Your grandmother scolded me for being silly, but I didn't care. I thought I was going to lose you, same as my friend Mabel lost her little girl."

Her mother rose from the bed, walked to the window, and pulled back the curtain. Her face looked like a ghost reflected in the glass as she stared out into the starless night. Olivia thought about her and Arlene's earlier behavior toward Helen. Her mother had never talked much about her relationship with Helen, or if she had, Olivia had not paid her any attention, and now hearing about the woman's kindness made her feel guilty.

"One morning I came in and found you just like you are now, buried in the covers like you were trying to keep the world out. It was then that I knew you were going to be all right," she said. Olivia was surprised to see her mother's hand creep up her face and wipe her cheek.

"Mom?" Olivia said. When her mother didn't answer, Olivia moved to get out of bed, but her mother turned to face her, eyes damp, a tiny smile on her lips.

"I should have made you get out of bed that day, but instead we spent the day reading and playing checkers. The next day, you woke up and got out of bed like the sickness had never touched you. Seems to me you needed that extra day then, same as you need it now."

"Mom, I'm not sick."

"Maybe not, but soup doesn't hurt either way, does it?" her mother said as she turned and walked out of the room.

"Guess not," Olivia said, reaching for the tray.

She had nearly finished the soup and was considering taking another nap when the doorbell rang. She barely had time to wonder who it could be before she heard Arlene's surprised voice. Olivia suppressed a laugh at the thought of Arlene and her mother being trapped together even for the few seconds it would take for her mother to show her friend inside.

Olivia had known Arlene from the time they'd started undergrad together, back when she still dated boys. Her mother had found Arlene charming in those days, just the kind of girl Olivia should befriend. That all changed when Arlene came out during their senior year.

After that, her mother had banned Arlene from the house and even threatened to stop paying Olivia's tuition if she didn't move out of the dorm room they shared. When Olivia refused, Arlene had taken matters into her own hands and moved off campus to live with her first girlfriend, making sure to send Olivia's mother a change-of-address card, along with a picture of her kissing her girlfriend.

Olivia swung her feet off the side of the bed and was preparing to stand up when her mother appeared in the doorway.

"You have company," she said, then turned and walked away before Olivia could respond.

"Thanks," Olivia said to her retreating back. She dragged herself from the bed and hurried downstairs into the living room.

Arlene sat on the couch, her body tense and leaning forward. As Olivia entered the room, the sound of the guest bedroom door slamming made both Arlene and Olivia jump. Their eyes met across the room, and they fell onto the couch, giggling like schoolgirls.

"Girl, I can't lie: that woman scares me. Why didn't you tell me she was here? You know I wouldn't have come anywhere near this place."

"Well, it's not like I knew myself. She just appeared out of nowhere."

"Damn, well, next time, please, send me an SOS or something. My nerves can't handle Minnie Blake without prior warning. What's she doing here, anyway?"

"I don't know. Like I said, she just showed up."

"Do you want me to leave? I don't want to cause any drama."

"Arlene, this is *my* house. You don't have to go anywhere. If she doesn't like it, she can leave." Olivia pulled the soft wool throw around her shoulders.

"All right then, girl, go on with yo' bad self," Arlene said, laughing.

"That's right, I'm a grown-up," Olivia whispered, laughing along with Arlene.

"I'm so glad to see you in a better mood," Arlene said, reaching out to grab Olivia's hand.

"So, how bad is it?"

"What?" Arlene said, an innocent look on her face.

"You know what. How bad is the gossip at the hospital?"

"Fine. Let's just say it couldn't be worse if you'd stripped butt naked and done a samba on Iso's desk."

"Damn it, what are they saying?"

"Well, I've heard everything from you had a meltdown and had to be carried away in a straitjacket to you attacked Sheldon Myers and were taken away in handcuffs. That didn't happen, did it? I mean, the Sheldon thing?"

"Almost," Olivia said.

"You lie! Girl, what the hell happened?"

After she'd finished telling Arlene everything that had happened outside Dr. Iso's office, her friend just sat, shaking her head.

"I'm sorry, Olivia. I wish I could have been there."

"It's not your fault. I played right into that asshole's hand."

"Did Iso see the whole thing?"

"The part where I almost slapped the holy hell out of Sheldon Myers? Yep."

"Damn."

"I know. I'm so mad at myself. I can't believe I let that bastard get under my skin the way he did. I could have killed him."

"You know he's going to try to make your life miserable from now on."

"He already has once. I won't let him do it again. I can't. He's a monster. Why can't anyone see that? I can't let him hurt her. I can't. You know what he did to us, to Carly. He's going to do it all over again. I have to protect Delilah," Olivia moaned.

She fell into Arlene's arms, soaking the front of her sweatshirt with her tears. Her friend held her close until she was calm again, never once trying to quiet the storm of her emotions. When she felt like she could speak again without losing control, Olivia sat up, leaning back until her head rested against the couch.

"Better?" Arlene asked.

"Empty," Olivia said.

"Good enough for now."

"Water?" Olivia asked.

"Sure," Arlene said.

Olivia took her time walking to the kitchen. By the time she came back carrying two bottles of water, Arlene was sitting on the couch, her legs folded up under her like she was intending to stay there forever.

"It's going to be okay, you know?" she said.

"I know. Sorry about your sweatshirt," Olivia said, tossing Arlene a bottle of water before she sat back down.

"Is there anything else you want to tell me?" Arlene asked as Olivia settled herself back onto the couch.

"I met Lisa," she said after taking a swig of water. The expression on Arlene's face was so comical that Olivia nearly gagged on her water.

"Come again?" Arlene said.

"You heard me."

"Wow! What happened? Was she pissed? Did she try and kill you?"

"Nothing. She was beautiful and cool, and she told me she's leaving, maybe going back to Kansas or something like that."

"What? How could you not have started with that? Why? Did she tell you? What did Brandon say? Jesus, you're the worst story-teller ever."

"I'm sorry," Olivia said, unable to stop herself from giggling at the pure outrage covering Arlene's face. "She just said it was time and that she knew he was going to need me, and she asked me to be there for him."

"What? I can't believe you. Why aren't you over there right now, comforting him?"

"Because she's wrong. Brandon's not going to be okay with her just leaving. Even if he does have some stray feelings for me, he loves her. If you saw her, you'd understand why. Hell, *I* might be in love with her." Olivia's heart twisted with misery as she thought about their meeting.

"Was she that pretty?"

"*Pretty* doesn't even come close. This woman makes Iman look like an average soccer mom. And that's without a glam squad at her disposal. Worse, she's a good person. Like, a really good person. I talked to her for five minutes and walked away feeling better than talking to my therapist for a year. Except for the guilt, that is."

"Shit," Arlene said, shaking her head. "Is she fat?"

"Shut up, Arlene."

"Sorry, I was just trying to help. Bad breath?"

"Not even. Let's just say Brandon will not be happy to lose her, especially if I'm the consolation prize."

"All right now, that's enough of that. I don't give a damn if she's Beyoncé mixed with Halle, with a little Toni thrown in for good measure. That has nothing to do with you and Brandon. And obviously, on top of all her other gifts, she's got brains, too, because she was able to see that. Listen, you don't have to go rushing over there right now, but don't wait too long. You need each other right now, and the universe has seen fit to give you a second chance. Don't blow it."

"Mama would say it's God," Olivia said.

"Whatever works," Arlene said, turning to take Olivia's hands in her own. "Seriously. I'm telling you this with all the love in my heart. Don't be a dumbass. Go get your man."

"I hear you. I promise. But I just need to take a breath and regroup."

"Yeah, okay. So, did Iso give you any idea as to what he plans to do?"

"With work? I don't know. He said I couldn't come back to the hospital for at least a week, then he would reassess the situation."

"Maybe things aren't as bad as you thought," Arlene said, evidently trying, but failing, to sound hopeful.

"Yeah, and maybe I can build a time machine and go back to this morning and behave like a perfectly respectable doctor and all-around intelligent human being."

"Come on, Livvy, don't be so hard on yourself. You've been under a lot of stress lately, what with this girl and everything."

"Everyone is acting like what happened to this poor child is her fault. This isn't her fault. Do you know they're going to release her within a week, to God knows where—a group home, a state facility, some foster home with people she doesn't even know or trust?"

"All right, don't get yourself all worked up. You've been through enough today. We can talk about this later. Right now, I'm going to get out of here before Minnie comes back. If you need anything, just give me a call. You know I'm here for you."

"Arlene, there is one thing," Olivia said, unable to bring herself to look her friend in the eyes. She knew she was wrong, knew it beyond a shadow of a doubt, but she had no choice. Arlene was her only chance.

"Yes?"

"I've been thinking."

"That's always dangerous," Arlene said.

"About Delilah."

"Uh-huh."

"I want to bring her here, to stay with me, just until they find her family."

"And if they never find her family?"

"I'll deal with that then," Olivia said, shrugging.

"You know getting approved to become a foster parent isn't exactly quick, especially when it's such a high-profile case. Didn't you say she was being released within the week?"

"I know. That's where you come in. I know it's out of line, and I swear under any other circumstances, I wouldn't ask, but I don't have any choice. Could you—"

"Olivia, please don't . . ."

"I know, I know, but it's the only way. I'm desperate. Please, will you talk to Melinda to see if there's anything she can do to help? Maybe she could fast-track my application, even if it's just an interview?"

"You know I can't. She's the case manager supervisor, for Chrissake. I can't ask her to risk her job, no matter how much I love you. I'm sorry, I can't."

Olivia leaned forward and buried her face in her hands. She had gone too far. She knew it, but she hadn't had any choice. Delilah needed her. Even now, with her whole world blowing up around her, all she could think about was keeping the girl safe. No one understood. No one really could.

"Livvy, are you okay?" Arlene asked.

Olivia felt her friend's hand on her back, tentative and unsure. She sat up, painting a weak smile on her face.

"It's okay. I'm okay," she said. "After the way I showed my ass this morning, Jesus Christ himself probably couldn't help. I'm sorry I put you on the spot. I just . . . I don't know. I'm sorry."

Arlene scooted closer and put her arm around Olivia's rigid shoulders. They sat together, not speaking, until Olivia's shoulders finally relaxed and she laid her head on Arlene's shoulder, her eyes dry, even though her heart felt like it was breaking into pieces.

"Olivia, do you think it's possible that maybe you're just a little bit *too* involved here? Maybe having Delilah live with you isn't such a great idea."

"Wow, Arlene. You know, it's been a terrible day, and I don't feel so good. If you don't mind, I'm going to go back to bed. You can see yourself out." Olivia pushed herself away from Arlene, jumped up from the couch, and hurried from the room, running up the stairs as the tears started to fall again.

Olivia hesitated at the top of the stairs, wanting to rush back downstairs and apologize to Arlene, but she couldn't force herself to move. Once she heard the front door snap closed, she looked down the hall at the guest bedroom and saw that the door was still shut tight. She wiped her face and walked over and tapped on the door. When her mother answered, she pushed it open. Her mom was sitting in bed reading her Bible by the light of the lamp on the nightstand, her reading glasses perched on her nose, an oversize scarf wrapped around her hair.

"Is that enough light?" Olivia asked.

"It's fine," her mother said, her shoulders tightening.

"Okay, well, I just wanted to make sure you were all right. I'm going to bed now. Good night."

"Olivia," her mother called as she turned away.

Though Olivia was tempted to act like she hadn't heard, she turned to face her, certain she didn't want to hear what she had to say.

"I don't think it looks right for a woman like Arlene to be in your house at all hours, especially since you don't have a husband around any longer."

Normally her mother's insinuations would have started a heated argument, but tonight she was too drained to respond.

"I'm a Christian woman, Olivia. God teaches us to hate the sin, not the sinner. I will pray for her, but there isn't any reason for you to risk your place in God's kingdom by knowingly associating yourself with immorality. I mean, seriously, Olivia, what must the neighbors think?"

"How's Daddy, Mom?" she asked. As soon as the words were out of her mouth, she wished she could call them back. She watched her mother's hazel eyes cloud with pain and knew she had gone too far.

Two years ago, her father had come home from work, sat down on the couch, and asked his wife to pour him a drink. By the time she'd returned with it, she found her husband bent over, sobbing into his hands.

After polishing off his drink in one gulp, he looked his wife of forty years in the eyes and told her that he was in love with his secretary, a man who'd been so close to the family that Olivia had grown up calling him Uncle Brian.

Her mother had packed her bags and somehow made the forty-five-minute trip from her home in Denver to Colorado Springs. Olivia had come home to find her sitting on the steps, eyes swollen from crying, hair standing on end as if she'd tried to pull it out strand by strand, and babbling like a wounded child.

For days she had lain in bed, refusing to eat or speak. Finally, after Olivia had threatened to have her forcefully committed, the story leaked out between uncontrollable sobs and wild laughter that had raised goose bumps on Olivia's body. When she was done, Olivia had crawled into the bed and wrapped her arms around her, holding her close as she cried.

The next morning, her mother had gotten up early and filled the house with the smell of fresh coffee and frying bacon. Despite Olivia's begging her to stay, she'd insisted that it was time to return home, making Olivia promise never to talk to her father about what she had told her. Her mother returned home that day like the conversation with her dad had never happened, and they'd never spoken about that night again.

"Good night, Olivia. Please shut the door behind you," her mother said now.

"Mom, I'm sorry."

"*Good night*, Olivia," her mother said, closing the Bible and reaching to turn off the lamp.

Chapter 21

Brandon sat at his empty kitchen table, holding the letter in one hand and a cup of coffee that somehow managed to taste too strong and too watery at the same time in the other. Making coffee was a skill that he had never mastered. Being forced to drink his own brew only made him miss Lisa that much more.

Since she left, he'd submerged himself in work, volunteering for any overtime that was offered. He worked so many hours that when he did finally drag himself home, he was too tired to think, and he often fell asleep without bothering to eat. Any spare time he had, he spent using all his contacts, including Smitty, to try to learn anything he could about Delilah. Maybe because he felt sorry for him, or just wanted to encourage him to join the force, even the LT ignored his constant presence in the squad room.

He told himself that he couldn't let go because he was the one who found her, but he knew it was far more than that. He acknowledged that a large part of not wanting to let go was because of Olivia and the haunted look in her eyes he was desperate to wipe away, but that wasn't the whole story. As much as he wanted to ignore that feeling, bury it even, he couldn't pretend he didn't see the similarities between this girl and his Carly, same as Olivia. But besides their physical similarities, he just couldn't see a connection.

He had managed to stay away from the hospital, not wanting to risk running into Olivia, not sure what he would say if he should see her. He loved her, he always had, he supposed, but he couldn't begin to think about a possible future with her before settling things between himself and Lisa. A letter would never be enough; Lisa deserved more than that.

He took a sip from the bitter, lukewarm coffee and weighed the letter in his hand. It felt light, no heavier than a postcard, certainly not heavy enough to end a two-year relationship. Setting the cup down, he ripped open the envelope. A single folded page of Lisa's lavender stationery slid to the table. As he reached for the paper, he noticed something sticking out from within the folds, and tears instantly stung his eyes.

He didn't have to open the letter to recognize the ribbon that Joe had made for Brandon's daughter so long ago. Suddenly he didn't want to read the letter. He slammed his open hand onto the table hard enough to make his palm sting and his coffee spill, and he jumped up and grabbed his jacket from the back of the chair.

He made it all the way out the door before he stopped. He stood on the second step, staring at his work truck. He could get in that truck, drive to work, stay there for the next twelve hours, and not think about anything. He could, but he was tired, so tired. He turned and looked through the still-open door. On the table the letter waited, along with the ribbon, intended for a child long gone from his life and, his heart told him, this world.

Turning his back on the waiting truck, he reentered the house, trudged across the kitchen floor like a man heading to his death, and slowly removed his jacket. He lowered himself back into the chair and picked up the letter, opening it carefully so the ribbon would not fall. Taking a deep breath, he began to read, not stopping until he came to the end. When he was done, he sat in the quiet room, not moving, barely breathing, feeling his heart hammer in his chest. If he moved, he would cry, he thought, and if he started to cry, he would never stop.

What seemed like a long time later, after his heart had slowed and his hands had stopped shaking, he picked up the note—because that's all it was, really—and reread it slowly, savoring every word.

Dearest Brandon,

Please know that although my heart yearns for you, our time together is done. I send prayers of gratitude to the fates for allowing me to walk your path with you, short though our time seemed. Now, it is time for you to go home, rejoin your wife, and bring healing to you both. The times ahead will be dark. Stay strong, Brandon, and let your light banish this evil back to the darkness whence it came. When your work is done, return to Kansas, and pay tribute to your friend for this token of love so honestly given. All will be well.

 Lisa

Brandon picked up Joe's ribbon and rubbed it against his face. Was he imagining the scent of pine and apple that always seemed to surround Lisa, no matter the season? He supposed he was, but still it made him feel a little less alone and just a little more hopeful.

Slowly he folded the letter and slid it back into its envelope. The ribbon he tucked into his wallet, where it rested on top of the last picture ever taken of his little girl.

"It's beautiful," he said out loud.

He wouldn't go to work today, maybe not tomorrow either. He would call his boss and ask for a leave of absence. Then he would sleep, and when he woke up, he would eat, and then he would go to Olivia, just like Lisa said.

Chapter 22

Fear. That's what Delilah felt. The only thing she felt. She didn't know how long it had been since Olivia had gone away. She'd tried to keep track of time by counting the nights, but they'd all seemed to run together ever since they started giving her the medicine every night. The new doctor said that it was supposed to keep the nightmares away and help her sleep, but the nightmares were still there, except now she was trapped, dragged so far down into the dark that she couldn't force her eyes open to let in the light. The policeman who used to sit by her bed and talk nice to the night nurses was gone, too, but Jacob was still there. He and Mother. They came to visit every night.

She hadn't spoken a single word since Olivia had stopped coming to see her, but she had heard plenty. The nurses said Olivia had lost it. They whispered about a lost child, a child who looked like her. Sometimes the mean man with the frog-like eyes would come in the middle of the night with a man who would ask her questions about where she came from and what had happened to her. They would stand over her and stare at her until she turned her head or closed her eyes. Sometimes, she would try to play like she was asleep.

Today she sat in the rocking chair, staring out into the bright sun, waiting for the social worker to come. The redheaded nurse had told her to be nice. She said that the social worker would help find her a home. All she wanted was for Olivia to come back.

She thought about the paper and pen the nurses had given her—to help her communicate, they'd said. If she had them now, she could send Olivia a message, but what would she say? The sight of those books had filled her with terror. Girls weren't meant to read or write, lest they become corrupted, so said Father, so said the Lord.

But that hadn't stopped Sunny from trying to teach her the little she knew, whenever she could. Even Jacob had tried, but still, Delilah could only write the letters of the alphabet and her name, and read a few small words. Even now, the thought of those books filled with shiny, slippery pages of nearly naked women displayed in obscene poses made her heart beat faster in her chest. She started to pray, begging for God's forgiveness over and over in her head.

Chapter 23

Olivia sat on the porch steps, staring into the empty street. It was the middle of the afternoon, and most people, she supposed, would be at work. It was strangely warm for an early January day, and bright sun shone on her face. Behind her, the door banged shut, and her mother appeared on the porch as if Olivia's thoughts had conjured her.

"You'll catch pneumonia sitting out here without any clothes on, and what'll that get you?"

"Mother, I'm fully clothed," Olivia said, keeping her reply simple in hopes that she would give up and go away.

"I hardly call your pajamas and a robe *clothes*. What must the neighbors think? Don't you think they're going to notice you sitting here in your bedclothes in the middle of the day like you don't have anywhere to go? How long do you think it's going to take them to figure out that you've lost your position and spread the news around the neighborhood?"

"Don't you mean nosy Ms. Helen? I don't care what she or anyone else has to say, and I haven't lost my *position*. I'm simply taking a few days off. Haven't you ever heard of a vacation?"

"Honestly, Olivia, you know how much Helen cares for you. It wouldn't hurt you to look in on her a little more."

"Mother, you know I don't have time to spend hours gossiping with Ms. Helen."

"Well, you sure seem to have the time to worry about a girl you don't even know. Helen is family."

"She's not *my* family," Olivia mumbled.

"That's not very Christian, Olivia. I raised you better than that."

"Why don't you go see her yourself? There she is now," Olivia said, raising her arm and waving at Ms. Helen's window, almost laughing out loud as the curtain snapped shut. "See, she's fine."

"Brandon called again. Don't you think you should give him the courtesy of hearing what he has to say?"

"Mother, please, can't you leave me alone for just a little while?" Olivia asked, lowering her face into her hands.

"It seems to me that's the last thing you need right now. I was thinking, since you don't have anywhere else to go, you should come stay with me and your father until you can pull yourself together." Her mother then turned and walked away before Olivia had a chance to answer.

"Oh God," Olivia said as the door slammed shut.

As she was dragging herself to her feet to follow her mother, Brandon pulled up in front of the house, parking his big black truck against the curb.

"Jesus H. Christ," she said as she sank back down onto the porch step. Glancing down at her worn black-and-white-checkered pajama pants and scruffy gray robe, she raised a hand to touch the two plaits she had braided her hair into, wondering if she could remove them before he noticed.

She watched him approach, his long strides cutting across the yard in no more than a few steps. She had just enough time to hope that she was dreaming before he stood in front of her, blocking out the sun, all too real.

"Hi," she said, offering a weak smile as she looked up into his scowling face.

"*Hi?*" he said. "Where have you been? I've been trying to contact you for days."

"I've been around . . . here," Olivia mumbled, dropping her eyes from his face to look at her feet, wishing again that she could reach up and at least loosen her hair.

"I see that. The question is, Why are you here? Why aren't you at work? I talked to Minnie. She told me you were fired. Is that true?"

"Brandon, why are you here? I don't think I can deal with this right now."

"I'm here because I was worried about you. When I heard what happened at the hospital—"

"Well, you don't have to worry. I'm fine, and no, I wasn't fired. I'm just taking a few days off, that's all."

"Well, I do worry—I can't help it," he said, lowering himself onto the stair beside Olivia. "I worry about you every day, especially since this whole thing with this girl started." He reached out to take her hand. "Are you okay, Livvy?"

Olivia felt the tears, hot and sharp, burning her eyes, and she fought, using all her strength, to push them back. She could fall apart right now, and Brandon would take her into his arms and make everything seem all right. He would, because he did worry about her; he always had. If she asked him to, he would stay. She could almost hear her mother's voice urging her on, but instead she steeled herself to the concern in his face and raised her dry eyes to meet his.

"I'm fine, Brandon. I'm just tired of everyone acting like I'm some fragile porcelain doll on the verge of shattering any damn minute. Yes, I had a bit of a meltdown at the hospital. I'm not the first, and I certainly won't be the last. And yes, Brandon, you were right. I did get too emotionally attached to this poor girl. But really, who could blame me? I'm human, aren't I? Tomorrow I'm going to get up, get dressed, and go back to work. I am, and I will continue to be, just damn fine."

She stood up and stalked across the porch into the house, almost knocking her mother down as she barreled through the front door. "Oh, for pity's sake, Mother, eavesdropping?"

"I was not eavesdropping. I was just coming to say hello to Brandon and see if you two needed anything. You didn't run him away, did you?"

"Yes, Mother. Yes, I did. I threw stones at him from the porch until he ran away crying. He's never coming back, never!" Olivia turned her back and stomped away, shocking her mother into silence, if only for a few moments.

"Honestly, Olivia, you're acting like a child," her mother called.

Olivia didn't bother to respond. Instead, she stomped up the stairs to her room and slammed the door. As she walked toward her bed, her eyes caught her reflection. Her mother was right. Not only was she in the midst of a teenage tantrum, but she looked the part.

"He *would* choose today to show up," she said to her reflection. "Hell, yesterday wouldn't have been any better." She sighed.

Turning away from the sorry reflection in the mirror, she riffled through her drawers for clean clothes before rushing into the bathroom to take her first shower in two days.

Chapter 24

Olivia crept down the stairs and through the house until she stood outside the kitchen door. Brandon sat at the table with her mother. Olivia could hear her mother's voice droning on and on, about what, she had no clue. She wondered if Minnie had stopped talking since she'd stormed out of the room. Maybe she thought that if she stopped, Brandon would leave. From where she stood, peeking into the kitchen, she could see Brandon, a plate with a thick slice of cake in front of him, sipping from a mug of coffee, occasionally nodding or grunting to show he was paying attention. If she didn't get back in there soon, he would probably never sleep again.

Taking a deep breath, she stepped into the kitchen. Minnie stopped talking in midsentence. No one spoke for a few moments, and then Minnie pushed her chair away from the table and stood.

"Brandon, it was lovely to see you again, and I hope to see more of you, but this old lady is tired," she said, not turning to look at Olivia. "I hope you will excuse me. I think I'll go visit Helen before I lay these old bones down. I want to make sure she's all right before I head home in the morning."

"Yes, ma'am," Brandon said.

"Mom, really, you don't have to go," Olivia said, hoping she sounded sincere but knowing she didn't.

"Yes, I do—your father needs me, and I've been gone far too long. I only came here to make sure you were all right, and I see you are."

"Don't you worry about Olivia, Minnie. I'll look after her. You need to go home to take care of Pops. You know the old man gets lonely without you."

Shame washed over her again as she saw the joy that Brandon's simple words brought her mother.

"You're a good boy, Brandon." Minnie bent down to touch her lips lightly to his cheek. "My daughter would be foolish to forget that," she said before walking out the door, leaving Olivia alone with Brandon.

"Are you okay?" Brandon asked. He stood up and pulled a seat out from the table for her.

"You mean besides being an ass?" Olivia asked as she sank into the chair.

"Yes, besides that."

"I swear I don't know how you do it. I'm in the room with her for five minutes, and we're trying to scratch each other's eyes out. You, you've got her eating out of the palm of your hand."

"Minnie's fine. She just loves you and has a really hard time show-ing it. She's worried about you, you know."

"Yeah, I know. I told her, I'm fine."

"Are you?"

"I will be."

"I know you will, but I had to check on you. If I didn't, Arlene was going to kill me." He grinned.

At the mention of Arlene's name, Olivia dropped her eyes to the table, hoping he didn't know about their fight.

"You know you were wrong, right?" he asked.

"God, can't anyone keep their mouths shut around here?"

"Olivia . . ."

"Fine. I was wrong. I was wrong about Arlene. I never should have asked her to ask Melissa to do anything that would compromise her professionally. I know that. I was wrong about Delilah. I should have passed her case on to someone else as soon as I saw her. I just couldn't. She needs me, Brandon. So, I'm wrong, okay? I admit it!" she yelled, dissolving into little-girl sobs as he stood and pulled her into his arms, molding her into his chest, smoothing her hair, and rubbing her back. A memory of him holding Carly in the same way after she'd had her first fight with her best friend over a jump rope flashed into her head, making her cry even harder.

"I want her back . . . I want her back . . . I want her back," she repeated over and over again, not realizing she was speaking the words until she felt Brandon's body shaking and looked up to see his face covered in his own tears.

"I do too," he said.

"I hated you," Olivia said calmly, looking into his face, not blinking away from the pain she saw in his eyes. "I hated you for not being able to find her."

"I blamed you," Brandon said. "You fell asleep, and I blamed you for not watching her."

"I blamed you too," Olivia said, then pulled away from him and walked to the sink, giving Brandon a moment to collect himself as she filled up two glasses with water, wishing it were her old friend vodka.

"I know. I blamed myself too."

"There was plenty of it to go around," Olivia said. She sat back down in the chair across from Brandon and slid him the lukewarm glass of water.

"I still remember every second of that day," he said. "I had a softball game on base. You and Carly were supposed to come watch."

Oh God, please make him stop, Olivia prayed.

"But you had one of your migraines, and you couldn't go. I didn't want to take Carly, because I couldn't watch her while I played ball and drank beer with the boys, so I left her with you. I knew you would fall asleep. I thought you'd already taken your medicine, but you said you'd be fine, and I told myself that I believed you would be. But really, I just didn't think it would matter. Carly was safe at home. I never believed . . . thought that there would be anything to worry about, not here," he said, his voice sounding like a plea. "I just never thought . . . and when I came back and she was gone . . ."

"I'm so sorry."

For a few moments, they sat, tears rolling silently down their faces, not touching, the only sound in the kitchen the sound of their breathing.

"I'm sorry," he said, finally reaching across the table to touch her hand. "I wasn't there for you when you needed me most. I was so filled with self-pity and guilt. I left you to handle all of this alone. It took me months of therapy to admit that to myself, and I should have told you this a long time ago: I'm sorry."

"I remember that day too," she said, her words breathing life into the ghost swirling around her heart. "I told you we couldn't go to the game because I had a migraine, but I was fine. It was hot and I was tired. It was my first day off in ten days, and all I wanted was to stay at home and be quiet. I lied to you.

"After you left, Carly begged to go outside and play, but I just wanted to have a glass of wine and read a book. I was so tired. I dozed off. I must have left the door open. The next thing I know, you were pulling into the driveway, and our baby was gone."

Olivia wanted to hang her head and hide her face from his eyes, but she didn't; instead she met his eyes with her own. "I'm sorry. I allowed you to carry guilt around that wasn't yours."

Brandon rose and pulled Olivia from her chair and into his arms. For a while they stood together, their bodies shaking with grief that had been locked away for too long. After the tears had subsided, he leaned down and found her lips with his own. When they were able to pull away, they looked into each other's eyes, both suddenly exhausted.

"Sometimes, when we're alone, I call her Carly," Olivia said. "I know it's not right or healthy, but I can't stop myself."

"I understand. It's why I've been trying so hard to keep my distance. She's not Carly. She needs you, but she needs you to be there for her, not as a fill-in for our lost child. I want to help her find her way home. I feel like that's the best way to honor our baby girl. Do you understand?"

"I do. I'm just not there. Not yet, but I'm trying."

"That's all you can do," he said. "I should go."

"Yes," she said, nodding, but she didn't step away from the circle of his arms.

"I'm sorry, I want to stay. I want to be with you—please believe me. But I think we need some time. Things just feel so raw between us in this moment. I want us both to have a chance to process everything and choose to be with each other for no other reason than because it's what we want. Do you understand?"

"Yes," she said again, this time stepping outside his grasp.

"I love you," he said simply, reaching for her hand.

"I love you too," she said, looking up at him, tears shining in her eyes.

Together they walked across the room to the door. Olivia was surprised to see that night had fallen.

"Where did the day go?" Brandon said, looking into the night.

"I was just wondering the same thing," Olivia said.

"Good night, Livvy," he said, bending down to kiss her lightly on the cheek.

"Please stay," she whispered to herself as he walked away from her down the stairs.

When he got to his truck, he turned to wave at her. In the dim light shining down from the streetlamp, it seemed as if time had magically rolled back, and he was her young husband again, his boyhood barely behind him.

"Good night," she called, raising her hand to wave at him as he got into the truck.

She stood there for a while staring into the empty night. As she turned to go into the house, a movement caught her eye from the bushes surrounding Ms. Helen's house. For a moment she thought she saw a shape, surrounded by shadows, silently watching her.

Fear seized her body, freezing her to the spot. She closed her eyes. When she opened them again, the only thing she saw was Ms. Helen's curtain twitching shut. On shaking legs, she turned and went back into the house, trying her best not to run, then slammed the door a little too hard once she was safely inside.

She tried to convince herself that she had imagined the silent watcher, but she was careful to check that the locks on the doors were secure, and all the windows were locked, before she turned out the lights and went to bed.

As she passed the guest room, she saw the light from under the door and paused. At some point, she remembered hearing her mother come in, but they hadn't spoken. She owed her mother an apology, she knew, but as she approached the door, her resolve failed her. After everything that had happened, she couldn't face the idea of a long emotional battle. She knew that what would start as a simple apology would end in a long, torturous fight. So she turned and walked away.

Chapter 25

Delilah stood silently beside the social worker woman, clutching the plastic bag given to her by one of the nurses. The bag held a pair of pajamas (complete with a pair of pink, fuzzy slippers), a change of clothes, and a stuffed monkey. The nurses had given her the things as a going-away present. Each one of them had signed a card, filling it with pictures of hearts and cartoon drawings, wishing her well as she moved to the El Paso County Group Home for Girls.

The bottom of the bag was filled with candy and other treats. Several of the nurses had tears in their eyes when they came to hug her and wish her well. She was grateful for their kindness, but all she wanted was for Olivia to come for her. Every time she heard someone approaching the room, her heart would jump, but Olivia never came.

"Do you have everything?" Mrs. Kovach asked as she finished signing the discharge papers. She walked toward the door, not bothering to check to see if Delilah was following.

"Wait, you know everybody must ride," the nurse said, wagging her finger in Mrs. Kovach's face. "You stay right there, and I'll have an orderly bring the wheelchair to give our little darling a ride out."

"Oh, for goodness' sake, how long is this going to take? I have other appointments, you know," Mrs. Kovach said as the nurse walked from the room.

Mrs. Kovach ignored the rocking chair and dropped into the hard, straight-backed chair beside the bed. She didn't look at Delilah. Instead, she pulled out her calendar and began writing furiously, stopping every few seconds to check her watch. Delilah stood helplessly in the middle of the room, clutching the plastic bag to her chest, silently begging for Olivia to come.

"Sit down, girl. You're making me nervous standing there like that. These people don't have any respect for people's time." As Delilah moved toward the rocking chair, the man with the mean eyes came into the room.

"Mrs. Kovach? I'm David Pierce, the executive assistant for the hospital chief of staff, Dr. Iso. I'm sure you've met him already." He reached out to shake Mrs. Kovach's hand. "It's wonderful to meet you. I thought I'd missed you."

"Mr. Pierce, I wish I could say it's an equal pleasure to meet you, but unfortunately, I am running extremely late, and no one in this hospital seems to care one whit about wasting my time."

"I'm sorry to hear that. Is there something I can do?"

"You can either allow me to walk out of here with this girl on her own two perfectly capable feet, or you can get us a wheelchair immediately."

"Yes, ma'am, I can take care of that right away. So, it's time for you to leave us, is it?" he asked, turning to Delilah. She recoiled, turning her head away from him to look out the window.

"Do you think that whatever happened to her struck her dumb?" David asked, turning back to Mrs. Kovach.

"I'm sure I don't know, nor is it my responsibility to know, and from what I understand, it's not yours either. My job is to deliver her safely to her new home, which I would like to do, if we can please get a wheelchair."

"Of course, but one more question, if I could. Has the state chosen a temporary home for her, or will she stay at the group home indefinitely?"

"Mr. Pierce, I'm sure you are well aware that I cannot answer that question."

"Sure, I know. I'm sorry. I'm just curious, like everyone else."

Mrs. Kovach didn't answer. Instead, she stood and walked toward the door. "Nurse, we are still waiting for a chair," she called down the hall. The young nurse looked over Mrs. Kovach's shoulder to where David stood.

"Yes, ma'am, right away," she said, after a nod from David.

A few moments later, an orderly pushed a wheelchair into the room.

"Your chariot," he said with a smile that reached all the way up to his eyes.

Delilah tried to smile back at him, but she was too afraid. The orderly stooped down on his knees until he was close enough for her to see the pain cross his face.

"It's time, little miss. These people have done all they can for you. Now you have to depend on the man upstairs," he said, lowering his voice so only she could hear.

Delilah leaned toward him as if she were going to kiss him. It was a good thing he couldn't get up easily, or he would have missed her whispered message.

"Olivia, tell her—" Delilah said, never finishing.

"I'll tell her," the orderly whispered as Mrs. Kovach approached from behind.

"What's going on here? Never have I had so much trouble getting out of a hospital," she boomed from over the orderly's shoulder.

"Time to go," he said, using the chair to prop himself up as he struggled to his feet.

Delilah walked to the wheelchair on shaking legs and sat down. As the man wheeled her from the room and through the winding hallways, she closed her eyes. The sun shining down onto her upturned face should have made her happy, but instead she was filled with dread as the security of the hospital fell away.

Chapter 26

Olivia sat in her office, staring down at the open files splayed across her desk. It had been weeks since she'd returned to work. In that time, she'd tried to regain her footing by submerging herself in cases. She spent twelve to fourteen hours a day at the hospital, partly to avoid going home to her empty house but mostly in an attempt to block out the pain of losing Delilah.

In the weeks since her return, she had not seen Brandon and had had only one short, strange conversation with him, in which he'd told her he was going to Cleveland to track down his old buddy Mike. When she'd tried to get him to tell her what he was up to, he put her off, promising to tell her everything once he returned. She received an occasional vague email, which she read over and over again, trying to glean any hint of what he was doing, or how he was feeling, especially about her.

She hadn't seen Arlene, either, mostly thanks to her skill in avoiding her by hiding behind her work. She owed Arlene an apology, one that she was afraid her friend wouldn't be willing to accept. Still, she knew she had to get it over with at some point. She and Arlene had been friends for far too long for her to lose her over her own foolishness. Glancing down at her watch, she was surprised to see it was lunchtime. A knock on the door made her jump, and before she could answer, the door flung open, and Arlene herself strode in, determination creasing her brow into a frown.

"Listen, I've been trying to give you your space, since I know that you're going through it between this girl and Brandon, but it's time you get over yourself," Arlene said as she walked across the floor before resting her knuckles on the desk.

"Well, hello to you, too, sunshine," Olivia said.

"Hi, yourself. Are you finished with your tantrum?"

"Yes, ma'am," Olivia said, nodding like a kid.

"Good, because if you weren't, I was going to kick your ass from one side of this hospital to the other."

"I was actually just on my way to find you," Olivia said.

"Find me? When was I lost?"

Olivia took a deep breath while Arlene sat down, the frown still firmly on her face, grumbling under her breath.

"I'm sorry," Olivia said in a rush as soon as Arlene was seated.

"What?" her friend asked, looking at Olivia, confusion replacing her frown.

"I'm sorry about how I treated you when you came by to check on me, and I am especially sorry for crossing the line by asking you to ask Melinda for such an inappropriate favor."

"Are you serious? Is this why you've been avoiding me like I was a bill collector? I know why you did what you did. I know what helping this girl meant—means—to you, and I understand that you had to try everything. I would have done the same thing if it were me."

Olivia nodded, not trusting her voice as Arlene sprang from the chair and rushed around the desk to throw her arms around her.

"I'm sorry," Olivia whispered, wrapping her arms around her friend.

"Yeah, me too. Have you heard anything?" Arlene asked, and this time it was Olivia who looked confused. "About Delilah and your application to be her temporary guardian?"

"What are you talking about? You know I didn't complete the application process. What would be the point? Everybody knows how unstable I am."

"Well, that's true . . . You are a little on the nutty side, but in a good way, I assure you." Arlene smiled.

"Yeah, well, tell it to the Colorado Department of Human Services."

"I did, and apparently they agree," Arlene said, slapping a thick folder down on the desk in front of Olivia.

"What's this?" she said, staring at the folder as if it could leap off the desk and bite her.

"Open it and see."

Slowly Olivia reached for the folder and opened it, all the while looking at Arlene.

"Look down, not at me, silly girl," Arlene said.

Olivia lowered her eyes to the open folder, her breath catching in her throat as she saw the completed CDHS application to care for children. On the bottom of the application, her signature had been signed, as well as if she had written it herself.

"Jesus." Olivia sighed, blinking back the tears that rushed to her eyes.

"Hey, Jesus didn't have anything to do with this. Just little old me," Arlene said, batting her eyes at Olivia.

"But what does this mean?" Olivia asked.

"It means that you have officially applied to become a foster parent. Apparently, the requirements to become a foster parent are far less stringent than actually adopting a child. Colorado only requires you to be over the age of twenty-one, have a home to live in and enough money to maintain it, and be able to provide emotional, physical, and mental support. The money and the house were no problem, and based on the number of recommendation letters you received, I think your character and ability to provide a nourishing environment for the child is without question."

"Recommendations? What recommendations?" Olivia said, her voice barely above a whisper. "I never asked for any recommendations."

"That's weird, because they're there—and a good thing, too, after that little show you put on. Lucky for you, Dr. Iso is a very understanding man."

Slowly Olivia lifted the application and started to look through the letters. Not only had Dr. Iso completed a letter, but the heads of all the departments, the director of nursing, and even Brandon had taken the time to sing her praises and vouch for her sanity, along with her ability to provide a stable home for Delilah. Olivia dropped her head into her folded arms on the desk and sobbed.

Once the harsh sobs had dwindled into sniffles and Olivia raised her head, she found Arlene smiling at her.

"You needed that," Arlene said.

"Yes. Thank you," Olivia said.

"You're welcome."

"What now?"

"Well, you have to go to the training class. If you pull out your orientation checklist, you'll see that your first class is scheduled for tomorrow night."

"Orientation checklist?"

"Yes, orientation. Melinda couldn't do much to push you forward in the process, but she was able to rubber-stamp the checklist, with the understanding that you will come over to the house and let her give you a one-on-one orientation, so you'll know what you're getting into. Plus, you'll have to have home visits with the appointed social worker, a Mrs. Kovach. I hear she eats nails for breakfast and takes zero crap. I suggest you get your house in order, because Melinda can't do anything about what she puts in her report either."

"Oh my God, Arlene, you didn't," Olivia said, her eyes growing misty again.

"Okay, enough blubbering. We have a lot to do if this is going to work out. Believe me, I didn't ask Melinda to do anything outside the rules. This was a small thing that she could do, and she was happy to do it," Arlene said, dropping her head to hide her own damp eyes.

"Do you know where she is?"

"Delilah?" Arlene asked.

"Yes, Delilah."

"Well, she's still in the state group home for girls. You'd be shocked to know how many foster homes are not eager to welcome an abused teenager who may or may not be responsible for killing a boy, especially now that the cameras have gone to chase the newest story."

"Arlene, stop. You know the police have cleared her of any wrongdoing. In fact, they believe that she was trying to save him."

"That may be true, but you know how people talk."

"Yes, I do. Those people are assholes. Don't be those people, Arlene."

"Fair enough, my friend. Lord knows, I've been on the business end of some of the idiotic wagging tongues. I offer you, and her, my heartfelt apologies." Arlene placed her hand over her heart.

"Is she okay?" Olivia asked.

"She seems to be fine, but Melinda says she still doesn't talk."

"Do you think I could see her?" Olivia asked.

"I don't see why not. She's not a prisoner." She added, "Do you think it's weird that she still won't speak?"

"She will when she feels safe."

Arlene asked, "Do you think you should wait to take her in until she feels safe enough to tell you a little bit more about what happened? Just so you'll have a better idea of what you're dealing with. I mean, I know you're a superwoman doctor and all, but still."

"I get what you're saying—I do. But I just feel this connection with her. I can't explain it. I feel like once I bring her home, she'll feel safe. Then she can start to heal."

"All right. I just want you to be happy. Oh, and tell me the details about your reunion with Brandon."

"I don't know what you mean." Olivia grinned.

"That's not what *he* said," Arlene said, laughing.

"What did he say?" Olivia asked breathlessly, loving the butterflies she felt in the pit of her stomach at the thought of their kiss.

"Wouldn't you like to know," Arlene said, making kissing noises as she stood to go.

"Oh my God, he didn't," Olivia squealed.

"Didn't what? I gotta go. I'll see you at the house tonight, and you can tell me all the juicy details."

"Give Melinda a kiss for me," Olivia said.

"Get your own woman," her friend said, and with a wave she was gone.

Chapter 27

Brandon sat on a bench, staring across the frozen pond at the majestic white building that housed Cleveland's art museum. Even on this gray winter evening, the tranquil setting was a wonder to him, set as it was in the midst of Cleveland's inner city. The backdrop of the museum, the beautiful trees, and the placid pond that he'd been told was home to a bustling population of ducks and fish made for a very romantic spot. He imagined that in spring and summer the place would be littered with strolling couples.

He'd been in Cleveland for two weeks, reviewing all the old files he could get his hands on from the 1988 cold case of Allison Moore. He couldn't have explained it to anybody who asked, but he was sure that this case was the key to the mystery of Delilah. His friend Mike had gone out on a limb and provided him with everything he could get his hands on. In his spare time, Mike chauffeured Brandon around the neighborhood where Allison and her parents had lived, where she'd gone to school, the fast-food restaurant where she'd worked, and where her then boyfriend lived.

With luck he could only attribute to divine intervention, the boyfriend, Tony Jenkins, still lived in the same house. His parents had passed away years earlier, and now Tony lived there with his wife and two children. When Brandon and Mike approached him initially, Tony had refused to talk to them, denying that he remembered anything about Allison Moore. Later that same night, Tony had contacted

Brandon and agreed to meet him alone, out in the open. That was how Brandon had come to find himself sitting alone at the duck pond for the last twenty minutes, staring into the cloudy gray sky, waiting for the promised snow to start, and losing hope that Tony would show up.

Thirty minutes past Tony's expected arrival time, Brandon stood, pulled his skullcap down, and raised his collar against the fat snowflakes that had started to drift from the sky. Disappointed, he walked from the park to where he'd left his rental car on the street. As he was about to get in, the door to the car parked behind him opened, and Tony Jenkins stepped out, motioning him toward the car. As Brandon walked toward him, Tony slid back inside.

Brandon was more than a little apprehensive as he approached the open window of the car. Instinctively he reached for his sidearm, remembering before his hand touched his empty hip that he was alone with a man who could be responsible for the disappearance of a teenage girl.

"Hey, man, what's up," Tony said as Brandon reached the window.

"Hey. I thought I missed you," Brandon said.

"Why you bringing the police around asking questions about ancient history?" Tony asked. His face remained impassive, but Brandon could feel the anger vibrating underneath the words.

"I'm sorry, man. I'm not trying to cause you any trouble, but you're the last person who spoke with Allison, and I know you cared about her. I just need to ask you a few questions. Is there somewhere we can go talk out of the cold?" Brandon tried his best to stop from shivering as a gust of wind blew across the water and smacked him in the face.

"All right, man. Follow me, but I ain't talking to no Cleveland police, you hear me? Them bastards cain't be trusted. I'm only talking to you because I owed Mike a favor. You can tell him I said we're square now."

"I hear you," Brandon said as he turned and hurried back to his car.

He had barely turned on the engine before Tony raced off, not bothering to check to see if Brandon was following.

After a short drive, Tony parked outside a diner located on the city's rail line. Without waiting, he walked inside, leaving Brandon to follow or not.

Brandon sat in the car for a moment, trying to get his thoughts together. He knew he would probably only have this one chance to speak with Tony, and the right questions could provide so many answers to the so-far-impenetrable mystery. From where he sat in his car, he could see Tony smiling and talking with the man at the register. He watched as they briefly clasped hands before Tony walked away from the counter.

Opening the door, Brandon stepped into the cold night and walked the short distance to the diner. As he opened the door, the wet heat mingling with the smell of strong coffee, fried potatoes, and greasy meat made his stomach rumble, reminding him that he hadn't eaten since early that morning.

"What can I get you?" the man at the register asked, quickly looking him up and down.

"I'll take a cup of coffee," Brandon said, nodding toward the booth where Tony sat.

"No problem," the man said as Brandon walked toward the back of the diner and slid into the seat across from Tony.

"Thanks for agreeing to meet me," Brandon said as the waiter approached the table.

"Y'all need anything else?" the waiter asked as he set down a steaming pot of coffee and two cups in the center of the table.

"I'm good," Tony said.

"Maybe later," Brandon said.

"Cool, the menu's right over there," he said, pointing at the plastic card tucked behind the salt and pepper shakers.

"Thanks," Brandon said.

"Holla if you need me," he said as he turned and walked away.

"So, what's up?" Tony asked. "What can I tell you that your boy Mr. Officer couldn't?"

Brandon decided not to waste any time tiptoeing around the subject, since he had no idea how long Tony would submit to his questions. He said, "I read what was in the file, but I was hoping you could tell me a little bit about Allison—the kind of person she was, and if you had any idea as to who could have taken her."

As Tony sat staring through the window at the empty train tracks, the TV blared from overhead, two old men talked smack as they played dominoes in the booth behind them, and the cook yelled out orders.

Finally, just as Brandon had started to believe he never would, Tony spoke. "Allison was an angel. She was the best person I ever met. I know everybody feels that way about the person they love, but in Allison's case, it was true. I can't tell you who took her, because I don't know anyone who would have wanted to hurt her, or her parents, for that matter. They were good people, and this shouldn't have happened to them."

"How long did you know her before she disappeared?" Brandon asked.

"I knew her before I was born," Tony said with a short laugh.

"I don't understand," Brandon said cautiously.

"I didn't expect you would. I'm sure that's not in your file."

"No, I'm afraid it's not," Brandon said, hoping he hadn't wasted his time with a crazy man.

"Our families had a lot in common. We both migrated to Cleveland from small Alabama towns. The Moores were from Selma, and my family was from Katherine."

As a train rumbled to a stop on the tracks outside the window of the diner, Tony turned and watched as people stepped down off the train, clinging to the handrails to stop from slipping on the icy payment. As the train pulled away, its whistle blaring through the cold night, Tony turned back to face him, taking a moment to sip his coffee before he started to speak again.

"My mom and Mrs. Moore got pregnant around the same time. They scheduled doctor's appointments together and even had their baby showers together, and when they found out they were having a boy and a girl, they started planning me and Allison's wedding."

Tony stopped and took another sip of his coffee. His eyes had a suspicious sheen as he stared out into the darkness.

"How did you and Allison feel about that?"

"At first me and Allison thought of each other as brother and sister more than anything else, and there was no pressure, but then around junior high, Allison's mom got sick again, and she'd spend days at my house when things were too hard for her at home. Her parents, especially her father, were grateful that she had somewhere to go, and I was glad she was there."

"When did your relationship change?"

"I don't know. In seventh grade we had our first real dance. She loved Michael Jackson, so we went as the couple from 'Thriller.'" His smile at the memory dropped twenty years from his face. "We did the 'Thriller' dance and won the dance contest, and I kissed her, for real kissed her, and from then on—"

"She was your girl," Brandon said. A picture of Olivia as she stood in her living room, waiting for him to take her to a dance, sprang into his head. She was dressed like Madonna's character from *Desperately Seeking Susan*, her hair a fiery cloud of unruly red curls. It was their first date.

"Yeah, she was my girl. After she disappeared, the cops tried to make it seem like I was some scum from the wrong side of the tracks. They tried to hype this argument someone told them we'd had. They spent weeks looking at me, while whoever took her got away without a trace."

"Why were you arguing?" Brandon asked.

"It's been twenty-five years. Why does that matter?"

"I don't know. Maybe it doesn't, but I have to ask. Any tiny detail could shed some light."

"I wanted to get married right then and there," Tony mumbled, staring down at the table.

Brandon felt his heart speed up. Tony was hiding something, or at least keeping something back. Brandon knew Tony wanted to tell him, but he could almost taste his fear. If Brandon let him, he would tuck it back away and maybe never say the words out loud, but with just the right nudge, he would tell him; Brandon was sure of that.

"Tony, this is the time—you may be able to help bring her home," Brandon said, not sure what to expect. "It's too late for her parents, but she deserves to be brought home."

"Do you think she's still alive?" Tony asked, his voice tinged with a hope that he'd probably kept from everyone, including himself.

"I don't know, but even if she's not, don't you need to know what happened?"

Tony let his head drop into his hands, not looking up as he nodded. "I just don't know how what I have to say will help with that."

"Maybe it won't, but don't you want to know that you tried everything in your power to find her?"

"Yes," Tony said, lifting his head from his hands to look at Brandon.

"Good. Why did you argue that day?"

"She said no."

"Why were you suddenly in a rush to get married in high school? You were so young . . ." Understanding shook Brandon to the core. "She was pregnant," he said.

Tony dropped his head again, staring at the table.

"You never told anyone?" Brandon asked after the silence had stretched on for several tense minutes.

"How could I? They were already trying to pin her disappearance on me. If they knew about the baby, they would've thrown me under the jail, evidence or not."

"Do you think it's possible that she ran away on her own? Maybe she was scared—"

"No way, man. If Allison was scared, she knew that she would always have me, her dad, even my dad. She knew we loved her too much to turn our backs on her. She wouldn't have run."

"Okay, did you notice anything strange—anyone just hanging around, maybe watching her, or someone out of the ordinary that she complained about before she went missing?"

"Naw, man, we were together every day. I would have known if there was anyone . . . except, I mean, it was nothing, but she did mention a customer that gave her the creeps. She called him Michael Myers—you know, from *Halloween*. She said he came into her job and was just standing there, staring at her. The manager made him leave, but when I came to pick her up that night, he was sitting on a bench outside the restaurant. He never said anything. He just sat and looked at us. I could see why she was creeped out, though. He was big, and just something about him didn't seem right."

"Do you remember what he looked like?"

"You wouldn't think so, after all this time, but I never forgot him. He was big. I mean *huge*, with a big mountain man beard. He had on a bulky coat. It looked dirty, but not street dirty—more like he worked on a farm or something. Or maybe I just thought that because of the hat he had on. It hid most of his face and looked like something a farmer would wear. It was definitely out of place for around here."

"Did you tell the police about him?"

"Naw, I mean we only saw him the once. He didn't do or say anything, and he never came back."

Brandon sat, trying to force all the pieces of information he'd learned into something that made sense. What could it mean? A pregnant missing teenage girl. A big man who seemed to have appeared and disappeared like so much dust in the wind. And a man still pining after his first love. Was he grasping at straws? Was it possible it was all a big coincidence that he was trying to force to have meaning to soothe his and Olivia's guilt?

"What's going to happen now?" Tony asked.

"I'm going to keep on looking. I'll let you know if anything turns up, if you want."

"Yeah, man, I want to know. I love my wife and my kids, but I'd be lying if I told you I didn't still miss her."

"Of course," Brandon said, reaching for the menu.

"Here, take this. I don't know if it'll help at all, but who knows," Tony said. He shrugged as he dug into his wallet and pulled out a photo, raising it to his lips before sliding it across the table to Brandon.

The school picture was of a teenage girl with reddish-blonde, tightly curled hair and wide, light-brown eyes. She was wearing an Aerosmith T-shirt with the word ANGEL written out in cursive across the bottom of it. In his head, he heard the song again, screaming out from the wrecked car. How had this car, meant to be a token of love, ended up as a coffin for the boy and almost for the girl, one who could have been a younger version of his own treasured child?

"'Angel,'" he said, tracing the letters of the word with the tip of his finger while his brain scrambled to understand what he was seeing.

"Yeah. She loved that damn song. Remember back in the day how they used to sell the cassette single?"

Brandon nodded, remembering he had been guilty of buying a girl or two a cassette single.

"I made the mistake of buying her that single the day it came out. It was her first tape for her car. God, she would just listen to it over and over. Drove me insane, but it always made me think of her." A smile touched his lips for just a moment. "Now, when I hear it, I still think of her, but I feel sick to my stomach." He shrugged again as he turned his head to look out the window, where another train was pulling up on the tracks.

Brandon sat staring down at the picture, unable to speak, as he thought of the girl, of Delilah. Of course, she wasn't Delilah. This girl was healthy, happy, and well loved. The photo showed the sparkle in her eyes and the mischievous, almost flirty smile barely touching her lips.

She wasn't looking directly into the camera, but slightly past whoever was taking the picture. Brandon would have gladly put money on the fact that Tony was somewhere nearby when the photo was taken.

Delilah had never known one bit of that kind of happiness. He'd bet on that too. But there was something, some connection. It couldn't be a coincidence that Allison, Delilah, and his Carly were so much alike. It was Delilah. Delilah held the key to everything.

"You good? You look shook."

"Yeah, man, I'm cool. It's just, she looks like someone I used to know. I'm sorry. I've been up all day, and I haven't had a chance to eat," Brandon said, sliding the picture into his wallet. "I'm good."

"If you say so," Tony said, but Brandon could tell he was already having second thoughts about deciding to trust him.

"Seriously, don't worry about it. It's been a long couple of weeks. I can't remember the last time I had a good meal. I'll be all right once I get some food in my stomach."

"Cool, then I'm about to be out. Don't forget to let me know if you find something, anything, about Allison."

"Promise," Brandon said.

"Bet. Try the breakfast," Tony said as he stood to leave, throwing his hand up at the waiter as he strode down the narrow aisle between the counter and the booths before pushing open the door and disappearing into the frigid night.

Brandon raised his hand to get the waiter's attention, both his head and his stomach in a whirl. It was time to go home.

Chapter 28

Olivia sat in the small drab office dressed in her best interviewing clothes, feeling like a kid in front of the school principal, asking for the impossible, for permission to move Delilah into her home. The social worker, Mrs. Kovach, was every bit as daunting as Melinda had described her.

Since Olivia had been ushered into the office, Mrs. Kovach hadn't said much besides the introduction. Instead, she had spent the last ten minutes studying Delilah's file, stopping every so often to scribble a note in the margins. Each time, Olivia wanted to lean forward to try to read what was written or simply ask, but she bit her tongue, burying her fingernails into the soft skin of the palms of her hands, while she waited, forcing herself not to fidget.

She wished Brandon were here with her, if not in the office, at least in the dingy too-hot waiting room, waiting to celebrate with her, or hold her while she cried, but he wasn't—maybe because she hadn't bothered to tell him about the appointment. There hadn't seemed to be any point. She didn't need to talk to Brandon to know what he would say, any more than she needed to hear the whispers floating around the hospital to know that everyone thought she'd taken leave of her senses. None of that mattered to Olivia. All that mattered was convincing this woman that hers was the best home for Delilah.

"Dr. Blake, are we ready to begin?" Mrs. Kovach asked as she closed the file and pushed it to the side, replacing it with a legal pad of paper.

"Absolutely," Olivia said, hoping her voice didn't sound as nervous as it did in her head.

"We'll start with some personal history. I understand you are divorced, no children, is that correct?"

"Yes, that's correct."

"I understand you lost a child under mysterious circumstances. Is that correct?"

Olivia supposed she should have expected the question or something like it, but the coldness of it left her stunned, staring at Mrs. Kovach, unable to respond.

"Dr. Blake, are you all right?" Mrs. Kovach asked, her brows knitted together in annoyance as she waited for Olivia to respond.

"Yes, I'm fine," Olivia said, the words coming out in a croak from her suddenly dry throat.

"Am I correct that you had a child that went missing under mysterious circumstances?" Mrs. Kovach asked.

"Yes," Olivia said, nodding in case the words never left her head.

"The case remains unsolved, is that correct?"

"Yes," Olivia said, wishing again that Brandon were there to hold her hand.

"Your child, was she approximately the same age as this girl?"

"No, she was quite a bit younger," Olivia said.

"Very well. You're a pediatric physician, is that correct?"

"Yes," Olivia said, the rapid change of subject leaving her feeling dizzy.

"How long have you been employed by the hospital?"

"I came on as a resident, fresh out of medical school, and have been here ever since."

"I have your age as forty-two, is that correct? You hardly look past twenty-five," she said, somehow making it seem more an accusation than a compliment.

"I am forty-two," she said, trying to hide her frustration at having to answer questions she knew Mrs. Kovach must have already known the answers to, given the amount of paperwork she had completed.

"Are you seeing anyone?"

For a moment, Olivia stared blankly at Mrs. Kovach, not understanding her question. Then, as she repeated the question in her head, she was unable to hide a giggle. "No, I'm not seeing anyone. It's been so long I wasn't sure what you meant."

"Do you have a roommate or anyone else who has regular access to your home?"

"No," Olivia said, unable to hide her confusion.

"I only ask because, as you are well aware, this is a very high-profile case," she said, tapping the tip of her pen against the paper on top of the pile. "Wherever she is placed has to have adequate security, and frankly, Dr. Blake, I'm not sure if a working single woman without any established support system in place is the right fit for this unfortunate girl. Surely you can see my point. I imagine that if you weren't so emotionally invested, you would more than likely agree."

Stunned, Olivia found that she couldn't speak. The idea of losing Delilah ripped through her, leaving her unable to defend herself.

"Well, then, Dr. Blake, I'm sure we have all we need," Olivia heard Mrs. Kovach say as she started to gather her belongings.

"Mrs. Kovach, please, let me say one more thing. I understand the seriousness of Delilah's situation. I understand that whomever you entrust to provide for Delilah's well-being will have to give her their undivided attention. I want to assure you that if you place Delilah in my care, I will take a leave of absence until her family has been located or she has found a permanent home."

"And the hospital, Dr. Blake, do you think they would agree to that, especially when you have no way of knowing how long the child would be in your care?"

"My concern is for the child, and I'll do anything to keep her safe," Olivia said.

"Well, thank you for your time and your candor today. I will consider everything I've learned and forward a recommendation to my supervisor as soon as possible. Good day to you."

Chapter 29

Olivia sat at the picnic bench, fidgeting with the gaily wrapped present in front of her. Kids ran around in a frenzy, chasing each other, falling over, even fighting. Harried chaperones did their best to manage the fray, but every now and again, one of the children would break away from the pack and approach Olivia, staring up at her with desperate, hopeful eyes before one of the women would gently prod the child back into the tangle of activity.

It was her first visit with Delilah since she'd left the hospital, and a part of her wanted to leave the gift and flee. She couldn't say why she was so nervous, but that didn't stop her from feeling slightly sick to her stomach. She supposed she was worried that Delilah would be angry that it had taken so long or, worse, that she didn't care at all. Even though no final approval to foster Delilah had been granted to Olivia, the group home administrator had kindly decided to update her on Delilah's condition, not that much had changed. Delilah still refused to speak to anyone, and according to the house mother, she spent most of the daylight hours sleeping or lying in a patch of sun in the yard, away from the other kids. Because of that, the attendants had taken to calling her Cat.

When she couldn't get outside, Delilah spent her time staring out the window as if waiting for someone. Although the house nurse had prescribed a sedative to help her sleep, she still suffered from night terrors, which caused her to wake up screaming. Because of this, she didn't share a room like most of the other residents, which made her placement into a private home even more urgent.

Olivia looked up as the house administrator stepped into the yard, her arm resting lightly across Delilah's shoulders. Delilah walked stiffly, her body as far away from the woman as the confining arm would allow, looking down at the ground instead of ahead, until the woman stopped and bent to whisper into her ear.

Delilah raised her head, her eyes widening as they fixed on Olivia. Olivia stood up from the table. Delilah stood frozen, staring at Olivia as if she couldn't understand what she was seeing. Suddenly, she sprang away from the woman's side and half ran, half shuffled across the space that separated them before coming to a stop in front of Olivia, head tilted back, her too-old eyes searching her face.

"Hello, Delilah. I've missed you," Olivia said, reaching out to take her hand. She guided her to the picnic table and helped her sit. "I brought this for you." She picked the gift up from the table and placed it in Delilah's hands.

Delilah held the package in her hands loosely, staring down at the shiny pink paper with a huge silver bow as if she had never seen a present before.

"It's yours, open it," Olivia said.

Delilah lifted the gift, carefully turning it over in her hands and running her fingers along the edges of the tape before peeling open the package, making sure not to tear even one bit of the brilliant-pink wrapping paper.

Olivia grinned at the expression on Delilah's face as she stared down into the package before lifting each piece of clothing from the box, handling them as if each were the most precious thing she had ever been given.

"I couldn't be sure of your style," Olivia said. "But when I was your age, I would've chosen a good pair of jeans over a frilly party dress, any day. Of course, a fresh pair of Chucks is essential for every young lady, if you ask me. If you don't like them, we can change or add things that are more to your taste. I hope you like them."

Delilah smiled at Olivia and raised a pink T-shirt covered in flowers to her face, rubbing the soft material against her skin.

"Thank you," she whispered, so low that Olivia barely heard her.

"You're welcome, angel," Olivia said, reaching out to touch Delilah's hair, relishing the feel of the soft curls against her palm. Not unexpectedly, an image of Carly sprang into Olivia's mind. Even though the memory brought some sadness, Olivia welcomed it as she sat in the sun with Delilah.

A part of her that had for so long railed against the reality of her loss had begun to crumble, and somewhere in the deepest recesses of her mind, she had begun to accept the unacceptable. Her beloved child was gone. Her heart knew it, and now her mind was starting to accept the truth of it too. She could not help Carly any longer. But this girl, this lost, beautiful girl. She could help this girl.

Delilah smiled, leaning against Olivia, resting her head against her arm. They sat that way, neither speaking, Delilah clutching the T-shirt to her chest, watching the other children play, until the administrator came to take her away, looking on in wonder as Delilah threw her arms around Olivia's neck, kissing her cheek as Delilah whispered goodbye.

The ride home was little more than a blur. Olivia could hardly believe it when she pulled up in front of her own house. She stepped out of the car and noticed Brandon's truck parked in the drive. When the front door opened and Brandon stepped out onto the porch, a dish towel hanging down the front of his pants and an oven mitt on his hand, the past and present collided.

Olivia closed her eyes against a wave of dizziness as the blood rushed to her head. She heard Brandon call her name from what seemed like a great distance, and then he was by her side, steadying her in his arms.

Chapter 30

Brandon paced around the living room, looking down at Olivia's strangely placid face, not sure what he should be doing. It had been less than a minute since he'd helped her into the house, his arm tucked around her waist as she leaned heavily into his side. Though her eyes were still too foggy for his liking, he was relieved to see the tiny smile that curved her lips.

"Brandon," she said.

"Livvy, you about scared me to death. Here, drink this," he said, grabbing the cup from the table.

"Well, you kind of took me by surprise too," she said, sipping from the cup of water.

"I was one second away from calling 911."

"You know I would have killed you if you had, right?"

"I'm glad it didn't come to that," Brandon said, sitting on the couch next to her, unconsciously resting his hand on her thigh.

✳

"I swear Ms. Helen must think she's won the lottery with all the goings-on over here lately. I bet she's scared to go to sleep for worry she's about to miss something," Olivia said, trying to ignore the effect Brandon's hand on her thigh was having on her heart.

"What happened?" Brandon asked.

"Nothing. I've just been pushing myself, maybe a little too much. I also forgot to eat today. I'm sure that didn't help."

"Well, fortunately, I've got you covered there," Brandon said, standing up and bowing toward the kitchen with a flourish.

"What's this?" Olivia said, swinging her feet off the couch.

"Oh no, you don't. I'm going to take care of you tonight."

"Um, Brandon, no offense, but I don't know that I'm up for hot dogs and frozen fries," Olivia said, biting down on her lip to keep from giggling.

"Oh, you are really pushing it, Doc, and after I slaved over this hot stove all day. You keep that up, and you're going to miss out on the best lasagna in Colorado."

"Wait, how did you get in here?" Olivia asked as Brandon came back into the living room, carrying two plates.

"Drinks, I forgot the drinks," he said, sliding the plates onto the coffee table before turning and rushing back into the kitchen.

"Well?" she said when he reentered the living room with two large glasses.

"Taste it," he said, handing her a glass.

Olivia took the glass from his outstretched hand, bringing it to her lips as he pulled a chair to the table so he was facing the couch.

Tentatively she took a sip, and as the sweet liquid touched her lips, tears sprang to her eyes.

"Orange and lemonade Kool-Aid with orange slices, our family drink," she said.

"Some things never change," he said, smiling at her.

"They don't." She smiled back at him as she took another sip. "Now how did you get in here?"

"You never changed the locks," Brandon mumbled as he wiped sauce from his lips.

"Shame on you, Brandon." Olivia laughed as his cheeks grew red. "It's a good thing you're right about the lasagna. This really might be the best lasagna in Colorado. Hell, maybe the whole West."

"I told you so," Brandon said with a wink.

"When did you get back?"

"Today."

"How was Cleveland?"

"Cold," Brandon said, but Olivia could tell he was holding something back.

"Is that all?"

"Well . . . why don't we talk about it after dinner?" he said.

"Okay. Is it bad news?" Olivia asked.

"No, it's nothing like that. I just want to run some things by you, and I would prefer that you weren't distracted by my unbelievable cooking skills."

"Seriously, Brandon, you know I have no patience. Why would you even bother to bring anything up if you weren't going to tell?"

"It wasn't me who brought it up."

"Whatever, just tell me. Is it about Delilah?"

"Maybe. Did you see her today?"

"Yeah," Olivia said, cautiously, as she glanced at Brandon, trying to gauge his reaction.

"How was she?"

"She was good. The house administrator had some concerns about her behavior. Apparently, she's still having the night terrors, so they're having to keep her pretty isolated. I hope I can bring her home soon."

"Good. I'm glad to hear it. You're a good egg, Dr. Hall," he said, sending a thrill through her body at the sound of their name on his tongue. "Hey, you know what this is missing?"

"A sprinkle of 'I don't give a damn,'" Olivia huffed.

"Wow, some things really don't change." Brandon laughed.

"Okay, fine," Olivia said. "I'm done, mmm, yummy, I'm full. Let's hear it."

"Fine, I'll go clean up and make us some coffee, and then I'll tell you all about it."

"I can help." Olivia jumped off the couch before he could stop her.

"I see you still haven't mastered the art of sitting back and allowing someone to look after you," Brandon said as she raced into the kitchen.

"You can take care of me when I'm old," Olivia called.

"With pleasure," Brandon said, following her into the kitchen with the dirty dishes.

Chapter 31

Olivia sat beside Brandon on the couch, a pot of coffee and two steaming mugs between them, looking down at the photos spread out on the coffee table. After they'd finished cleaning the kitchen, Brandon had lit a fire in the fireplace before he began to tell her about his trip to Cleveland. Now the room was silent except for the occasional popping of dry wood as Olivia tried to digest everything. Brandon leaned forward, gazing into her face. He looked anxious.

Olivia picked up the picture of Allison Moore. Just like Brandon, she felt that sensation of staring into a future that would never be. He was right. This girl, Allison, she could be an undamaged version of Delilah, or the Carly who could only live in their dreams.

"I'm not sure what to say," she said, dropping the picture back on the table and wrapping her arms around her body, which suddenly felt too cold, even with the heat from the fire filling the room. "Do you think that this girl is somehow connected to Delilah?"

"She has to be, doesn't she? How could this be a coincidence?"

"Okay, let's say you're right—and for the record, I believe you are—what does it mean? Obviously, Delilah can't be Allison Moore; she's too young. She's only twelve, thirteen at the most, so she couldn't even be the baby this poor girl was carrying when she disappeared."

"I know you're right, but I've been thinking: What if she did run away? Maybe Tony or her parents didn't know her as well as they thought they did. She wouldn't be the first teenage girl to keep a boy, or even a man, secret. Maybe she fell in love with someone no one knew about. Maybe the baby wasn't even Tony's. Maybe they ran away together to live happily ever after. If she did, it's possible that she got married, moved to Colorado, and had other babies . . .'"

"Other babies like Delilah," Olivia said.

"Could be—it makes sense if you think about it."

"That's a lot of maybes, and yes, I guess it's possible, but as far as making sense, I'm not so sure."

"Why not?" Brandon asked.

"Think about it. When she disappeared, she was fifteen. I buy that a fifteen-year-old could've made the decision to run away with a secret boyfriend, but she didn't stay fifteen." Olivia got up and poured another cup of coffee for herself, then held the pot over Brandon's cup, but he shook his head. "At some point she grew up, and I can't believe that all this time later she wouldn't have reached out to her family, especially if she was happily married and raising her own child." Olivia sat back on the couch, watching Brandon's face work as he chewed over his thoughts.

"Maybe she didn't have that kind of relationship with them. You know that sometimes the people who are supposed to care about you the most can cause the most harm."

"Maybe, but from everything you've told me about her, it doesn't fit."

"That's true, but everything isn't always what it seems, and people don't always tell the whole truth in these situations." Brandon stood up from the couch and paced around the room.

"But why would the boyfriend lie?" she asked. "He went out of his way to meet with you, and again, it's been twenty-five years. What would be the point now? Allison Moore's disappearance literally destroyed this family. They looked for her until it killed them. Does that sound like a family that would have turned their backs on this girl for any reason?"

"I guess not, but I know there's a connection between Delilah and Allison Moore. I can feel it. Then there's Carly. You don't want to say it, but I know you see it too. If Carly—"

"Please don't."

"Olivia, I'm not trying to hurt you. I'd do anything not to, but we can't hide from it anymore. Delilah could be an older version of Carly, same as Allison Moore could be of Delilah, or at the very least her sister."

Olivia leaned forward and picked up the picture again. He was right, she knew it. If she laid the pictures of all three girls side by side, they would look like sisters. What were the odds of three beautiful biracial-looking girls, with golden-red curls, disappearing and ending up in the same place after so long? Virtually impossible.

"Okay, I can see your brain churning away. Go ahead, tell me what you're thinking. I'm a big girl; I can handle it," Olivia said, surprising herself with how strong and sure she sounded, when her brain felt like it was in a blender.

"Well, maybe the answer is exactly as it seems," Brandon said. "Suppose the police had it right all along. Maybe she was taken, but not killed, as everyone assumed. Maybe the person who took her wanted her for more than a quick thrill. Maybe he kept her."

"You mean, you think she's still alive?" Olivia asked.

"It's possible, isn't it?"

"I suppose so, but what would this girl be like after all these years?"

"Well, she wouldn't be a girl anymore," Brandon said.

"Oh God, it might not be right to say, but I hope you're wrong. There are things worse than death."

"Yeah, you're right about that."

"What are you going to do?" she asked.

"I don't know. Turn it over to the police, but I can't think about it anymore tonight." He gathered the pictures and the reports into a pile and stuffed them back into the envelope.

"I think you should go home and get some rest. You must be exhausted."

"I am. Olivia, I don't want to push you, and I know we're taking it slow, but I was wondering if I could stay here, just for tonight. I'll stay on the couch. I just don't want to go back to that empty house, not tonight," he said in a rush.

Before the last words were out of his mouth, Olivia was throwing her arms around his neck. "Yes," she said, kissing his lips as they curved into a smile.

Rising from the couch, she took his hand and led him to their bedroom.

Neither of them said a word as they undressed and slid into the bed that had always been theirs. As Brandon pulled her close to him, Olivia felt safe.

Chapter 32

Olivia paced back and forth across her office, waiting for Arlene to arrive. She supposed she could drive herself, but the way she was shaking, she was pretty sure that any attempts at driving would land her up a tree. She'd gotten the call that morning. The court had approved her temporary fostering of Delilah, and she was scheduled to pick her up this afternoon from the group home. The last time she'd felt this giddy sense of joy and nerves had been when they'd brought Carly home from the hospital.

She wished Brandon had been able to share her excitement, but despite her continued attempts to reassure him, his wariness continued in all matters regarding Delilah. He wouldn't even tell her what was going on with the investigation anymore. Last night, as she'd watched him pack up all the things that had managed to migrate to her place from his in the past few weeks, he'd continued to warn her to try to keep some distance. She'd promised she would, but they both knew it was far too late.

Sinking into her chair, Olivia dropped her head into her hands, trying to calm herself by closing her eyes and taking a few deep breaths. If she arrived to pick up Delilah in her current state, they'd probably send her away.

She'd almost regained control of her nerves when a sharp knock at the door startled her, making her jump in her chair and bang her knee under the desk.

"Fuuudge," she cried, grabbing for her knee as the knock repeated. "Come in," she yelled louder than she intended.

"Is everything okay? I thought I heard a scream," David said as he stepped into her office.

"Everything's fine. What do you want, David?"

"I need your signature on your leave paperwork."

"Fine, let me have it." Olivia barely glanced at it before signing her name.

"Good luck, Olivia. I hope you know what you're doing," he said as she handed him back the paperwork.

"What is that supposed to mean?"

"Nothing. I mean this is a very unusual situation, and I hope you've thought this through." He lowered himself into a chair and crossed his legs, as if he intended to stay for a while. "It seems risky to take this girl into your home with so many unknowns."

"I'll be fine—sorry to disappoint you," she said, the words sounding like those of a sulky teenager to even her own ears.

"Believe it or not, I'm not wishing you ill. It's just, you can't know what could happen, do you? Lord knows you don't need another tragedy. Honestly, I don't know why you'd put yourself in this situation."

"Thanks for your concern, David. I'm sure I'll be fine."

"I hope so, and I hope this girl will be too," he said. He stood and marched across the room, nearly knocking Arlene down as he walked out the door.

"What bug done crawled up his ass?" Arlene asked as she stepped into the room.

"Who knows? Let's go," Olivia said as she got up and walked around the desk, her stomach feeling like she had just gotten off a roller coaster.

"Wait," Arlene said, placing her hand on Olivia's arm to stop her from moving away. "You're a good person. And you're doing a great thing. Don't ever doubt that, okay?"

Olivia nodded, not trusting herself to speak, knowing if she did, she would start crying and maybe never stop.

"All right, then, let's go. Delilah awaits," Arlene said, giving Olivia a quick squeeze.

On the ride to the group home, Olivia fidgeted in her seat like a two-year-old in need of a nap, alternating between babbling about nothing and staring out the window. When they were a few blocks from the group home, Arlene pulled over to the side of the road and turned to face Olivia.

"Honey, you have got to get a grip. You're acting like a maniac, and I don't mind telling you I would have serious doubts about releasing any child into your hands in your current state. Calm down. It's going to be fine."

"I know, I know. I don't know what's wrong with me. Am I that bad?"

"Yes, yes, you are. You're sweating, babbling, and generally making me nervous, to be honest."

"I'm sorry."

"It's cool. We're going to sit here for a few moments," Arlene said. "You're going to breathe in and out, and then we're going to go pick up this child, and you're going to take her home and take good care of her. Okay?"

Olivia shook her head, not trusting her voice. She stared past Arlene out the window, watching cars go by, fighting back the tears that always seemed so close to the surface these days.

"Arlene, do you think I'm doing the right thing?" she asked. After a few moments of silence, she said, "Never mind, I guess I have my answer."

"Listen, I don't know if it's the right thing, but I do know that there is no way you can turn your back on that girl when she obviously needs you so much. I just pray that we can find out who she is soon."

"What would you think if I told you I almost hope we never find out where she came from?" Olivia said, admitting out loud for the first time what Brandon, and probably Arlene, already knew.

"Yeah, it wouldn't exactly be breaking news," Arlene said, smiling at Olivia.

"But you still love me."

"You know I do. Are you ready?" Arlene asked.

"I'm ready."

Chapter 33

Olivia and Arlene were greeted by Mrs. Kovach and Odessa Pickett, the house administrator, when they entered the group home. Mrs. Kovach's face wore the stern expression of a displeased principal, while Odessa's offered a tentative smile.

"Dr. Blake, we've been waiting," Mrs. Kovach said, glancing down at her watch.

"I'm sorry. We ran into a little traffic," Olivia said.

"Well, glad you could make it. Please step into the office. There are a few things we need to discuss."

"Is everything okay?" Olivia asked.

"Fine. Please follow me," Mrs. Kovach said, turning her back and walking toward the office.

"Don't worry, everything's fine," Odessa said softly.

"Ms. Pickett, if you don't mind, please escort Dr. Blake's friend to the waiting area while we talk."

"Is that really necessary?" Olivia asked.

"Yes, it is, due to privacy concerns. I'm sure you understand."

"It's no problem. How about I just wait in the car?" Arlene said.

"No, it's freezing out there," Olivia said.

"Let me show you to the waiting room," Ms. Pickett said as she led Arlene away. "It's comfortable enough, and I could get you a cup of coffee while you wait."

"Please sit," Mrs. Kovach said, gesturing to the chair. "Dr. Blake, I don't mind telling you that I disagree with the decision to allow you to foster this girl. Your unreasonable attachment can not only cause harm to Delilah, but to yourself as well."

"I'll be fine," Olivia said.

"Maybe. I hope so. I know the trauma you went through with the loss of your own child. Can you honestly say that you've recovered enough to take on this very delicate situation?"

"The board obviously decided I could," Olivia said, her lips barely moving as she forced out the words.

"Let's not be coy, Dr. Blake. I'm sure you agree that this is clearly a circumstance of who you know, not what's best for anyone involved in this situation."

Olivia forced her face to remain calm and her hands to stay still before speaking. "Be that as it may, Mrs. Kovach, the decision has been made. Now, are you going to turn over Delilah to my care or not?"

"Are you ready for me?" Ms. Pickett asked from the door.

"Of course, Ms. Pickett. Please update Dr. Blake on the events from last night."

Ms. Pickett entered the room and sat in the chair beside Olivia.

"Is Delilah all right?" Olivia asked.

"She's fine now, but sometime last night, after all the children were supposed to be in bed, Delilah somehow managed to get outside. She was found in the yard under the tree. It appears she crawled out the window of her room."

"Oh my God. It was freezing out last night. How did this happen?"

"We don't know. The night security guard found her under the tree, not very far from her room window. She couldn't have been out there for more than a few minutes, since it had only been about five minutes since he passed the spot where he found her on his rounds. Fortunately, she didn't suffer any ill effects from the cold, but there was some injury to her hands. It looked like she had been hitting the tree, or clawing at it, judging by the state of her fingernails."

"Did she say anything about why she was out there?" Olivia said.

"No, all she would say was 'Hurt.' She was treated on the premises, just a bandage and something for the pain and to help her sleep. She slept through the rest of the night without incident, but we did have to increase the patrols. If she were staying, we would have to take more precautions."

"I understand," Olivia said, trying to hide how upset she was.

"Do you, Dr. Blake?" said Mrs. Kovach. "This is a very serious issue. I did recommend that Delilah remain here, where she can be more closely supervised. Against my recommendation, the department believes it would be less disruptive to place her in a private home, so we will release her to you today. But understand, this girl needs intense help, Dr. Blake. This is just one incident, but it's not the only issue this child has. Are you aware that she seems to have a compulsive need to pray? She has to be prompted to eat. She has no idea how to interact with other children, or if she does, she refuses to. She seems terrified of men. Have you even thought about what you will do about her educational needs? Obviously, she's not ready to attend school."

"With all due respect, I am a pediatrician. I can assure you, I'm perfectly capable of providing a safe space for Delilah."

"I know you believe that, Dr. Blake, but if you find that you cannot handle this situation, please, for your sake and Delilah's, don't try to be a hero—bring her back."

"Mrs. Kovach, I appreciate your concern, but I'm not interested in being a hero. If I find myself in a situation that I feel even remotely uncertain about, I will contact you or Ms. Pickett, and if it's determined it's best to bring her back, then I will."

"Well, then, that's all we can ask, isn't it? Ms. Pickett, please bring Delilah."

"May the Lord cover and protect you," Ms. Pickett said as she walked from the room.

Chapter 34

The interior of the car was silent as Arlene drove back to Olivia's, both hands gripping the steering wheel. Every now and then she glanced into the rearview mirror at Delilah, who sat huddled in the back seat as close as she could get to the door, her eyes fixed, unblinking, on the back of Olivia's head. The intensity of Delilah's stare sent a shiver through Arlene's body. She understood why Olivia was so attached to Delilah, but Arlene couldn't shake the feeling that whatever had happened to her wasn't over. Not for the first time, she wondered if she had made the right decision in helping Olivia bring Delilah into her home.

As Arlene drew closer to Olivia's house, she slowed down, wanting to prolong the ride as long as possible, not wanting to leave Olivia alone with the girl. Although Olivia seemed to have forgotten the circumstances surrounding her arrival into their lives, Arlene could not forget the still-unexplained corpse of the boy found with Delilah.

Arlene pulled into the driveway at Olivia's house and turned off the car. As she started to remove the keys from the ignition, Olivia reached out to still her hand.

"Hey, thanks for the ride, but I think it's best if I get her settled in alone. I'll call you later." Olivia pushed open the car door and stepped outside before Arlene had the chance to say more.

"Okay, but can I talk to you a moment before you go?" Arlene asked as Olivia reached back to open the door for Delilah.

Without bothering to stop to look at Arlene, the girl took a few steps away from the car, stopping at the stairs that led up to the porch of Olivia's house.

"Arlene, I know what you're going to say. I'm fine."

"You can't blame me for worrying. I feel sorry for Delilah, I do, and I understand how you feel, but someone tried to kill her, did kill that poor boy. She hasn't told us anything about what happened. Liv, it just makes sense to think they could still be out there. Can you at least consider an alarm system, or hire some security? I know a guy." A small smile replaced the worry in her eyes for just a moment.

"I promise. I'll look into it—now stop worrying. Everything's going to be all right. Seriously, I have to go. I'll call you later tonight."

"You better, or I'm coming over here," Arlene said.

"I wouldn't expect anything less," Olivia said with a grin.

"I hope you know what you're doing," Arlene said as Olivia closed the car door.

"I do, and thanks for being here for me, Arlene." Olivia leaned over into the window and blew Arlene a kiss.

"I always am," Arlene said.

✳

Olivia held her breath as Delilah stood a few feet from the front door, her back and shoulders stiff, her head slightly bent to the side, reminding Olivia of a deer sniffing the air for danger. Olivia wanted to reach out and touch her, but she wasn't sure that Delilah wouldn't panic.

Seconds ticked by, with nothing but the sound of their breathing filling the space between them until Delilah's hands uncurled and her shoulders relaxed and she took a step inside, walking around the room, touching the chairs and the sofa, her fingers skimming lightly across the coffee table, before bending to sniff the flowers in a vase.

Olivia went to lock the door. When she turned back around, Delilah stood staring down at a heavy silver-framed picture she'd picked up from the end table. Arlene had taken the picture of Carly and Brandon building a snowman, while Olivia made a snow angel. Heavy snow had been falling, making it appear as if they were inside a snow globe.

"My family," Olivia said, fighting back the tears that were so close.

"Family," Delilah said, returning the picture to the table.

"I'm sorry, I know you must miss yours," Olivia said, crossing the room to put her arm around Delilah, surprised to feel her body trembling.

"And then the Family will come," the girl said, as if reciting a lesson, sending a chill racing up Olivia's spine.

"Oh, a goose walked over my grave," Olivia said, trying to ignore the sudden unease Delilah's words had caused. "Time to get you settled," she said, taking the girl by the hand.

Chapter 35

Brandon sat with his feet on the desk while Amy buzzed around her office, headphones covering her ears, seemingly oblivious to his presence. Every now and then she would sing a couple of lines to a song at the top of her lungs without any signs of embarrassment, and Brandon would grin in appreciation.

He'd been in the office for most of the morning, thinking. Occasionally, when he had a thought or a question to bounce off Amy, he would write it down on a yellow legal pad on her desk, to be discussed at their scheduled noon meeting.

So far, he was frustrated because no matter how hard he tried to organize his thoughts, the question he needed to ask kept slipping away. As soon as he thought he had it, it would disintegrate into confusion. He didn't need anyone to tell him that he was running out of time; every nerve ending in his body seemed to be on high alert. If he didn't figure this puzzle out soon, it was going to be bad news for everybody.

Taking out his phone, he opened his email and scrolled through the many unopened messages, searching for any from his boss. He was lucky that he'd been able to take personal leave. But, since his absence was so unexpected, he'd promised to keep an eye out for any problems that might crop up that his employees couldn't handle. Thankfully, everything seemed to be going smoothly during his absence. He only hoped things would stay that way until this situation was resolved.

The beeping of his watch told him that noon had arrived. Without glancing at the clock, Amy removed the headphones, picked up the legal pad, walked to the desk, and slid into the chair across from Brandon. He let his feet fall from the desk and sat up in the chair, looking across the table at Amy, waiting for her to speak.

"Hi, Brandon, how are you doing today?"

"I'm great. How are you?"

"Well, here you are sitting across from me, looking as tense as a guitar string ready to pop, trying to sell me some BS that you're fine. Other than the fact that I hate being lied to, because it hurts my baby's ears, I'm fine."

"Come on, Amy, you know I love you. Don't give me a hard time."

"Don't feed me BS."

"Okay, okay, I'm a little . . ."

Amy raised an eyebrow and cracked her knuckles.

"Fine, I'm a lot nervous," Brandon said.

"Okay, now we're talking. Why are you nervous?"

"You know that I don't believe in all this mumbo jumbo about having feelings like something is going to happen, but damn it, I got this sick feeling that something bad is coming, and I feel like the only way to stop it is to figure this thing out with this girl."

"Okay."

"I know it sounds stupid."

"I did not say that. My mother told me, 'Always trust your gut,' and my mama is never wrong," Amy said. She picked up a lime-green Beanie Baby and tossed it from hand to hand before setting it back down.

"Okay, so what am I supposed to do about it?"

"Sounds to me like you need to solve this thing."

"Shit . . ."

"Watch the language—growing ears over here. Do you really want your godchild's first word to be *shit*?"

"Godchild? Really? Oh wow, thank you. I didn't think . . . ," Brandon said, grinning at Amy.

"Of course you didn't. That's what you have me for." Amy picked up the legal pad he'd been scribbling on and studied it for a moment.

"I wrote down all my questions and pretty much everything else I was thinking," Brandon said.

"You said, 'I need to find Allison Moore. What happened to Allison Moore? Who is Allison Moore? What happened to Allison Moore's baby?' Sounds like you're focused on Allison Moore," Amy said.

"I am. I can't explain it yet, but I feel like she's the key to this whole thing."

"Why do you think so?"

"For a couple of reasons, number one being my gut tells me she is, plus the car. And I can't get over the resemblance between her, Delilah, and . . . well, never mind that," Brandon said, though he could tell by how Amy looked at him that she realized he'd almost said *Carly*.

"So, what's your next step in finding Allison Moore?"

"That's the problem. I don't know."

"Well, it's a good thing you have me now, isn't it?" Amy said.

"You know how to find her?" Brandon asked, sitting up straight in his chair.

"Not exactly, but I know somebody who might be able to help. While you were stressing yourself out brainstorming, I did some research online.

"During the original investigation, there was a reporter named Dorothy Hines, who was as obsessed about the case as you are now. She wrote dozens of articles about Allison Moore. She works for CNN now, but she hasn't forgotten about the case. She has a blog called *Cold Case Hunter*, where she devotes time to researching old cold cases that have been abandoned by law enforcement and the media. She and her followers have had some success in breaking some pretty high-profile cases.

"Remember the Bobby Sanford case, where the little boy went missing at one of those pizza play places designed as heaven for kids and hell for adults? Well, their research and letter-writing campaign got the attention of a witness on Facebook, who remembered seeing a guy talking to the boy the day he went missing. That witness catapulted the story back onto the front pages for just long enough for others to come forward. Two weeks after Dorothy Hines got involved, they found the boy's body and caught his killer."

"You wouldn't happen to have her number, would you?" Brandon asked, feeling hopeless.

"I'll do you one better. I have her number and her email, and she's waiting for you to contact her."

"How . . . I mean, what . . . how did you do that?" Brandon asked.

"Well, one of my friends that I volunteer with at the women's shelter is a member of Dorothy's blog community, and her best friend. Thanks to the miracle that is instant messaging, I was able to chat with Dorothy, and she wants to speak directly to you. She may even be able to convince CNN to run a piece on it, especially with the interest in the girl."

"Amy, you're like a superhero. Seriously, I would marry you today if you would just say yes."

"I know, right? I amaze myself sometimes."

"Should I call her from here, right now?" Brandon asked, hopping up from the chair.

"You'd better."

As Brandon pulled his phone from his pocket and dialed the number, he sent up a silent prayer that this reporter could somehow help him find new information. He had failed Carly, and it had nearly destroyed both him and Olivia. He couldn't fail this girl too. If he did, there might not be any coming back for Olivia, or himself either. He, or rather they, needed answers.

Chapter 36

Olivia sat on the couch, flipping through the channels on the TV. She wished more than anything that Brandon could be there with her, but she knew that even if he could, he wouldn't. He couldn't understand how important it was for her to protect Delilah. She recognized that he was partially right when he'd accused her of being so attached because of Delilah's resemblance to their lost Carly, but it was more than that. Delilah needed her. She couldn't explain it, but she knew that she was the only one who could help Delilah and had to be there for her. "When the time comes," she whispered into the empty room.

Olivia didn't know what had gotten into her. It wasn't like her to be anxious or jittery, but lately her nerves were strung so tight she felt like she was going to snap at any moment. Just the other night, a cat, or maybe even the wind, had knocked over Ms. Helen's garbage can in the middle of the night, and she'd nearly had a coronary.

She'd even started seeing things that weren't there. Twice now, when she'd gotten up in the middle of the night to check on Delilah, she'd looked out the window and sworn that she saw a hulking figure of a man hiding in the shadows of Ms. Helen's house. Even when she'd stared at the spot for what seemed like hours and it hadn't moved, her mind hadn't been convinced enough to let her go back to sleep.

Tonight, she was determined to ignore her own paranoia. But she'd still checked every door and window in the house twice to make sure they were locked. Giving up on finding anything on TV to distract her, Olivia reached for the phone and dialed Brandon's number before she could chicken out. As soon as it rang, Olivia moved to hang up, but before she could put the phone down, Brandon's voice filled her ear, sounding sleepy and concerned.

"You okay?" he mumbled, without saying hello or asking who it was.

"How'd you know it was me?" she asked, relaxing for the first time all night.

"Caller ID."

"Oh. I'm fine. What are you doing?"

"It's two o'clock in the morning—do I really need to answer that?"

"Guess not. I couldn't sleep."

"Hmm," he said.

"What does that mean?" she snapped.

"Nothing. Have you tried some warm milk?"

"Warm milk? How old do you think I am, nine?"

"Okay, fine. How about counting sheep?"

"Good night, Brandon. Sorry I bothered you."

"You didn't." He sighed. "To tell you the truth, I've been having trouble sleeping too. I miss you."

"I miss you too. You know you can still come over."

"I will, but I don't want your new roommate to feel uncomfortable. I know she's still in a fragile state. I don't want to upset her."

"Are you planning on staying away as long as she's here? Because who knows how long that could be," Olivia said, trying to imagine his face. Was it tense, or did he have that resolved look he got when he knew arguing was futile?

"Liv, please, don't ask me stuff like that right now."

"Fine, but I think you should think about it, don't you?"

"Why? Do you plan on keeping her?"

"I don't know. If her family doesn't come for her, and the state allows it, then yes, probably. If I do, will you walk away from me again?"

As the words left Olivia's mouth, she wished she could pull them back, but instead she waited in the silence, listening to him breathe, knowing that she had hurt him.

"Liv, I'm not having this conversation right now. Go to sleep. I'll come by tomorrow, and we can talk then."

"I can't sleep, remember?"

"Why? Are you afraid of the boogeyman?" he asked.

"Yes, I think I am," she said.

"I think I am too. Do you want me to sneak over there and climb in your window and take advantage of you?"

"Yes, I do."

"I'll be there in twenty minutes."

"You'll give Ms. Helen a heart attack," Olivia said with a laugh.

"I think she'll be all right. I'm on my way."

"No . . . no, don't come. I mean, I wish you could, but it's already so early, or late, and I don't want to risk upsetting Delilah."

"Shouldn't she be asleep?"

"She is. At least I think she is, but sometimes I'm not sure. After everything she's been through, she sleeps pretty light."

"Of course," Brandon said.

"Come tomorrow, please, will you?"

"Of course I will." Brandon sighed. "I have to check on my girl."

"Thank you; I know you don't understand why I'm doing this."

"No problem," he said, but she could tell he was still angry.

"If it makes you feel better, I think I can sleep now."

"It does. I'm sorry for being such an ass. I just want to be with you."

"I understand. Good night, Brandon."

"Good night, Liv," he said as she hung up the phone.

On her way to bed, Olivia stopped to look in on Delilah. She lay with her back to the door, curled into the fetal position, the clothes that Olivia had given her as a gift folded neatly at the end of the bed, as if she didn't want them too far away from her. The sight of them hurt Olivia's heart. And she made a silent promise that she would do whatever she could to make sure this girl would never want for anything that she had the power to provide.

Chapter 37

Brandon sat in his truck outside Olivia's house for about twenty minutes, watching Delilah sitting on the steps. He knew she knew he was watching her, but she refused to acknowledge him. Instead, she sat there on the stairs, staring across the street at Ms. Helen's house.

He shook his head and turned off the engine. No sooner had he shut the truck door and turned toward Olivia's house than Ms. Helen's door opened and the old woman stepped outside, wearing a fuzzy bathrobe and clutching her purse as if she were on her way to run an errand. Before Ms. Helen could speak, Brandon raised his hand in a wave, then walked over to the porch and stood in front of Delilah.

"Hello, Delilah," he said. He saw her chest rise as she sucked in a deep breath, her eyes staring down at her feet. "Mind if I sit down?"

As Brandon lowered himself down beside Delilah, she jumped up from the steps and ran inside.

"Brandon Hall, you come here right now," Ms. Helen yelled from across the street. "There are some mighty strange things going on around here, and I want some answers."

"Good afternoon, Ms. Helen," Brandon said as he stood and walked over to her porch.

"Good afternoon to you, too, Brandon. I want to know what's going on around here. Who is that girl staying with Olivia?"

"Don't you worry about that. She's only going to be there for a short time."

"Well, I do worry. I've been seeing and hearing some mighty strange things around here at night, things I have never heard before."

"Like what, Ms. Helen? Aliens again?" Brandon said, trying to hide a smile.

"Every night I've been hearing something in my yard."

"It's probably just prairie dogs scavenging for food. Maybe they're like us and just want to stock up on snacks before the storm comes."

"I know what animals rummaging through my trash sound like. Besides, what animal do you know has a shadow about seven feet tall?"

"It could have been a bear. If you see it again, you should probably call the police. A hungry bear can be pretty dangerous."

"I told you it wasn't an animal."

"Well, whatever it was, you call 911 if you see it again. Okay?"

"Fine," she said as Brandon turned away and approached Olivia's house.

Olivia opened the door and stepped onto the porch, a worried frown creasing her forehead. "What were you doing talking to that nosy old biddy?"

"Nothing. She wanted to know about your guest."

"Did she really ask you that?"

"She did."

"She has some nerve," Olivia said, shaking her head while holding the door open for Brandon to enter.

"She's old, with nothing better to do. What do you expect?"

"Common courtesy."

"She wasn't rude, just concerned. Believe it or not, she cares about you."

"Well, I think it's pretty rude to spy on someone in their home and then ask questions about something that is none of her damn business." Olivia turned her back on Brandon, walked into the living room, and plopped onto the couch.

"She also said there's been someone lurking around her yard at night. I didn't want to tell her, but I'm thinking it's probably a reporter," Brandon said as he sat on the other end of the couch, facing Olivia.

"That makes sense . . . ," Olivia said.

"What do you mean?"

"Well, lately I swear someone's been watching me. Just the other night, someone knocked over Ms. Helen's garbage can. I tried to convince myself it was the wind, but I have to admit I was freaked out. It never even occurred to me that it could be a reporter. What do they possibly think they're going to find in the middle of the night?"

"Something scandalous. Maybe they hope to catch you sneaking in a man or yelling at the kid. Who the hell knows with those people? They're vultures."

"Yeah, you're right. What am I going to do?"

"The only thing you can do. Ignore them and wait for them to go away."

"That's what I told Arlene, but I have to admit, it's a little easier said than done." Olivia sighed.

"True, but I guess it's to be expected when you take the only survivor from Colorado Springs' biggest mystery into your home."

"Thanks, smart-ass."

"Hey, don't bite my head off for telling the truth," Brandon said.

"Well, you don't have to be so damn smug about it."

"You know what? I think somebody needs a nap. Why don't you call me when you feel like being bothered?" Brandon pushed himself up from the couch.

"I'm sorry, please don't go. You're right—I'm super cranky, and I apologize for taking it out on you. Please stay."

"Fine, I'll stay, but you owe me a home-cooked meal once this is all over with," he said as he sat back down on the couch.

"You think it ever will be?"

"That's the reason I wanted to see you. Where is she?"

"Probably in her room. Why?"

"Just wanted to make sure she wasn't in hearing distance," Brandon said, scooting closer to Olivia.

"What is it?"

Brandon told her his idea about sharing Delilah's and Allison's stories on Dorothy Hines's blog. He could see the mixture of hope and dread in Olivia's eyes and he felt bad for her, but he was determined to find a way to locate Delilah's family. That stubborn unwillingness to give up, even after it seemed every possible avenue had been exhausted, was one of the main reasons he had been so successful as a cop. He hoped it would help him now.

"I know it's a long shot, but it's something," he said.

"Wow. I don't know what to say," Olivia said, shaking her head.

"It's pretty amazing, huh?"

"Don't take this the wrong way, but what do you hope to accomplish with this story?"

"Someone might know or remember something, anything."

"After twenty-five years?"

Brandon stood up and looked down at Olivia. He was disappointed and a little angry at her reaction, but he understood how terrifying the idea of losing Delilah to some long-lost relative of Allison's must be for her. He wished there were something he could say to reassure her, but he realized in this case, the truth was the best option.

"I'm going to try everything to find this girl and bring her home. A lot has changed. Back then, most people didn't have cable. Allison's story may not have been heard outside of her own neighborhood. With the internet, and cable, satellite TV, you never know," he said.

"I'm sorry. I honestly don't know what the hell is wrong with me—overtired, I guess. Of course I want you to find Allison, and I will help any way I can."

"Thanks. The best thing you can do right now is get some sleep," Brandon said with a smile.

"Yes, sir," Olivia said as she stood and gave him a hug and a quick kiss as he looked down at her.

"I miss you, Liv."

"Not even close to how much I miss you."

"I feel like it's going to be over soon," he said.

"I hope you're right."

"When have I ever been wrong?" Brandon said as they walked to the door.

As Brandon hugged Olivia goodbye, he looked over her shoulder. Delilah stood in the doorway of the living room, staring at him. Brandon smiled at her, raising his hand to wave. But as he loosened his hold on Olivia, Delilah faded back into the hallway, disappearing as quietly as she had come.

Chapter 38

Olivia watched, riveted, as Dorothy Hines recounted the story of Allison Moore's disappearance. What started as a blog post had evolved into a national news story, and Olivia couldn't help but fear what this new attention to Allison's story would mean for Delilah. She wrapped her arms around herself to ward off the chill that crept over her body when the picture of a young Allison Moore flashed onto the screen.

"Crap," Olivia whispered. After turning off the TV, she made her way down the hall to check on Delilah. Brandon had planned a picnic for tomorrow, in hopes of making Delilah feel more comfortable with him being around. But suddenly, all Olivia wanted was to crawl into bed, close her eyes, and quiet her racing brain.

As she approached the room where Delilah spent most of her time, she was surprised to see light spilling from the partially opened door. She pushed open the door and stepped inside the room, gasping in shock.

Delilah sat in the middle of the floor, a photo album chronicling Carly's short life sprawled open in front of her. Pictures of Carly, which Delilah had removed from the album, surrounded her. As Olivia took a step into the room, Delilah extended her hand to Olivia.

Olivia looked down at the photograph in Delilah's hand. In the picture, taken the morning Carly disappeared, Carly had been staring up at Olivia, the sun turning her curls into a ring of fire surrounding her pale face, her cheeks as red as fall apples.

"Sunny," Delilah said, her voice sounding rusty and old in the quiet of the room.

Olivia stared blankly at Delilah, unable to understand.

"Sunny," Delilah repeated.

Olivia stumbled over to the bed and flopped down, never taking her eyes from Delilah.

"Hurt," Delilah said, and there was no denying the fear in that one word as she lowered her voice to a whisper.

Olivia felt her head grow light and her body sway. She would faint if she didn't get ahold of herself. Closing her eyes, she bent forward and placed her head between her knees until the ringing in her ears dissipated and the room grew steady again. Slowly she raised her head and looked at Delilah. The girl sat, unmoving, her eyes locked on Olivia's face, as if she could wait forever.

"Sunny. Hurt," she repeated, holding the picture out to Olivia.

"Carly," Olivia said softly, taking the picture from Delilah, not noticing the tears that slid down her cheeks.

"Hurt," Delilah repeated.

"Yes, hurt," Olivia said, clutching the picture to her heart.

A frown creased the smoothness of Delilah's forehead as she picked up a different picture, this one showing Carly running through the leaves at the farmers' market. A pain, sharp and cruel, pierced Olivia's gut as an image of that day sprang into her mind. It had been the first real cool fall day, and a goat was there. Carly had tried goat cheese, and Olivia and Brandon had laughed at the look of surprised disgust on her face.

"Sister," Delilah said, hugging the picture to her own tiny chest.

"You have a sister?" Olivia asked, keeping her voice calm, even as her heart raced with excitement at Delilah's words.

"Sister," Delilah said.

"What was your sister's name?"

For a long moment Delilah said nothing. She only stared down at the picture, tracing the face with her fingertips as if trying to touch the girl behind the image.

Olivia resisted the urge to push Delilah; instead she sat quietly and watched her study the photos.

"Sunny. My sister's name was Sunny," she finally said.

"What did Sunny look like?" Olivia asked, wanting to pull back the question even before it had fallen from her lips.

"Sunny," Delilah said, pointing to a smiling picture of Carly.

"Sunny looked like Carly," Olivia said, pushing aside her feelings.

"Gone," Delilah said.

"Where did Sunny go?" Olivia forced herself to ask, though she was sure she didn't want to know the answer to that question, or any others, while sitting alone with Delilah in the heart of the night.

"Father took her away," Delilah said, tears shining in her eyes.

A loud crash, followed by the sound of breaking glass, filled the room. Olivia screamed and dived from the bed, folding Delilah into her arms. Putting a finger to her lips to warn Delilah to stay quiet, Olivia stood, holding on to Delilah's trembling hand. Quietly she hurried across the floor and eased open the closet. It was a poor hiding place, but Olivia hoped it would keep Delilah safe long enough for help to arrive.

"Stay quiet until you hear my voice or see the police," Olivia said, bending down to whisper in Delilah's ear. "Nod if you understand."

Delilah bobbed her head up and down, once, but as Olivia turned to shut the door, Delilah clung to her hand, refusing to let go.

"Shh, angel, don't be afraid. Everything is going to be all right," Olivia said, hoping it was the truth.

As she turned to close the door, she saw a wooden bat that Brandon had bought for Carly one year, when he was sure she was going to be the first professional ball player in the family, just because she'd watched a game with him and remembered one of the players' names. Carly had played with the bat exactly one time, and it had probably been in the same place ever since. Now Olivia grabbed it and firmly pushed Delilah back in the closet and shut the door.

Murmuring a quick prayer, she crept from the room, holding the bat close to her chest. The noise had come from the kitchen, but she had no way of knowing where the intruder was in the house. Once she left the confines of the narrow hallway, she would be exposed and vulnerable to an attack. She thought of the cell phone she'd left lying on her nightstand. She could almost hear her mother's voice in her ear, nagging her about keeping it close. Probably why she never did. To reach it, she'd have to make it all the way upstairs, leaving her cut off from Delilah. To get to the house phone, she'd have to make it unseen past the kitchen, all the way across the living room. Also not a good option.

She eased her way down the dark hall to the kitchen, where the noise had come from. Standing at the edge of the hallway, her tongue stuck to the roof of her dry mouth, the sound of her own heartbeat filling her ears, Olivia took a ragged breath and leaped into the living room, swinging the bat, screaming like a banshee until she tripped over her own feet and fell, banging her head on the floor as the bat flew from her grip, knocking over a lamp.

Olivia lay still, waiting for the intruder to step from the shadows and attack. When nothing moved in the dark room, she dared to open her eyes. Taking a deep breath, she waited for her heart to slow to a normal pace before trying to sit up. As she rose from the floor, she became aware of a rustling sound coming from the kitchen. Her body stiffened as she looked around the room for the bat.

As her eyes grew accustomed to the shapes in the familiar room, she saw the kitchen curtain fluttering in the breeze from the open window.

"Shit," she whispered, grabbing the back of a chair as her legs grew weak. A shaky laugh escaped her lips as she silently chastised herself for her nervousness. As Olivia walked into the kitchen to close the window, she saw that the noise that had nearly stopped her heart had been caused by a flowerpot that had blown off the windowsill and now lay shattered on the kitchen floor. Had she opened the window?

A small noise drew her attention back toward the hallway, and she whirled around, a scream on her lips. Delilah stood looking at her from the doorway, the fear in her eyes making a lie out of the determined press of her lips. Olivia's heart caught as she looked at Delilah, so ready to stand with her against the monsters that held so much terror for her. Forgetting about the mystery of the open window, Olivia raced across the kitchen and bent down in front of Delilah, taking her into her arms.

Delilah's eyes never left Olivia as she watched her shut and lock the window and then sweep up the broken ceramic pieces.

Once the floor was clean, Olivia reached to turn out the light.

"No," Delilah said clearly, pulling Olivia away from the light switch.

"Okay," Olivia said. If anyone had asked, Olivia would have said she left the light on to appease the girl, but if she were forced to be honest, she would have to say she was grateful for the request.

"Bedtime," Olivia said.

"Bedtime," Delilah repeated, bringing a smile to Olivia's face.

Olivia felt the tension drain from her body as Delilah turned away from her and walked into her bedroom.

Olivia had taken a few steps away from the room when she heard Delilah's voice, void of any emotion, drifting through the open door and into the hallway. Olivia's feet stuttered and she froze, goose bumps raising her flesh as Delilah's words became clear and she realized the girl was praying.

✳

Ms. Helen stood staring at the demon come to life. She could feel the evil roll off him, sure as she could feel the snow coming. She stood as still as the trees in her own yard, praying to God he wouldn't turn and catch her spying. She was eighty-five years old that day and couldn't remember a time when she had wet her own pants, but when he turned his eyes on her, Ms. Helen felt her water let loose and run down her legs. A whimper like a hurt dog escaped her throat, but she was powerless to move, even as she watched him come for her. "God save me," Ms. Helen said as her heart stuttered in her chest and darkness claimed her.

Chapter 39

The phone rang beside Brandon's head and startled him into full aware-
ness. As soon as his hand touched the receiver, he knew it would be
Olivia, just as the hairs standing at attention along his neck let him
know something was wrong. A glance out the window revealed a morning sky that looked closer to twilight than dawn.

Brandon snatched the phone and sat up in one jerky motion,
smashing the receiver against his head in his hurry.

"Hello?" he nearly yelled.

"Brandon, it's me, Olivia. I'm sorry to wake you."

"That's okay, I'm here."

"Can you come over?" she asked, and Brandon could hear the
quiver in her voice she was trying to hide.

"Are you okay?"

"I'm fine. It's just been a long night. I know you must be on your
way to work—"

"I'm on my way," he said, hanging up the phone as he jumped out
of bed.

Brandon raced around the room, throwing on clothes as he went.
He barely brushed his teeth before racing toward the door, only to
realize at the last moment that he'd forgotten to turn off the water in
the bathroom sink. Olivia had tried to hide it, but she was terrified. He
hadn't heard that tone in her voice since the day she'd told him Carly

was missing. Then the terror had been on display for the entire world to see, but this barely subdued version was somehow worse.

Brandon jumped into his truck and peeled out of the driveway, praying he wouldn't get stopped before he could reach Olivia. Taking a deep breath, he forced himself to slow down enough that if he did get stopped, he wouldn't be arrested. Fighting the urge to pick up the phone and call Olivia back, he gripped the steering wheel with both hands and tried to empty his brain and focus on the road.

When he pulled up, he was a little surprised to see that it looked exactly the same as yesterday. There were no flames, police, or news crews, just the house where he and Olivia had once lived their life together. Seeing it wrapped in the peaceful quiet of the morning immediately slowed his heart. Sucking in a deep breath, he stepped out of the truck, enjoying the feel of the cold air cutting across his cheeks. The snow would be here soon, he thought as he walked up the porch stairs.

As he raised his hand to knock, the door flung open. Olivia stood in front of him, her hair and clothes disheveled, dark circles growing under her eyes. He'd started to let his arm fall back to his side when Olivia launched herself into his arms, almost knocking him backward.

"Whoa," he said, squeezing her tightly into his chest.

"I'm sorry, I'm sorry. It's just the window, the wind, Delilah . . . ," Olivia said, her voice breaking, the last words disappearing into sobs.

Brandon loosened his grip on Olivia and guided her into the house, patting her gently on the back. As they stepped into the house, he let go of her long enough to turn and shut the door. He fully expected to see Ms. Helen peeking from her window, but for once her curtain remained still as he locked the door.

"I guess everybody has to sleep sometime," he mumbled.

"What?" Olivia asked.

"Ms. Helen, she's not at her post."

"Oh," Olivia said as she walked into the kitchen and reached for the full coffeepot.

"What happened here?" Brandon asked, looking around the kitchen.

"I feel like a silly fool," Olivia said, splashing coffee onto the table as she tried to fill two cups.

"Here, let me." Brandon took the coffeepot from her hand and guided her to the chair.

"Oh my God, you're going to think I'm being such a baby."

"Why don't you let me decide? Tell me what happened."

As Brandon sipped his coffee, Olivia told him everything that had happened during the night, from Delilah starting to talk to the mysterious shattering of the flowerpot. By the time she'd finished, her hands were steady and her voice was strong, but an embarrassed smile hovered on her lips, making Brandon want to reach out and kiss her.

Instead of fighting the urge, he leaned across the table and lightly touched his lips to hers.

"You're not being a baby," he said.

"I'm not?"

"No, but I should have never left you alone."

"Thank you for coming back."

"Thank you for calling," he said, reaching out to touch her cheek.

"Suddenly, I'm so tired. I feel like I could crawl right up on this table and go to sleep."

"Why don't you go to bed, and when you wake up, I'll make you some lunch, or even dinner if it comes to that."

"I wish I could, but Delilah . . ."

"Don't you worry about that; I'll take good care of her."

"I don't doubt it, but you know she's not comfortable with anyone but me yet."

"That's true, but she doesn't appear to be going anywhere anytime soon, and neither am I, so I say it's time that we start to get comfortable, don't you think? Besides, you're only a room away."

"Yes, sir." Olivia stood and reached for him. He relished the feeling of having her wrapped in his arms and wished he could pick her up and carry her to the bed they had once shared. As if she felt what he was thinking, she reached up to kiss him, and he let his hand drop below her waist to caress her backside.

Olivia pulled back to look into his eyes and jumped out of his arms like a kid who'd been caught stealing a kiss by her parents. Brandon whirled around, following Olivia's eyes.

Delilah stood in the door, staring at them. Her eyes were blank and unmoving.

"Delilah," Olivia said, her voice shaking. She stepped in front of Brandon and walked over to where the child stood. "Good morning, angel," she said, bending down to hug her.

For a moment it seemed Delilah would not answer, but then she spoke. "Good morning, Olivia," she croaked.

To Brandon, it sounded as if Delilah were just getting over laryngitis, her voice was so rough.

"Can you say good morning to Brandon? He's a friend," Olivia said, putting an arm around Delilah's back.

Delilah lowered her eyes to the floor as Brandon smiled.

"Good morning, Brandon," she said.

"Good morning, Delilah," Brandon said, kneeling down in front of the girl until they were eye level. "I had a beautiful girl, just like you. Her name was Carly. I couldn't protect her, but I will protect you and Olivia. I promise."

Delilah's head snapped up, and instead of avoiding his eyes, the girl gazed at his face in wonder.

"'The king will slay the dragon with his magic sword and rescue me from the evil castle, and we'll all live happily ever after,'" Delilah said.

"'At your service, milady,'" Brandon said, tears flooding his eyes as he bowed down on one knee, repeating the words from the play he and Carly had written together, then performed for Olivia, one Mother's Day. Carly had loved it so much that adding to the story had become a favorite rainy-day pastime, allowing it to branch out like so many limbs on a tree, a special project between father and daughter.

"'Your loyalty shall be greatly rewarded, good knight,'" Delilah said, her hand covering her heart as she bent her knees in a quick curtsy.

※

Olivia thought her heart would break into a million shards as the words once spoken from daughter to father fell from Delilah's lips. She reached up to touch her own face and was surprised to find her cheeks not only dry, but as cold as if she'd just come in from a winter's storm.

She watched as Brandon stood, his dazed eyes searching hers. She couldn't hear what he wanted to say, whether he would convince her of a coincidence or allow himself to hope that Carly was still alive. Either choice was unbearable.

Turning away, she left Brandon and Delilah alone in the kitchen, staring at each other.

She wouldn't remember walking down the hall or crawling into her bed, but she would always be grateful for the merciful darkness that soon enveloped her, protecting her, even from dreams as she slept.

Chapter 40

Brandon could have said any of a thousand things, but as he stared into Delilah's wary, too-old eyes, his heart spoke for him.

"Do you know my girl? Have you seen my Carly?"

Delilah stared at him long enough for centuries to pass, it seemed, before she spoke.

"Sunny," she said, and then reached out to touch his face.

Brandon wanted to let it go. He felt his world teetering on edge. If he didn't push, he could continue with Olivia as they rebuilt their lives together, maybe starting their own family anew. And if that new family must include Delilah, he could accept that, too, in time. All he had to do was dismiss Delilah's words as a strange but meaningless coincidence.

The girl took a step back, her eyes clouding with caution as she looked past him to where Olivia had disappeared down the hall.

"I'm sorry. I didn't mean to scare you, but this is very important, and I need your help," he said.

"Help?" Delilah asked.

"Come with me," he said, reaching for her hand as he stood up, the idea of not knowing for sure suddenly too much for him to bear. All he needed to do was show Delilah a picture of his Carly, and he would know, they would know, once and for all.

For a moment he wasn't sure if Delilah would follow him. She stood staring at him as if trying to see right through him. When she reached out her hand, he folded it in his and guided her down the hall.

As he stepped across the threshold and into the room that had once been his daughter's, for a moment his mind slipped, and he was sure the child's hand he was holding was his Carly's, and he was only walking her to bed. The momentary lapse hurt even worse than the initial blow, and Brandon almost turned and fled, leaving the memories buried in the past, where they belonged.

Suddenly the urge for a drink was so strong he could almost taste it. Delilah tugged on his hand, leading him to the bed, where the photos lay spread out. He didn't want to see. He didn't want to hear what Delilah had to say. He wanted to shove the question back into the darkness where it belonged, but Delilah pulled him onward.

When they stood in front of the bed, she pointed at a picture of Carly, taken while she was playing make-believe in the yard, unaware that her parents were spying on her from the window as she held a conversation with her make-believe friend over the fence.

"What's your friend's name?" he had asked her.

"I can't tell you, Daddy—he's my secret friend. He's going to bring me a pony."

"Well, no ponies in the house; you make sure you tell your friend that," he had said, swooping her up into his arms and making her giggle as he swung her around.

"Sunny," Delilah said, pointing at the picture, and Brandon's world collapsed around him.

Chapter 41

Brandon sat in the dark alone. Olivia was asleep again, and so was Delilah. He would have to tell her everything the girl had told him—well, almost everything. He knew he would. All evening, as he'd stood beside Olivia, looked her in the eyes, joked with her, even kissed her a couple of times, he had managed to look like he was sane, but all the while his mind had been splintering apart.

Outside, the wind whipped itself into a fury, and small flakes of snow drifted against the window. "Father": that's what Delilah had called her captor, with the same tone of horror reserved for all monsters who stalk the nightmares of young children.

"Sunny was disobedient, and Father had to punish her. He said Sunny was cursed with evil, so he locked us in the Teaching Room. Follow the path from the house through the woods, and that's where you'll find it."

All night, he'd used all his strength to hold back the emotions that threatened to crush him. Now, as he sat alone in the dark, the tears flowed down his face, hot against his cold cheeks. He didn't reach up and brush them away. Instead, he let them soak his chest as he stared out the window, reliving Delilah's words.

"She went with him?" Brandon had asked, unable to stop himself, though he knew the answer would kill what was left of his soul.

"Sunny said he would come to her and talk to her through the fence," Delilah had said. "He told her that he had magic powers that made him invisible. He warned her not to tell her parents, or they would become angry and never let her see him again, and then she would never get the pony that she wanted so badly. She wanted to see the ponies."

He should have made her stop then, but instead he'd listened until all the words were gone.

"Where is home?" he asked.

"High up in the mountains, right under God's nose," she whispered, as if worried about someone overhearing.

"How did you get away, Delilah?"

"It was Jacob. Jacob and Mother."

"Can you tell me about it?"

Brandon barely breathed as he waited for her to speak. When she started to talk, her voice was as flat and cold as a machine.

"I never knew there was anything but the mountain, Mother, the Family, and Father, not until Sunny came. Jacob was mad at Sunny at first for telling me about down here. That's what he always called it. He said it would only start trouble. He said Father would never let any of us get away, but Sunny wouldn't listen; she begged him to help her escape, to help her get back to you. He shoulda told Father what Sunny was up to, but he couldn't; he loved Sunny, more than his own life, and so he helped."

"How?" Brandon said, fighting back the nausea swirling in his stomach.

"Anytime Father and Mother went visiting the Family, Jacob would come and work on the old car, trying to make it run. He was going to teach us how to drive it, in case something happened to him, but before he could, the snow came and wiped out the mountain road. Sunny wanted to take our chances and go anyway."

"Why didn't you?" Brandon asked, nearly choking on the bitterness that filled his throat.

"Jacob thought we had more time, but one morning even before the rooster crowed, Father came and took Sunny away. When she came back, she wasn't Sunny anymore. She wouldn't eat and she wouldn't talk and she didn't laugh no more. She just cried, unless she was asleep. Then she screamed. Father called the Family together and told them that the Lord had blessed Sunny with his greatest gift, a baby."

"Oh God," Brandon moaned, covering his mouth with his hand, trying to hold back the scream that filled his head. "What happened to her? Where is Carly, Delilah?"

"She drank the medicine that Jacob made and killed the baby. Father said she'd broken God's law. He said she was ruined. He called the Family and hung her from the whipping tree until she was dead, as God willed. Soon he'll be coming for me. He's going to take me home, and I'm going to be punished just like Sunny and Jacob."

"What is your father's name?" he had asked, but Delilah could not, or would not, answer. He'd pushed Delilah until she'd completely shut down. Olivia wouldn't have approved of his tactics, but like it or not, Delilah was the only link he had to the monster.

A crash from outside startled Brandon, and he stood and walked to the window. The streets were deserted, as they so often were before a storm. Snow devils chased each other down the street in swirls, picking up the lids from garbage cans and tossing them in the streets.

Was he out there tonight, this Father, watching, waiting for a chance to take Delilah back? A shiver raced down his spine.

"You're safe here, Delilah. Do you understand? Olivia and I will keep you safe. No one will ever hurt you again. I promise."

Delilah stared at him, her eyes clouded with uncertainty and fear, saying nothing as she studied his face. Finally, she nodded. He resisted the urge to pull her into his arms, instead reaching for her hand and giving it a gentle squeeze.

Tonight, he would slip into bed with Olivia and hold her close to him, grateful that, at least for now, she was ignorant of their daughter's fate. Tomorrow the hunt would begin.

Across the street, one dim light blinked on inside Ms. Helen's house, and he made a mental note to check on her in the morning. As if hearing his thoughts, the curtain twitched shut, and the light faded out.

Chapter 42

"I'll be back as soon as I can, I promise. I wouldn't go, except I've had this meeting scheduled for weeks, and it's an important client. Considering how cool Bob has been about letting me take off without any notice, I thought I'd at least try to get this done," Brandon said, but Olivia only heard he was going. She knew she was acting like a baby, but ever since she'd heard Delilah repeat the words from Carly's play to Brandon, she felt like a bomb, one wrong move away from an explosion that would send her into oblivion forever.

All morning Delilah had hidden herself away in Carly's old room, mostly with the door shut, coming out only when Olivia had insisted that she join them for breakfast, where she'd sat, silent, her head bowed, pushing the plain white toast that she favored from one side of the plate to the other.

More than once, Olivia had seen her stealing glances at Brandon, who pretended not to notice, filling the room with light chatter, even managing to coax a brief smile from Delilah as he regaled them with a tale about a pack of wild pigs running amok down I-25. But now Brandon was leaving, and Olivia would be forced to be alone with Delilah. Delilah, who knew words that had been special between father and daughter. Words that only the two of them should have known.

Brandon, in his infinite kindness, had understood that she was not ready to face the truth and allowed her to hide, at least for the time being, and she was grateful.

"I'm afraid," Olivia said, slamming down the coffee cup she'd been holding, but not drinking, for the last ten minutes.

"You're afraid of Delilah?" Brandon asked, startling her.

"Brandon, don't patronize me."

"I'm not. I just don't know what you're getting at. Look, I know you're kinda freaked out, with good reason. I'm not going to lie: so am I." He walked to the window and looked out at the still-clear street. "That's odd."

"What?" Olivia asked.

"Nothing . . . I guess every time I look out this window, I expect to see Ms. Helen looking back at me, but this morning her curtain is closed tight," he said, a frown on his face as he turned around to face Olivia.

"I guess old busybodies need rest too," Olivia said.

"The last couple of weeks have been hell on both of us, and Delilah, too, I'm sure. I was thinking that maybe we could take some time to get away once this is all over."

"What if it's never over?"

"Then I guess we'll wrap ourselves in the safety of this house and never leave," he said, walking around the table to put his arms around her.

"I'm sorry, it's just that something doesn't feel right. I don't know what it is, but I feel like every nerve in my body is on red alert," she said, resting her head on his chest.

"I know what you mean," he said, stroking her back. "Listen, there's no reason for me to go rushing into the office right this minute. I'm sure a call would work."

"You don't mind?"

"Absolutely not—I'll reschedule to after the storm passes."

"Thank you. I know I'm being a baby, but I just have this feeling."

"Why don't you go check on Delilah, and I'll go check on Ms. Helen. When I get back, I'll make you ladies lunch, and we can watch the snow come down together."

"That sounds wonderful."

"I'll be right back," he said, kissing her lightly on the lips.

"Take your time," she said as the door closed.

✳

After she'd cleared the table and put the few dishes into the dishwasher, she left the kitchen and walked down the hall. Carly's door was almost closed. Olivia gently pushed it open. Delilah was buried under the covers, her head resting on the pillow. Her body rose and fell as she slept. Since she'd come into her home, Olivia had never seen Delilah so at peace. Instead of waking her up, she sank into the overstuffed story chair, as Carly used to call it, and watched Delilah sleep. Outside, the snow started to fall, and Olivia felt her own eyes grow heavy.

Chapter 43

Brandon walked outside and closed the door behind him. As he stood at the top of the steps, he tilted his head upward and watched the snow fall. Without thinking, he stuck out his tongue and caught a new snowflake, laughing at his own silliness. In a little while, there would be enough to make a decent snowball. Kids would fill the street, building snowmen and snow forts, while Ms. Helen spent countless hopeless hours trying to shoo them out of her yard. With a grin, Brandon realized he was just a little jealous.

He lowered his head, strode off the porch, and walked the short distance to Ms. Helen's house. He wasn't surprised to see that someone had already thrown salt on the sidewalk in front of the house as well as the walkway. As crotchety as she was, everyone in the neighborhood still looked after her.

"She ain't there," a voice said as Brandon raised his hand to knock on the door. He turned, his hand still hanging in the air, to see who had spoken.

Otis Williams stood at the foot of the stairs, a shovel slung over his shoulder, his heavy coat swallowing his small frame, and a furry hat, which looked as if it could have been an actual animal only a few moments prior, jammed down on his head.

Otis had been taking care of Ms. Helen ever since her husband had died in a bar fight. People half joked he was more than just a handyman to the lonely widow. If he was, no one had ever made a stink about it, even before the time when the idea of a black man and a white woman keeping company was acceptable.

"Mr. Otis, you nearly gave me a heart attack," Brandon said.

"Well, if yo' heart is that weak, you deserve it," he said, dropping the shovel from his shoulder to the ground.

"I guess you have a point there," Brandon said.

Otis didn't speak; he just nodded and leaned on the shovel, looking up at Brandon expectantly.

"Where did she go?" Brandon asked.

"Don't know. Showed up here once the snow started, to clear the walk and see if she needed some things from the sto', and I ain't git no answer."

"That's odd," Brandon said.

"Sho is. Ms. Helen don't go nowhere no more, and she sure don't go nowhere without telling me. She knows I worry," Otis said.

"Did you try and call her?" Brandon asked.

"I did. She ain't there."

"Maybe her daughter came and picked her up. You know she does that sometimes."

"She not supposed to come until two days fo' Easter. They bring her back Easter night. That way they can show them church folk they done their duty. Only reason they even do that 'cause they think she sitting on a bunch of money and they scairt they gone get left out her will."

"Well, I don't know anything about that," Brandon said.

"Do you visit yo mama?" Otis asked.

"Mr. Otis, you know my parents are both dead."

"What that got to do with you visiting?"

"I guess you're right about that."

"Sho I am."

"When is the last time you saw Ms. Helen?"

"It's been a couple days, 'cause I got the croup and was laid up for a minute, but Minnie told me she talked to her and she was fine."

"Minnie?"

"Yeah, Minnie—you know, Minnie more like a daughter to her than them two she gave birth to."

"When did Minnie talk to her last, then?" Brandon asked.

"I cain't be certain—my mind slipping, especially when I'm sick—but she called me, said Helen fine."

"Well, the news has been going on and on about this storm coming. Maybe Minnie contacted her daughters and had them come pick her up until it's over. She'd be worried sick if Helen stayed down here by herself. Especially if we lose power, like they say we may."

"I suppose so, but look like she woulda told me if she did."

"I'll tell you what, Mr. Otis. I'll get in touch with Minnie and see what I can find out."

Grumbling under his breath, Mr. Otis slung the shovel over his shoulder and shuffled away.

Brandon turned and stomped back across the street, all the delight from the impending snowstorm forgotten.

Chapter 44

The house was quiet when Brandon pushed open the door. He'd expected to find Olivia sitting on the sofa, waiting impatiently for his return. He opened his mouth to call her name but stopped himself at the last moment. After closing the door, he walked down the hall, careful not to make any noise.

When he reached Carly's open door, he swallowed sudden tears. Olivia was curled up in the story chair, sound asleep, a blanket tucked carefully around her. Delilah lay as close to her as she could get without falling out of the bed. He couldn't count the number of times he had come home and found Olivia and Carly in those exact same positions. Brandon stepped into the room, blinking the tears from his eyes, and bent to kiss Olivia's warm cheek.

As he stood, his phone buzzed in his pocket, sounding like a jackhammer in the quiet of the room. As fast as he could, he yanked the phone from his pocket and was surprised to see the number for the lab.

"Amy, is everything all right?" he whispered, not bothering to say hello as he rushed from the room.

"Brandon, thank God you answered. You have to come here now."

"What's wrong?"

"Seriously, Brandon, I can't talk to you on the phone. You have to get here as soon as you can, okay?"

"I can't. Not right now. Olivia has been freaked out all morning, and to tell you the truth, I'm feeling a little odd myself. I can't leave her right now. She and Delilah are finally asleep. I don't want them to wake up and find me gone."

"Brandon, you know I wouldn't ask if it wasn't that important. Hell, if you don't want to leave them, bring them with you. It's that important."

"How long will this take?"

"Not long, I promise, but you have to come."

"Amy, why can't you just tell me?"

"If I could explain it, I would. All I can say is, it may be the answers you're looking for."

"Okay, I'll be right there. But seriously, I have to come right back."

"That's fine. The sooner you get here, the sooner you can get back, so come on." She hung up the phone before he had a chance to respond.

Brandon hesitated for a moment, considering whether he should wake Olivia. *I'll be back before she wakes up,* he thought as he rushed out of the house, making sure to lock the door behind him before driving toward the station as fast as the streets would allow.

Even though he drove the truck as fast as he could on the already-icy streets, he felt like it took him forever to make it to the station. Worse, he couldn't push away the feeling that he'd made the wrong decision in leaving Olivia and Delilah alone.

As Brandon pulled into the parking lot, his phone buzzed again. He fully expected it to be Olivia, calling to find out where he had gone, but he was shocked to see it was Minnie. Instantly, he remembered that he'd forgotten to call her about Ms. Helen and guessed that Otis must have found her first.

"Minnie," he said, trying to keep the impatience from his voice as he exited his truck.

"Brandon, don't worry, I'm not going to keep you. I see on the news that a storm is heading your way. I just wanted to make sure that Olivia is all right. I tried to call the house, but I got a busy signal, and you know she doesn't ever answer that cell phone." Brandon could almost see Minnie's hands curling and uncurling, as she did when she was nervous or frustrated. "I swear I don't even understand why she has one. With her being a doctor, I'd think she'd need to keep it near her at all times. Plus, I need you to check on Helen. I haven't been able to get her on the phone in days."

"She's on leave, Minnie. It's been *days*?" Brandon asked, trying to keep his tone light.

"Yes, days. Can you hear me, Brandon? Why is the phone at the house getting a busy signal?"

"I'm sure it's because the snow probably built up on a line and brought it down. Olivia is fine. I just left her, and I'll be going back over there as soon as I can."

"I know you and Olivia are back together, though neither one of you had the decency to tell me, so stop acting like you were just visiting. I may be old, but I'm not stupid."

"What's age got to do with it," Brandon muttered.

"What did you say?"

"Nothing, Minnie, I'm sorry. I have a bad connection here. I'll tell Olivia to call you as soon as I talk to her."

"Very good, and don't forget about Ms. Helen."

"Are you sure her daughter didn't pick her up?"

"Of course I'm sure. Her daughter is not picking her up one minute before she has to, which is two days before Easter, and they think that's too soon."

"I'll go check on her as soon as I can, but I've got to go right now," Brandon said. He could have told her about the conversation he'd had with Otis, but he knew if he did, he'd never get off the call. So he ignored the twinge of guilt the omission cost him and hung up before she had a chance to veer off into another conversation.

Brandon sprinted into the building, bypassing the crowded squad room, where troopers had started to gather before hitting the streets. He took the stairs two at a time, nearly knocking Amy over as he burst through the stairwell door.

"Hey, what are you doing standing in front of the door like that? That's dangerous."

"Only if people crash through it like they're being chased," Amy said, standing with one hand at the small of her back, looking tired and pale under the harsh light.

"Are you okay?" Brandon asked.

"I'm lovely, except this little boy is choosing today of all days to act up," she said, patting her belly.

"You should be at home with your feet up."

"You're right about that. As soon as we're done here, that's exactly where I'm going," she said, her face twisting with pain.

"Maybe I should take you to the doctor. It might be time."

"He wouldn't dare. My husband is halfway across the world, and this is supposed to be the worst storm in Colorado history. No way am I having a baby today."

"If you say so, Your Majesty. So, what was so important that I had to come see you right now?"

"I'm sorry for dragging you all the way down here, but these people came a long way to tell their story. I thought you'd want to hear it in person. I think they may hold the key to all of this."

"What people?" Brandon asked, looking over Amy's head into the deserted hall.

"Right this way," she said.

Brandon followed Amy down the hall to her office and opened the door. An older black man and woman sat in the two chairs facing Amy's cluttered desk.

"Henry and Sadie Jessup, this is Brandon Hall. He's a friend, and he's been looking into Allison's disappearance."

Chapter 45

Inside the silent house, Delilah sat up straight. Olivia was sound asleep in the chair. Delilah slid from the bed as quietly as she could. Wrapping the quilt around her, she crept from the room and pulled the door closed. She walked to the front door, pausing to look back at the house that could have become her home. As she hesitated, Sunny appeared beside the couch, beckoning to her, her dead eyes pleading with Delilah not to go. Delilah wasn't surprised to see her. Sunny was always there in one form or another.

"He will kill her if I don't go. You know he will," she said. The ghost shook her head, reaching out her hands toward Delilah.

Delilah wished she'd been able to kiss Olivia goodbye, but she couldn't risk waking her. Refusing to look back, she stepped out into the frigid air. Although the clock said it was barely two in the afternoon, the sky had darkened, making it seem much later. Heavy, wet snow fell, high winds whirling it through the air, hiding the street in a blanket of white.

Standing on the porch, wrapped in only the quilt she'd dragged from the bed, her body shaking and teeth chattering uncontrollably, Delilah looked toward the house across the street where he waited. She had seen him in her dreams as clear as day, sitting in the old woman's house. Now she could feel him calling her, as sure as if he were standing beside her, whispering in her ear.

Sunny's father had promised that he could keep her and Olivia safe, but she knew he was wrong. She had prayed every day on her knees for mercy. She had resisted the temptation of gluttony, keeping as close as she could to the food of Mother's table. She had turned away from the obscene books the nurses had put in front of her. Still, the Lord had ignored her pleas. Father was here, and the devil himself would not stop him from returning her to Hurt Mountain.

She wished she were still asleep. She wanted to be brave but could not stop the hot tears from sliding down her cold cheeks as she walked down the stairs and trudged across the street. As she reached the foot of the steps of the house, the front door opened. Father stood looking down at her, holding out his hand.

For a moment, panic took over, and she took a step backward, fully intending to run back to Olivia. A laugh, cold as the snow falling from the sky, came from the doorway. An image of Olivia, her neck snapped like a broken twig, rushed into Delilah's head. She forced herself to move forward again. Once she was on the porch, she stole one quick glance back toward the house. It was mostly hidden from view now by the swirling snow. Inside, Olivia was safe, and that was enough.

As she stepped across the threshold into the waiting house, Delilah retreated to the dark comfort of her mind, allowing the blackness to swallow her as Father reached out to pull her into his arms.

Chapter 46

Brandon looked down at the older black couple, dressed in what looked like their Sunday best, sitting on the edge of their seats and staring up at him expectantly.

"Well, is anybody going to say anything?" asked the older man, whom Amy had introduced as Henry Jessup.

"Nice to meet you," Brandon stammered, taking an awkward step into the room.

The man stood up and walked toward Brandon, his back straight as a ruler, his dark skin seeming to glow against the crisp white shirt he wore buttoned up to his neck.

"Nice to meet you, too, sir. Are you the one gonna find out what happened to our girl?" he asked, looking Brandon in the eye without blinking.

"I'm sorry?" Brandon said, turning toward Amy.

"Let me catch you up, Brandon," Amy said. "Mrs. Jessup saw Dorothy Hines's story on CNN—"

"The cable box wasn't working right, so it was the only channel we could get in the house," Mrs. Jessup explained.

"Yes, ma'am. Anyway, they saw the story—" Amy started before she was cut off by Mrs. Jessup again.

"At first I didn't know what you was talking 'bout, 'cause I had the volume turned down low," Sadie Jessup said.

"But when Mrs. Jessup saw the picture of Allison—"

"We have the same picture of Allison in our house, hanging over our mantel. It was the last picture she took," Sadie said.

"Sadie Bell, let the woman tell him what happened," Henry said.

"Yes . . . yes, you're right. Go ahead, honey." Sadie nodded toward Amy.

I bet she used to be a teacher, Brandon thought.

"Yes, well, when Mrs. Jessup saw the picture, she recognized her niece—"

"Well, of course I did. Who don't recognize they own kin? Allison's been missing for twenty-five years now. I almost fell out when I seen her picture up on that screen."

"You almost broke your foot," said Mr. Jessup.

"I sure did, running across the room, trying to get to the TV to turn it up before you went off."

"Mrs. Jessup copied down the number you left and called in to the station," Amy said. "They traveled all the way here from Selma, Alabama, to talk to you about their niece, Allison Moore."

"Lord, help us," Mrs. Jessup said, tears shining in her eyes.

Brandon's head felt like a Tilt-A-Whirl as he listened to the Jessups' words.

"That girl, Jane Doe, as you call her, sure looks like she could be our kin too. Mr. Hall? Can you tell us what happened to Allison?"

"I'm going to do my best, Mr. Jessup. It's been a long time, and there wasn't a whole lot of information, same as with Jane Doe." *Or Carly either,* he thought.

"Well, maybe this will help some," Mr. Jessup said, handing Brandon a large envelope thicker than the file he'd gotten from the Cleveland Police Department.

"What is this?" Brandon asked, his heart going wild in his chest.

"The stuff the private investigator gave us before he quit trying to find Allison."

"You hired a private investigator?" Brandon asked, taking the envelope.

"Yes, we would've done anything to find our girl, but the Lord . . ." Mr. Jessup shook his head, leaving his statement unfinished.

"The Lord don't make no mistakes," Mrs. Jessup said, reaching for his hand.

"Maybe not, but it sho is hard to accept sometime," he said.

Mrs. Jessup nodded in agreement as silence fell on the room.

"Was Allison's mother your sister, Mr. Jessup?" Brandon asked after a few moments had passed without anyone speaking.

"Bessie was my only sister. My mama and daddy always expected me to look after her, and Lord knows I tried, but I couldn't stop her from leaving Selma. She said it wasn't no place for someone like her there."

"What do you mean, 'someone like her'?" Brandon asked.

"It's hard to explain, but black folk can be more color struck than whites most times."

"I'm sorry. I don't follow."

"I reckon you wouldn't. Anyhow, for reasons nobody can explain, my sister was born looking as white as you. I reckon that would've been fine, except her family and everybody around her was as dark as me," he said, tapping the deep-mahogany skin of his face. "She went through a lot, with the teasing at school and at home too. When I was a kid, I thought it was just funning. I didn't know how bad it hurt her till she was much older. By then she was so bruised and lonely, we couldn't hardly reach her."

"Lord, yes," Mrs. Jessup agreed, bobbing her head up and down.

"Poor Bessie, she didn't feel like she belonged nowhere. She was too white for her own people, and she was the white folks' worst nightmare. A black woman that could pass for white."

"And she couldn't change the color of her skin," Brandon said.

"Sure, you right. So, when Black Joe came courting, we all felt like it was a blessing. He loved Bessie and treated her like a queen, he did. They got married right out of high school, and Bessie talked him into moving her up north to Cleveland. She never came back to Selma 'cept for when it was time to bury our folks."

"Did you keep in touch with her in Cleveland?"

"Of course I did. She was my baby sister. She was happy in Cleveland. Joe was a good honest man. He worked hard to give her a good life. When she got pregnant with Allison, I ain't never seen a woman so happy."

"We all were," Mrs. Jessup said.

"Yes, that's right," Mr. Jessup said.

"See, the Lord never saw fit to bless us with a child, so when Allison came, we just poured all our love into her. I guess you can say she was the family baby."

"I talked to the police in Cleveland," Brandon said. "They said that Bessie had some . . . um . . . struggles with depression. Did you know anything about that?"

"I knowed about it, but not from no police. Joe tried everything he could to make Bessie happy, but something happened to her after Allison was born. It's like a giant sad cloud just swallowed her up. She had her good days, but Joe couldn't never find any way to bring her all the way out of it, not for too long anyway. He was so worried about her, he hired a neighbor woman to keep watch over her."

"What about her relationship with Allison?"

"Well, it was mostly good. Allison could sometimes drag Bessie out of her funk when nobody else could. I don't know why living was so hard for Bessie, but I know that after Allison come up missing, it became impossible."

Brandon pulled a picture of Allison Moore from the envelope that Mr. Jessup had handed him and laid it face up on the desk. In the picture, Allison looked around the same age as Delilah. She was standing in the front yard of the house that Brandon had visited. She wore a simple white dress, the kind that young girls wore for graduation or church. Her hair shone in the sunlight, turning her curls fiery red. She could have been Delilah, Carly, or even Olivia, Brandon thought, feeling sick to his stomach.

"Brandon, are you all right?" Amy asked.

Brandon forced himself to close his eyes and breathe slowly. Delilah could be Allison Moore's child, he supposed. In fact, he thought, it was more probable than not. If she was, it would mean she belonged with the Jessups, as devastating as that would be for Olivia to accept. It would also mean that Allison could still be alive, or that she had been for years after she was taken. What had happened to the child she'd been carrying when she disappeared? Had there been others? Thinking of what she must have gone through all those years made him sick.

"Brandon?" Amy called.

"I'm fine," he said. "I'm sorry, Mr. and Mrs. Jessup, I can't answer any questions concerning Allison or Jane Doe yet. Amy will collect some DNA from you, and we'll know for sure soon enough."

"How long will it take?" Mrs. Jessup asked.

"Not too long," Amy said. "I'll go get some swabs." She stood up and waddled out of the room, leaving Brandon alone with the Jessups.

Chapter 47

The Jessups sat watching Brandon, neither saying a word as he sifted through the information they'd collected over the past twenty-five years. As he sorted through the collection of documents, separating the photos into one pile and removing the documents that were duplicates from the Cleveland police file, he paused, then picked up a stack of papers held together with a paper clip. After a few sentences, it was clear that the detective who'd completed the investigation had found it important enough to compile a thorough report. As he read, Brandon felt his heart start to race, and he raised his eyes to meet the Jessups'. The pair sat stiff as schoolchildren, waiting to be called on by the teacher.

"Did you read this?" Brandon asked, careful to keep his voice steady so as not to alarm the couple, even though his own mind struggled to make sense of what he was reading.

"We did. The PI said he tried to get the police to investigate, but nobody wasn't interested, so he just included the report in Allison's file. 'Just in case,' he said."

"There was another family, another girl gone missing, like Allison, like Del . . . Jane Doe?"

"Yes, sir, her mama looked just like our girl too," he said, pointing to a picture half buried under some papers that Brandon had put to the side.

Brandon noticed, with some surprise, how steady his hands were as he picked up the picture of a young woman, the triumph on her face shining through the exhaustion in her eyes as she grinned into the camera from a hospital bed, holding a brand-new infant.

"What happened to her?" Brandon forced himself to ask, even though a part of him knew he didn't really want to know.

"It's all in the report, but from what the detective said, that young couple—"

"The Mercers. That's their name, the Mercers," Mrs. Jessup said.

"That's right, the Mercers," Mr. Jessup said, reaching out to pat Mrs. Jessup's hand as he nodded. "Anyway, the detective said she was taken from her stroller in a grocery store in Cleveland right out from under her mama's nose. The mama had to run out to the store to pick up some diapers. Of course, she took the baby with her."

"Baby's name was Aliyah, such a pretty name," Mrs. Jessup said.

"Why do you think the detective thought this case was connected to Allison's disappearance?" Brandon asked.

"Look," Mrs. Jessup said, leaning forward and searching through the pictures on the desk. She handed Brandon a picture of a young girl, her hair pulled back into a reddish-blonde ponytail. Her light-brown eyes smiled into the camera, full of mischief. "That's Anne Mercer at thirteen years old."

Brandon stared at the picture of the young Anne Mercer, which could easily have been a picture of Delilah today, trying to organize his scrambled thoughts.

"Did the police ever have any leads?" he asked, breaking the silence that had fallen over the room.

"Nothing that ever panned out. Everything he could find out about the investigation, he put in the file," Mr. Jessup said. "It wasn't much. Mrs. Mercer says everything was pretty normal, except for the young girl."

"Young girl?" Brandon asked.

"Yes, sir," Mr. Jessup said. "Mrs. Mercer said the baby got fussy, like they do, and a young girl came out of nowhere and asked to see the baby. The report says, Mrs. Mercer thought she might be sick, she was so frail, so she said no, said something about the girl made her nervous."

"Did she say how old the girl was?" Brandon asked, struggling to keep all emotion out of his voice.

"All the report says is she was a teenager," Mr. Jessup said.

Could it have been Allison? Brandon wondered.

"What month did the Mercers' baby go missing?" Brandon asked as he flipped through the report, more to himself than the Jessups. "Was the young girl alone?" he added.

"The detective didn't know for sure. Mrs. Mercer thought she may have seen a man, a big man, standing nearby in an aisle, but she couldn't swear it. She only saw him for a second, and later she was so distraught, she wasn't sure if she just made him up in her mind, especially since no one else saw him."

"The police believe it was this girl who took the baby?" Brandon asked.

"I don't know what the police thought, but the detective sure did," Mr. Jessup said.

"But how would she have been able to take the baby without her mother seeing her?" Brandon asked.

"The restroom," Mrs. Jessup said. "She had to go to the restroom, but the stalls were too small for her stroller, so she had to leave her alone while she was in the stall. When she came out, her baby was gone."

The room fell quiet again as Brandon and the Jessups worked through sorting the private detective's file. When they were done, they had approximately twenty photos and a stack of notes that the private investigator had made from interviews with potential witnesses.

Brandon was stunned by the quality of the investigator's work. He may not have found Allison, but it was clear his investigation had been far more thorough than the one the police had conducted. Brandon studied the pictures while the Jessups watched him closely.

Most of the pictures appeared to be of Allison at various ages, probably given to the investigator by the family. More than likely, the investigator had intended to use them for possible identification purposes, but one picture was a grainy black-and-white photo, the kind that would have been taken from a security camera.

Brandon barely breathed as he reached for the photo. The picture was so fuzzy it was impossible to make out a face, but the image of a large man wearing the kind of hat that a farmer might wear in the fields was clear. Brandon thought of what Allison's boyfriend had said about the strange man who'd appeared to be watching Allison shortly before she disappeared. This must be that man.

Brandon turned the picture over, hoping there was a note, but the only thing on the photo was a date of April 1988, one month before Allison had gone missing.

"Mr. and Mrs. Jessup, do you know anything about this picture?" Brandon asked. He handed Mr. Jessup the picture.

"Just what the PI told us. He said that he got the picture from the manager where Allison worked before she went missing. Said he told the police about the tape, but no one ever came for it," he said, handing the photo back to Brandon.

Brandon stared at the photo, reluctant to put it down. Something about that image gnawed at his brain, but he couldn't grab hold of it. He continued shuffling through the pictures of Allison, capturing her in various moods, with different groups of friends. If nothing else, the pictures showed Allison had been a happy, well-loved girl.

At the end of the stack, Brandon's hand froze. The last picture staring up at him from the table was also taken from a security camera. In this one a large man and a girl were standing in a convenience store. The man clenched the girl's hand in his. Unlike in the grainy photo from before, the man appeared to be looking directly into the camera. The girl stood, her shoulders hunched, her head hanging low, as if preparing to duck a blow, but Brandon had no trouble recognizing Allison Moore.

"I need you to tell me everything you know about this picture."

"It ain't much," Mr. Jessup said, shuffling through the pile of notes. "The PI said this was probably the last picture of Allison ever taken. It was at a gas station on I-70, a couple of days after she went missing. The owner said Allison had been traveling with the man you see there and an older woman, who said Allison was her granddaughter. The owner say he knew something wasn't right, but he didn't find out about Allison being missing until almost a week later, and remembered how scared she looked. They had one of them tip lines set up, so he called it."

"The Mercers' daughter, Aliyah, was taken in May?" Brandon asked, shuffling through a stack of papers they had just finished sorting.

"Yes. May 2003, I believe. Why? Does that matter?"

"I don't know. Maybe it's just a coincidence," Brandon said, trying to keep his voice calm and his face expressionless. "How far would you say the Mercers lived away from your sister, Mr. Jessup?"

"Not far. According to the report, no more than a few blocks. Shaker Heights is pretty small," Mr. Jessup said.

"Who is he?" Mrs. Jessup asked as Brandon continued to stare down at the picture, the face staring back up at him, an itch he couldn't scratch.

"I don't know," Brandon said, shaking his head.

"You look like you do," Mr. Jessup said.

"It almost feels like I do; something about him just seems so damned familiar," Brandon said, tapping his forehead.

"You think the same monster that took our Allison took their baby girl," Mr. Jessup said. The words were more of a statement than a question, a statement Brandon couldn't bring himself to deny.

"If Jane Doe is their lost child, do you think our Allison could still be alive too?"

Two pairs of eyes stared at Brandon, waiting for him to answer. He stood up and walked around the desk before placing his hand on Mr. Jessup's shoulder.

231

"Mr. Jessup, I wish I could say yes, but I just don't know. I promise that I'm going to do everything I can to find them," he said. "If you don't mind, I'm going to take these with me so I can go through them a little more carefully. I'll get them back to you once I'm done."

"You keep it—everything but the pictures of Allison, that is. We'd like them back. As for the rest, this is it. After this trip here, we're turning it over to the Lord," Mr. Jessup said. Mrs. Jessup nodded in agreement.

"I understand. Where are you staying; can I give you a ride?"

"We staying at a motel not far from the airport, on Aerotech Drive," Mr. Jessup said, reading from a piece of paper he pulled from his coat pocket. "We rented a car, so we're fine."

"How is everything going in here?" Amy asked from the doorway.

"I reckon we got what we come for."

"Well, the storm has really picked up steam. If you plan on getting back to your hotel before they close the roads, you better hurry."

"We better get going," he said, reaching out his hand to help his wife rise from the chair.

"Before you go, Mr. Jessup, would you mind if I sneak some of your DNA?" Amy said.

"Don't know how much sneaking's got to do with it, but you welcome to it if it helps us find Allison."

As Amy quickly gathered a sample from the inside of Mr. Jessup's cheek, Mrs. Jessup watched intently.

"What happens if the DNA proves the girl is kin to our Allison?" Mrs. Jessup asked, turning toward Brandon.

"I don't know," he said.

"Can we see her?" Mrs. Jessup asked.

"I'm not sure . . . maybe . . . I'll have to check," Brandon said, turning to Amy, silently pleading for her help.

"The girl has been through a lot," Amy said. "Even if she is your kin, she's going to need some time. Right now, the court is responsible for her well-being. Please, you've been through so much—be patient for just a little longer."

With a nod of his head, Mr. Jessup started out of the room, his wife and Brandon following behind him. Brandon turned and mouthed "Thank you" to Amy as he followed the Jessups out of her office.

Chapter 48

A loud banging pierced the heavy fog of sleep, dragging Olivia out of the warmth of her dreams. For a moment she lay still, confused. She was cold, and darkness surrounded her. The noise, louder this time, snapped her fully awake, and she sat up straight in the chair, twisting her head to look at the bed where Delilah should have been.

The bed was empty. Ignoring her stiff neck and stiffer knees, Olivia jumped from the chair.

"Delilah! Brandon!" she screamed, running from the dark room.

When no answer came, she stumbled down the hall, feeling along the wall for the light switch. She remembered she'd been sitting in the chair watching Delilah, and somehow, she'd fallen asleep.

"Delilah, Brandon," Olivia wailed again, feeling the panic starting to overtake her as her hand bumped against the light switch.

Olivia flipped the switch, and when nothing happened, she remembered the storm.

"Shit," she whispered, leaning against the wall, trying to stay calm enough not to dissolve into a puddle of useless tears. The banging sound echoed through the house. She crept down the dark hall toward the sound, forcing herself to take slow, even breaths in an attempt to stop herself from hyperventilating. It wouldn't do anyone any good if she passed out.

When she stepped into the living room, the composure she was working so hard on flew right out the front door, which had been left

---

wide open to swing back and forth in the wind, slamming into the wall, causing the banging noise that echoed through the house. Olivia stood, her mouth hanging open, staring around the deserted living room.

Snow had swept in from outside and was collecting in small piles around the room. Outside the door, the world looked as if it had been wiped away, and Olivia suddenly felt as if she were the last person left on earth. A cold blast of wind blew snow into her face, shaking her from her stupor, and she rushed across the room to slam the door shut.

Brandon. Surely, he must have taken Delilah with him. He must have thought he was being kind by allowing her to sleep. Of course he had. He knew better than anyone how tired she was. "Of course," she said out loud, racing across the room to grab the phone. Sweet or not, she would kill him for scaring her so badly, she thought as she dialed his number and raised the phone to her ear.

"No . . . no . . . no," she moaned, throwing the dead phone at the wall. Hot tears swelled in her eyes and ran down her cheeks without her noticing as she dashed across the room, tearing back the curtain to look into the unrelenting white swirl.

Ms. Helen, she thought, staring across the street where her neighbor's house should have been. Ms. Helen would have seen Brandon leave. Turning from the window, Olivia snatched her coat and slid her feet into her sneakers before rushing outside. As she reached the edge of the porch, a gust of wind pushed her sideways onto a patch of ice. Too late, she reached for the railing, but her feet flew out from under her, and she landed with a hard thud on her back.

At first, she felt nothing as she lay there staring up into the sky, snow landing on her upturned face. It took only a few seconds for the pain shooting from her ankle to reach her brain. She screamed, panicking as her voice was carried away by a strong gust of frigid wind as she imagined lying there, unable to move, freezing to death in the snow.

Olivia closed her eyes against the drifting snow. An image of Delilah, as she'd been found, covered in blood but fighting to stay alive, burned into her feverish brain, and she felt ashamed. In spite of everything, Delilah had fought for her own survival, and here Olivia was lying on her back, ready to surrender because of a sprained ankle.

Biting down into her lip, numb from the cold, Olivia rolled over onto her belly. Steeling herself against the expected pain, she pushed herself onto her feet, first balancing most of her weight onto her unharmed ankle. Gingerly she shifted her weight onto the injured ankle and was surprised to find that although it was tender, she was able to walk with only a small amount of pain.

She limped across the street, tucking her head down away from the wind, realizing the jacket she had grabbed in her hurry was doing no more to protect her from the elements than the canvas sneakers that covered her feet.

Grateful to have made it across the street, she looked at Ms. Helen's house and frowned. From where she stood, it appeared the door was open. Olivia trudged forward, hoping what she was seeing was a trick of the waning light. As she made her way up the snow-covered walkway, her foot caught on something, and her already-weak ankle gave way. With a yelp of pain, Olivia fell forward, landing on a hard object buried beneath the snow.

"Son of a bitch," she grunted, pushing off the object and lifting herself to her knees.

Olivia's breath caught in her throat as she looked down and saw that the snow where her hand rested was stained a brilliant red. Carefully, she leaned forward and started scraping. In seconds, she was looking down into the open, dead eyes of Otis. Except, he barely looked like the Otis she had known for as long as she could remember. At first glance, it looked as if half his head and face was just gone, but then she realized she was wrong. His head had suffered a savage blow, *just like the boy's.*

Olivia felt her stomach turn. She flung herself backward, away from the corpse, and scrambled to her feet, ignoring the pain in her ankle as she climbed the stairs onto the porch. Mr. Otis was dead. Standing in front of Ms. Helen's open door, staring into the darkness, shaking with fear, Olivia fought not to turn and run away.

She knew even before stepping across the threshold that Ms. Helen would not be able to help her, or anyone else. Still, she stepped inside and slowly made her way through the house, not bothering to call out. When she stood outside the closed bedroom door, she turned the handle, barely breathing as the door opened.

Ms. Helen lay on the bed, her head twisted at an unnatural angle, her unseeing eyes staring at the door, where Olivia stood frozen in horror.

Chapter 49

Father drove carefully through the swirling snow, a smile on his face as he hummed along to the gospel song playing on the radio. He took his eyes off the road long enough to look over at where Delilah sat huddled in the seat beside him. She wished she could be brave like Sunny had been, but when he reached out and laid his hand on her, terror spread throughout her body, making her stomach ache.

She tried not to move, but when his hand moved across her bare flesh, she couldn't stop herself from flinching away from him. Tears filled her eyes as he slapped her thigh, laughing out loud as she cried out in pain.

The truck slid on the icy road, threatening to turn sideways. She saw a car slide off the side of the road and land in a ditch, but Father did not pause. At the start of the road that led into the mountains, Father paused and looked down at her. By now Olivia would have discovered that she was missing. Maybe they had found the old woman too. None of that mattered now.

"Be home 'fore long," Father said.

She didn't answer, but that didn't matter none either.

Chapter 50

Brandon stood knee deep in snow, his teeth clenched hard enough to make his jaw ache. He tried his best not to let fly the string of curse words on the edge of his tongue. As predicted, the early-spring storm had quickly morphed into the worst blizzard in recent Colorado history. Already local meteorologists were gleefully trying to outdo each other in naming the storm while comparing it to every storm in their memories.

The unlucky tourist whose vehicle had slid off the road and become lodged in the snow-filled ditch chattered on, seemingly unaware that Brandon had long since stopped responding to his incessant questions.

It had been hours since he'd been able to contact Olivia. Just as Minnie had said, the house phone rang busy, and her cell phone went straight to voice mail. Out of desperation, he'd tried Ms. Helen but received the same busy signal. He'd been on his way back to Olivia's when he saw the tourist stranded in the ditch, and he'd had no choice but to stop. He'd already called the police, who'd promised to send help as soon as possible.

That was a full hour ago, and still there was no sign of even a tow truck. Since neither he nor the unlucky tourist was injured, Brandon knew it could still be quite a while before anyone showed up. By then, regardless of his truck having four-wheel drive, it could be impossible for him to get home until after the plows and salt trucks had caught up, which could be hours, or maybe even tomorrow, depending on how long the thick snow continued to fall.

"Sir, I don't mean to be a nervous Nellie, if you will, but I feel like we need to do something here. The snow is picking up, and we've been here for quite a while. I don't suppose anyone is coming."

Brandon didn't answer immediately, only stared into the snow, hating it as much as any adversary. He knew the man was right; he didn't have a choice. It was impossible to leave him alone here. If he did, he had no doubt the tourist would be dead by the time someone else showed up.

"Fuck," Brandon said under his breath.

"I'd say that was a pretty fair assessment," the man said.

"Sir, I apologize; please get back to the truck. I think it's best if I take you to the police station."

Trudging up the embankment behind the unlucky traveler, Brandon tried to convince himself that the panic gnawing in the pit of his stomach was just a result of his overworked imagination, but his senses would not be fooled.

"Where are you, Olivia?" he whispered into the wind as he watched the man climb into his truck.

Brandon watched as an old truck rambled by, going a little too fast for the conditions. If the driver didn't watch it, he'd also wind up in a ditch, he thought. As if the driver had caught his errant thought, Brandon saw the truck's brake lights flicker; the truck slowed, as if the driver considered stopping before continuing on.

"Thanks a lot," Brandon grumbled as he topped the embankment and carefully maneuvered himself across the ice.

He'd started to pull open the door when he looked down the road and saw flashing red-and-blue lights approaching in the distance. He turned to watch the cruiser, praying it was coming for them. When it pulled up behind his truck, Brandon let go of the handle and sank against the truck in relief.

He watched with a grin on his face as Hector Martinez, a recent transplant from Miami, gingerly inched his way across the frozen road, a scowl covering his round brown face.

"God damn this snow—I nearly died a hundred times trying to get here. I tell you what, I'm going back to Miami, land of sun and fun. This right here just ain't for me."

"Aw, come on, man, you gotta give it a chance; you just got here. Wait until summer, when the sun is out and you don't have to worry about one hundred percent humidity and bugs as big as your fist. You'll be loving it then."

"They call that winter at home," Hector said.

"It'll be over before you know it."

"Your lips to God's ear," Hector said.

"Well, I'm glad you made it. I was getting worried."

"Yeah, sorry about that, man. I couldn't drive any faster than ten miles per hour in most spots. The road is really slick. You better go while you can."

"Thanks, I'll leave Mr. Grossman in your capable hands. Mr. Grossman, Officer Martinez is going to take care of you from here," Brandon said, willing the fussy little man to hurry out of the truck.

Once they were safely in the squad car, Brandon got in his truck and pulled away, slowing down when the vehicle shivered against the slick pavement.

Chapter 51

Olivia stood in the middle of her living room, gasping for air, her chest rising and falling so fast that it soon hurt to breathe. She'd practically crawled across the street to escape the mausoleum that was Ms. Helen's house. Every limb and every nerve trembled, and though she could see her own breath in the cold room, she felt hot all over.

Otis was dead. Ms. Helen was dead. Delilah was gone, just like Carly. Was Brandon dead too? Olivia stumbled to the phone. With shaking fingers, she picked it up, praying that she would hear a dial tone. When she put the phone to her ear and heard nothing, she felt her control slip and bit down on her lip, hard enough to taste blood on her tongue.

Cell phone. The thought appeared in her head as bright as a new penny. Unlike everybody else in the world, she hated the constant intrusion of the digital age, especially the cell phone. The only time she even carried one was if she was on call. Her mother had given her one for her birthday that seemed to be more computer than phone. She had spent more than an hour programming it and explaining everything it could do, with Olivia only half listening. Since she'd been on leave, the phone had sat, ignored, on her nightstand, plugged in, she hoped.

On shaky legs, she stumbled through the house and burst into her bedroom, sweeping everything off the nightstand in her desperation to find the phone.

"Please, God, please."

Just as she was sure that the phone was somehow lost, she pushed aside a book and saw it sitting right where she'd left it.

"Thank you," she whispered, reaching out with trembling hands. As she picked up the phone, the power cord slid away and landed on the floor.

"No," she said as her eyes followed the cord to where it was still plugged into the wall.

"No," she said again, shaking her head.

It could still be fully charged. It could have charged before the plug came loose. I only need enough power for one call . . . surely, she thought as she held down the power button, tears forming in her eyes.

"Just as dead as Otis and Ms. Helen and maybe Brandon too," she said, covering her mouth with her hands. In the movies, someone would slap her to get her under control, or give her a drink, she thought.

"God," she screamed, tossing the dead phone across the room.

She reached up to touch her face, surprised to find that her cheeks were dry under her fingers. She walked down the hall, each step feeling like her body weighed a thousand pounds, and entered the bedroom that she and Brandon had shared in the beginning of their marriage, right after they'd first moved into the house. It was smaller than the master bedroom, but at the time they'd been so in love that they'd opted for the smaller room to keep them closer together. Less than a year later, they'd moved into the master.

After their move, Olivia had used the smaller room as an office. She'd spent hours sitting at the garage-sale desk Brandon had bought for her, telling anyone who would listen how she was writing her masterpiece. Two months and twenty pages in, she'd put away the book, and the room had turned into a kind of storage area.

Now Olivia entered the small, cluttered room and walked straight to the desk. Bending down onto her knees, she yanked out the bottom drawer—the *sacred drawer*, they had jokingly called it—and reached all the way to the back and pulled out a bottle of unopened vodka. She had always thought that if she fell off the wagon, she'd feel anger or even pain, but all she felt was numbness as she cracked open the bottle and raised it to her lips. With every swallow, the pain seemed to fall further away, until Olivia felt nothing.

She wouldn't remember how long she sat in the little room, or how much she drank, or even how she managed to get back to the living room, but somehow, she crawled onto the couch and sank gratefully into the darkness.

Chapter 52

As Brandon pulled up in front of the house, the unease that had been growing in his gut turned into a full-on panic. He stared through the window, his hands clutching the steering wheel. The house stood silent and empty, as if long deserted. He felt his pulse quicken as he noticed that the door of Ms. Helen's house was slightly ajar.

Brandon turned his head and looked down the street, taking note of the lights shining from the windows of every other home, except for Olivia's and Ms. Helen's. Whatever power outage had struck the neighborhood seemed to have affected only those two houses. When he reached the front yard, he stood staring at the dark, empty windows of Ms. Helen's house. The open front door seemed almost to be taunting him, daring him to come on in.

Shoving his hands into his pockets and tucking his head down, he walked across the street, pushing against the wind that cut into his face. As soon as he stepped up onto the sidewalk, the snow stopped as suddenly as if someone had turned off a machine. He looked up into the night sky. Not even a stray flake fell.

He lowered his head and stumbled backward into the street. An eye, filled with snow, staring into nothing, looked back at him. He looked around for anyone, but it felt like the whole neighborhood had disappeared. Stepping forward, he could make out the outline of a body, mostly covered by the snow. He bent down and used his hands to uncover the face, his stomach clenching into a painful knot as he recognized Otis. He reached into his coat and dialed 911 for the second time that day.

After disconnecting from the dispatcher, he rushed past Otis's body and up the stairs, bracing himself for what he was sure he would find. Snow had blown inside through the open door and piled up in corners, leaving a fine covering over the furniture in the empty living room.

The chair where Ms. Helen had sat by the window and watched life go by remained where it was, but another chair faced the door, as if whoever had sat in it had been waiting for someone to enter through the front door. A shiver raced down Brandon's spine as he thought back to earlier that afternoon.

"Ms. Helen?" he called, feeling foolish at allowing that tiny amount of hope.

The door to the bedroom was wide open. Ms. Helen lay in the bed, her dead eyes staring into forever. As horrific as the scene was, Brandon's eyes fixed on the quilt covering her body. Carly's quilt.

Whenever the police were able to get there, they would find two murder victims, one covered in a quilt that had last been in Olivia's possession. His mind snapped back to the feeding frenzy that had happened once the press had decided that they were responsible for Carly's disappearance. It had almost killed Olivia then. He was sure it would this time. He stepped into the room and carefully removed the quilt from Ms. Helen, then quickly left the house and hurried back across the street. Olivia was his concern now, he thought as he closed the door.

Moving as fast as he could across the snow-packed yard, he grabbed hold of the railing to stop himself from sliding backward down the ice-covered stairs. He reached out to touch the door and was surprised that it swung open beneath his hand. Olivia hadn't left a door unlocked since Carly had gone missing. He stepped inside, stopping in the foyer to give his eyes a few moments to adjust to the dim room. Inside the house was as cold as outside, if not colder.

He stepped into the living room and saw Olivia lying unmoving on the couch. Her eyes were closed, a thin fall jacket her only protection against the cold. She didn't respond when he called her name. When he touched her skin, she felt like an ice sculpture. Brandon fumbled to find a pulse.

As he bent down to place his ear against her chest, the distinct smell of alcohol rose from her open lips.

Brandon held his breath as he waited, listening, refusing to accept that he could have lost her. He choked on a sob as Olivia's chest rose slowly. He ripped his coat off and wrapped it around her body.

"I'll be right back," he said, forcing himself to leave her to find more blankets. He made it all the way to Carly's room before it hit him that Delilah was gone. An image of the large dark man appeared in his head, as clear as if he were standing in front of him.

"God help us," he whispered as he hurried to get the blankets.

When he returned, he wrapped Olivia in three blankets and kissed her lips before standing and sliding back into his coat. He hated to leave her alone, but he knew he needed to get the power back on.

Carefully he made his way down the stairs and trudged around to the side of the house, where the ancient circuit breaker box was located.

He and Olivia had often talked about remodeling the old house to move the breakers inside but had never gotten around to it. As he came around the corner of the house, he saw the door to the box hanging open. He stepped closer and saw that each switch had been flipped into the off position.

As he flipped the switches back on, light streamed from the windows, and he could hear the power cycling back on. After closing the door to the circuit breaker, he turned and tromped back through the snow, which had formed drifts against the side of the house.

When he stepped back inside, he was grateful to hear the old furnace coming to life. He imagined that the room had already started to warm. Color was returning to Olivia's pale skin, and her chest rose and fell as if she were merely asleep. He reached out to touch her face, wiping away tears that had gathered in the corners of her eyes. Bending down, he gently kissed her lips before walking down the hall and spreading the quilt across the bed.

Chapter 53

The house was full of people coming and going: the state police, the FBI, CSI, and every other acronym in the book. K-9 dogs sniffed around the house, their barks and whines piercing the air. News crews filled the once-quiet street, making it appear as if a big-budget movie were being shot instead of a double homicide / kidnapping investigation. Brandon still didn't understand how they'd been able to respond so quickly. Apparently not even Mother Nature was a match for determined reporters with their bloodlust up.

Brandon sat at the kitchen table, taking turns sipping the cold cup of coffee that someone had shoved in front of him and gnawing the inside of his jaw. He wanted to get to the hospital to be with Olivia, but so far, the best he'd been able to do was alert Arlene, who had rushed to her side.

He would have thought that the fact that he had a solid alibi for his whereabouts would have been enough to answer any questions, but the FBI insisted on treating him like a suspect—or *witness*, as they called it—requesting that he not leave the scene until all their questions had been satisfied. Brandon had complied, especially since the request came from Lieutenant Webber, but his patience was running thin, and his need to be with Olivia was nearly unbearable.

Brandon slammed the coffee cup onto the table, leaped to his feet, and yanked his jacket from where it hung on the back of the chair. He'd taken no more than two steps toward the door when it swung open and Sheldon Myers stepped inside.

"Son of a bitch," Brandon said.

"Mr. Hall, so sad to meet again under these circumstances," Sheldon said.

"Why are you here?"

"Well, I, like everyone else, was concerned when I heard the news. I just wanted to make sure that you and Dr. Blake were all right. Is there anything I can do to help?"

"Mr. Myers, it seems that if you really wanted to help, you would've stayed as far away from here as possible."

"Brandon, I want you to know that, despite what she may think, I do care about Dr. Blake, but it's also my job to make sure the stories I report are fair and balanced. Sometimes that may hurt people I genuinely care about. Still, after the last unfortunate situation, I think you understand how important it is to manage the press. I can help you with that. But if you'd prefer to go it alone, I will leave you to your own devices."

"To you, the kidnapping of our daughter is an *unfortunate situation*?" Brandon asked, standing so close to Sheldon that he could feel his breath on his face.

"You misunderstand. I'm merely offering my assistance as a spokesperson who can attest to Dr. Blake's impeccable character."

"You mean like you did before? Will you insinuate that Olivia killed this child too? That is what you told the media during the other *unfortunate situation*, wasn't it, or am I mistaken?"

"That's not fair. I'm sure you know how the media works. My comments were taken completely out of context."

"In what context is 'Based on all the evidence I've seen, it appears that Dr. Blake is responsible for the disappearance of her own child' a good thing?"

"There was more to it than that."

"Of course there was. There was the interview you gave where you accused Olivia of killing our child and hiding the body. What was the context for that?"

"Brandon Hall . . ."

"You know, I don't know how you got the nerve to walk through that door, but I suggest that, before I have a chance to raise my hands and wrap them around your throat, you get out."

"Mr.—"

As soon as Sheldon started to speak, Brandon raised his hands, but before he could make good on his threat, the reporter turned and rushed out the door. Brandon stood in the doorway and watched as he stood on the lawn, surrounded by other journalists hungry for any scrap of information he was willing to share. Brandon turned away and slammed the door.

He knew Olivia needed him, but Delilah needed him even more. He couldn't stop his mind from imagining the hell that she must've been experiencing. How long had he been gone? He glanced down at his watch and was shocked to see it was past 6:00 p.m. Hours had passed since he'd left Olivia and Delilah, safe and happy. Outside, the snow had stopped, but the wind still howled, creating drifts and making it feel twenty degrees colder than it was.

Yanking on his jacket, he turned and headed for the basement, where he could slide out the window and escape unseen. He reached into his pocket to search for his gloves, but instead his fingers closed around the picture that he'd taken from the Jessups' file. He had intended to show it to Olivia and maybe Ms. Helen, too, but none of that mattered now, he thought, the image of Ms. Helen's dead eyes springing into his head as he looked down into the face of the man staring into the camera.

"Who are you?" Brandon asked, that feeling of almost knowing making his skin crawl. "I'll find you. I promise I will."

"Find who?" Hector Martinez asked from the door, where he stood looking at Brandon.

"Hector, I didn't hear you come in. Shouldn't you be off duty by now?"

"The LT called an all hands. Nobody goes home until we make sure we've done everything we can to help."

"Thanks, man, I appreciate it."

"No thanks necessary."

"Still . . ."

"What you got there?" Hector said, pointing at the picture in Brandon's hand.

"Nothing, I guess."

"Judging by the look on your face, I wouldn't want to be whoever that is when you find him."

"You ever see somebody and know them from somewhere, but can't place them?"

"Yeah, man. It'll drive you wild if you let it."

"Come take a look at this photo. I know him, I swear I do. I can't help feeling that if I could figure this one thing out . . ." Brandon handed Hector the picture.

Hector looked at the picture for a long time without saying anything. Finally, he shook his head and handed the photo back to Brandon.

"I see what you mean. Something about him does seem familiar, like 'every boogeyman you've ever seen in a scary movie' familiar, but I can't say I've ever seen him in person. I think I would have remembered. He gives me the willies."

"Maybe that's it. Hell, I don't know. My brain is so damn fried at this point, I'm not sure if I would recognize my own mother if she walked right through that door."

"Hey, I'm sorry about your wife. Is there anything I can do for you now?"

"Well, there is one thing." Brandon hesitated.

"Name it."

"I need to get to the hospital now, but the feds are being, well . . ."

"Pricks?"

"Exactly."

"Cool. How you wanna do this?"

"How about you meet me around the corner, and I'll figure out the rest?"

"All right, I got you."

"Hector, you know you could take some heat for this."

"For what? Giving a friend a ride to the hospital to see his wife? Far as I know, you're not under arrest, and nobody ever told me giving a buddy a ride in his time of need is not okay. We are here to protect and serve, after all. So I'm only doing my duty."

"I owe you one."

Hector tapped his palm to his heart and bowed his head before turning and walking back outside. After closing the door tightly but making sure to leave it unlocked, Brandon hurried downstairs into the basement. He knew it wouldn't be long before someone came to check on him.

As he pulled himself through the window and stepped into the backyard, he paused to look up into the dark, cloudless sky. A chill that had nothing to do with the cold raced down his spine, and again he wished he had his weapon.

Chapter 54

Delilah sat in the middle of the Teaching Room, her head and shoulders slumped forward, eyes closed. Her legs and arms were bound closely to the chair, so that even if she had thought of moving, she could not. Although the silence made her feel as if she were the only person left in the world, she was not alone. Father lay stretched out on the floor near the door, like a slumbering bear protecting his cave, and Sunny, or rather Carly, sat at her feet, staring up at her with her mournful eyes.

Delilah wanted to take refuge in the darkness, which had become her friend, but the pain from the wounds that crisscrossed her back, reopened by Father's whip, denied her even that relief. Useless tears fell from her eyes, but no sound escaped her mouth for fear of waking Father, and then the lesson would begin again.

The ghostly Sunny shook her head sadly, reaching out to cover Delilah's hand in hers.

Delilah's thoughts drifted to Olivia. She would be sad at her disappearance, but she was alive, and that was something. Delilah knew she would either die here in this room, maybe even tonight, or she could beg forgiveness, and he would remove her binds and tend to her wounds, and then the baby making would begin, again.

Outside, rain began to fall, filling the room with the sound of hundreds of tiny drums as it beat down on the tin roof. As if the rain carried a spell crafted by some witch out of a fairy tale, Father continued to sleep, and eventually, so, too, did Delilah.

Chapter 55

Olivia lay on her back in the narrow hospital bed, her eyes squeezed shut, trying her best to appear asleep. Nurses and doctors entered the room and hovered over her, their whispered words floating around her ears. Arlene sat in the chair beside the bed. Even though she refused to open her eyes, Olivia could feel her waiting, but she was determined to wait her out. She couldn't talk to anyone, not now.

Delilah was gone, probably as dead as Carly by now, and it was Olivia's fault. She knew Arlene would try to convince her differently, but if she hadn't insisted on bringing Delilah home, wouldn't the girl still be safe? She thought so, and no amount of comforting by her friend would change that.

The noise from the hall outside her room suddenly receded, and Olivia heard the door click shut. She did not open her eyes immediately but continued to lie still in the bed. Several moments passed with no hint of sound or movement, and Olivia allowed her eyelids to sneak open enough to look through the slits into Arlene's face.

"I'm not leaving, you know. It doesn't matter if you never speak to me—I won't leave you."

Olivia squeezed her eyes back shut, refusing to abandon her only defense against reality.

Arlene reached over and folded Olivia's hand in hers.

When Arlene refused to release her hand, Olivia opened her eyes and squeezed Arlene's hand.

"I'm so sorry," Olivia said, dissolving into sobs as Arlene folded her into her arms.

"Honey, what are you sorry for?" Arlene said, stroking her hair.

"She's gone. I was supposed to take care of her. I promised her I would, and she's gone. She's gone," Olivia cried, her voice climbing with each word.

"Stop," Arlene said, shaking Olivia hard enough to keep her from descending into full hysteria.

Olivia's sobs quieted, and she pulled away from Arlene's embrace, sinking back into the bed and wiping the tears from her eyes.

"She's gone," Olivia said quietly.

"I know, honey. We're going to find her."

"Like we found Carly," Olivia said, all emotion drained from her voice.

"You've got to stay strong, Liv, please."

"I wish Brandon was here," Olivia said.

"Your wish is my command," a voice said from the door.

"Well, aren't you a sight for sore eyes," Arlene said as she walked to the door to meet Brandon, leaning into his embrace.

"How's our girl?" he whispered in her ear as he pulled her close, still within earshot of Olivia.

"Hanging in there," she whispered back.

Chapter 56

As Brandon approached Olivia, she reached out her hand for him. Her fingers felt like ice as he held them and bent to kiss her lips.

"I'm sorry, Brandon," she said, turning her face away from his eyes.

"For what?" he asked.

"I couldn't keep her safe . . ."

"Olivia, Delilah needs us to be strong."

"It's just like Carly all over again," Olivia said.

"It doesn't have to end that way. We can still help her."

"How? How can we help her? We couldn't save our own daughter. How can we help *her*?"

"Olivia, I need you to try to calm down and take a look at these and tell me if you've ever seen him before," Brandon said. "I don't know, but there's something. I just can't put my finger on it."

He handed Olivia the pictures and leaned back in the chair. He didn't know he was holding his breath until she screamed.

"Hurt! Oh my God, it's Hurt. Hurt Mountain Farm, the donkey, the farmer. Oh God. Oh God! I saw him. He was here."

"Here? What do you mean? When?"

"I don't know. He was looking for . . . no, I asked him if he wanted the emergency room. He was hurt. I mean, he had a scar on his face." Olivia traced her finger from the corner of her eye to her mouth.

He felt, rather than saw, Arlene rush past him. Saw her snatch the photo from Olivia's limp fingers, her eyes filling with shock as she recognized the face in the picture. Then it all came back to him in a horrific rush.

Hurt. The creepy farmer from the farmers' market, with the decrepit-looking donkey. Hadn't he and Liv laughed at how he'd looked? Olivia had said he gave her the heebie-jeebies. That's what she had said: the heebie-jeebies. But hadn't they—no, he—insisted that Carly not be rude and say thank you to the nice man who'd given her a candy apple on that beautiful day they'd taken her to the market, even though she'd tried to hide behind Brandon's legs? Hadn't he given her a very stern lecture about being polite? Wasn't he the one who'd told her the foolish story about the toad who was really a prince?

Olivia was still moaning, her words jumbled and incoherent now. A nurse rushed into the room. Brandon watched as she shot something into Olivia's IV.

"The farmers' market guy? The one who sold the candles, the goat's milk soap, and the homemade candy? He's the one? I remember him," Arlene said, openly crying now, the picture clenched in her hand.

Hurt of Hurt Mountain Farm had taken their daughter. Now he had Delilah, again. If Brandon didn't find her soon, Hurt would kill her, or worse.

Brandon's legs felt unstable as he stood looking down at Olivia. Whatever the nurse had given her had worked quickly. Now she lay quietly, fighting to keep her eyes open.

"Stay with her, Arlene. Whatever happens, stay with her. When the feds show up, you tell them, tell them about Hurt."

Arlene nodded before giving Brandon a hug. She didn't ask what he was planning. She didn't need to. He was sure the answer was clear on his face.

Chapter 57

Brandon rushed through the doors of the police station and up the stairs, running past several troopers without stopping to answer their questions. When he reached Amy's office, he was stunned to find it dark and the door locked.

"She's on the way to the hospital to have the baby," a voice said from behind him.

Brandon whirled around to face Lieutenant Webber.

"Is there something I can help you with, Brandon?"

"Sir, how did you know I was here?"

"It's hard not to notice when someone tears through a police station like a man on fire. So, where's the fire, Brandon?"

"Nowhere. I didn't see you."

"Funny thing, Brandon. I just got off the phone with my boss, Commander Redwood. It seems he got a very angry call from the FBI about a civilian who may hold some valuable information regarding a very high-profile investigation. The commander is understandably reluctant to crap on the FBI, so he asked that I handle the situation. I assured him that your integrity is unimpeachable and that you would not withhold information about a crime from the police. I hope I didn't speak out of turn."

"No, sir," Brandon said.

"Good. What do you have there?" Lieutenant Webber asked, pointing at the file clenched in Brandon's hand.

"It's everything I've gathered on the Jane Doe investigation. I was going to turn it over to Amy, so she could add her input before passing it on to you, sir."

The lieutenant reached out his hand, and Brandon handed over the file, feeling like a kid in the principal's office as he waited for him to flip through each page.

"Is he our guy?" he finally asked, looking down at the picture of Hurt captured by the convenience store camera.

"Yes," Brandon said.

"At any moment this office is going to be crawling with federal agents, all wanting to speak with you. I need you to talk with them, tell them what you know—"

"Lieutenant, please, I have—"

"Brandon, you don't need to say anything else. We all know how badly you want to catch this monster. We all know what it means to find this girl, for her and for Olivia too. Every trooper that could get here is already marshaling downstairs, and more are on the way from all over Colorado. The feds will run their investigation their way, and we'll run ours, but your job right now is to do your duty and tell the feds what they need to know, and when you're done, I promise we will run this mad dog to ground."

"I understand," Brandon said, turning away from his lieutenant.

"Brandon," Lieutenant Webber called.

"Sir?"

"We'll get him."

"I need to go call Olivia and let her know what's going on," Brandon said, leaving Lieutenant Webber standing by the elevator as he ran back down the stairs, ducking out a rear door to avoid the jumble of voices coming from the squad room.

Brandon sat in his cold truck, with the key in the ignition, while Lieutenant Webber's words buzzed around inside his head like angry bees. He knew that what the lieutenant had said was right, but his heart told him that if he didn't leave now, he would never see Delilah or Hurt again. *Olivia would die.* He didn't know if he'd heard the words or simply thought them, but he recognized them for the truth they were and turned the key in the ignition, slowly backing out of his parking space and leaving the police building behind.

He drove until he'd reached a convenience store and pulled into the parking lot. Once he was parked, he pulled out his phone, praying for a decent connection as the little circle spun slowly, as if trying to decide if it would grant his wish.

When the search engine opened, he began to breathe again and typed, "Hurt Mountain Farm, Colorado Springs." When nothing came up, he bit back the urge to scream. Instead, he took a deep breath and closed his eyes, combing his memory for any piece of information that would give him the answers he needed.

The voice beside his ear was so clear that he flinched as if he'd been slapped.

"Freedman Hurt," Carly said.

Afraid of what he would see, he turned his head toward where the voice had come from. For the tiniest moment he saw her reflection in the steam-covered window, and then she was gone, a mirage or a delusional mind, except his heart told him it wasn't. A sob caught in his throat, and he swallowed it down, blinking away the tears that blurred his vision as he typed in the name.

Before he could even finish typing, the words popped on the screen as if it had been waiting for someone to come along and ask for the information. It took only a few moments for Brandon to find an old news article about a home in Old Colorado City where Freedman had lived with his parents and sister. A tragic fire had apparently burned down the house, killing his father, sister, and invalid mother.

He continued to search and found that not only had Hurt inherited the property in Old Colorado, but there was also a deed in his name for a piece of land located miles above the city, on Pikes Peak. There was no record of a house, just coordinates and size, but he knew without question that this was where he would find Freedman Hurt and Delilah, and maybe he'd finally bring Carly home to rest, once and for all.

Brandon looked out the window of the truck into the snow. As bad as the roads were in the city, conditions would be that much worse on the road that led into the mountains. He had chains, which would help some, but he'd need a lot of luck, and maybe some divine intervention too. As he put his foot on the brake and put the truck in gear, raindrops began to fall from the sky, slowly at first, but within moments the drops had become a steady stream, then a heavy deluge, washing away the snow.

Brandon stared out the window, amazed.

"Hurry, Daddy," she said.

Brandon started the car and pulled out of the parking lot.

"I'm coming, baby," he said, his mind blank save for one thought: *Kill Freedman Hurt.* "Daddy's coming."

Chapter 58

Freedman Hurt opened his eyes and stared into the dark, not moving. His back and arms felt sore, and he had a crick in his neck. As his eyes adjusted to the darkness, he saw the shape of the chair in the center of the room, and he smiled.

Delilah was home. He had rescued her and returned her to her righteous place, as his God demanded. The fire had died down in the hearth, and the room had begun to grow cold. He lifted himself from the floor and turned his attention to the dying fire. As warmth crept into the room, he shrugged out of his heavy coat. Outside, the wind tore through the barren trees, and the steady sound of rain drummed down on the roof.

He walked over to the door and wrenched it open. Rain fell in sheets, washing away the snow that would have protected him and Delilah, at least for a while. He immediately thought of the police officer. He would come; Freedman was sure of that. When he came, would he bring help, or would his pride lead him to come alone?

"Pride goeth before the fall," he said aloud.

Yet he couldn't be sure. He didn't doubt he could handle the man if he was alone—he would even enjoy the task—but to stay and chance losing his Delilah was too great a risk.

"Lord, the devil is strong. Please lead me to your will," he said.

Thunder seemed to shake the ground beneath Freedman's feet as a bolt of lightning tore across the sky. He shook his head and turned away, closing the door against the sudden rainstorm. He would be obedient to God's wishes and move Delilah to safety.

Chapter 59

Delilah watched, careful not to move even an inch as Father rose from sleep. Her breath caught in her throat as he turned to look directly at her, only breathing again as he turned his back on her to tend to the fire.

Outside, the storm continued to rage, as if it intended to rip the building from the ground and fling it into the trees. She heard Father speak but could not hear what he said. As she watched, he turned from the door and walked slowly toward where she sat.

She tried to be strong, as Sunny had begged her to, but fear took over and she whimpered as he reached for her, the light from the fire glinting off the knife he held in his hand. It was the same butcher knife Mother had used to cut the dead chickens into pieces for their dinner, the same knife Father had used to kill her for helping to set them free. Now, it seemed, he would use it to kill Delilah too.

Delilah closed her eyes, only having time to pray that death would come quickly before she felt the cold steel brush her arm, and suddenly her arms were free. Father bent over and swiped the knife downward, cutting the rope from her ankles. When he stood, he didn't speak, just stared at her like he didn't recognize her at all.

Delilah focused all her attention on not crying out as blood flooded into her arms and legs. Father tossed the knife away into the darkness. Delilah listened as it bounced off the bed and landed on the dirt floor with a thud.

"Get up," he said.

Delilah tried to push herself up, but her knees buckled under her weight, and she fell back into the chair.

Father reached down and grabbed her by the hair, dragging her off the chair and onto the floor. Delilah screamed and pitched forward, landing on her side as she reached for her knee, ripping her hair from Father's hand.

She saw Father reaching down to grab her, and without thinking, she rolled away from him into the shadows outside the reach of the light of the fire. Father roared his anger, kicking outward, trying to find her with his foot.

The room was too small for Delilah to stay hidden for any amount of time, even in the dark. A few seconds and a few steps forward were the only things that separated her from a life indistinguishable from hell. In a flash of certainty, Delilah knew that she would rather join Sunny and Jacob and all the nameless girls and women who had come and gone than live one more torturous moment as Father's hopeless slave.

Knowing the time to free herself was almost gone, Delilah hurried toward the bed, where the knife had landed. Tears mixed with sweat as she crawled across the floor on her hands and knees, searching for the knife. When she felt the hand close around her ankle, she screamed. She expected to be yanked to her feet, but instead Father dragged her across the floor toward the fire. Terror gripped Delilah, and she tried to kick herself free.

"No . . . Father, no . . . please," she cried, but he didn't stop until he stood in front of the hearth, where he stared into the waiting flames.

"Father, forgive me, I have sinned. I was led astray by sinners, and I was weak," she said, hating the words as she said them but too afraid of the fire not to give him what he wanted.

Father looked at her, as if trying to decide. Delilah held her breath and prayed for a miracle, too afraid to even beg for her life lest her voice send him over the edge. Finally, he nodded, a smile like a jack-o'-lantern creasing his face.

"God hears you, girl. He forgives your sin, no matter how heinous. He will welcome you in his kingdom when the time comes," he said, nodding again as he let go of her wrist.

Delilah dropped her eyes to the ground, afraid of what he would see in her face.

"Drop down to your knees, girl, and thank the Lord for your forgiveness," he said, his hand dropping onto her shoulders, pushing her to her knees.

Out of habit, Delilah clasped her hands together as she bowed her head. She heard the rustle of the wood as Father stirred the fire. She knew what was coming next. The Lord may have forgiven her, but Father had not. He would dole out punishment after all, and shame on her for having dared to hope that she would be spared. She watched as he raised the poker, glowing red hot from hours resting in the flames.

"Please," she whispered as he reached for her, not knowing who she was talking to. It didn't matter.

Father stood in front of her as she knelt on the floor in front of the fire, his eyes closed, mumbling to himself.

"Run now!" Sunny screamed inside her head, sending her stumbling forward on her hands and knees.

She heard Father grunt, but she didn't stop to see where he was.

Delilah knew the knife under the bed was her last chance. He wouldn't bother with punishment now. If he caught her, he would string her up from the hanging tree and whip the life out of her body.

She had just managed to reach under the bed when she felt his hand grab her ankle again. Delilah screamed as he yanked her backward. Suddenly, more than anything, she wanted to live. She allowed her body go limp as he dragged her toward him. As soon as he'd flipped her over onto her back and released her ankle from his grasp, Delilah focused all her remaining strength into her foot, praying it would find its mark, knowing that if she failed, there would be no second chance. Calling upon all the force she could muster, she raised her leg as he lunged forward, driving the heel of her bare foot into his nose with all her might.

She felt the bone crush beneath her heel. Blood spurted from Father's nose, splashing onto her foot. For a moment, Father continued forward, seemingly unaware of the damage, but then he rocked backward, falling sideways as he grabbed for his face, sounding more like a wounded bear than a human.

Delilah rolled over and scurried back toward the bed on all fours. As she searched, she could hear him coming. Her fingers skimmed across the wooden handle of the knife just as his hand fell onto her leg, and he once again dragged her from under the bed and into the center of the floor. Enraged, he let go of her ankle and reached down and grabbed a handful of hair and lifted her from the floor, ignoring her screams as the roots separated from her scalp, her feet dangling in the air.

"Father, forgive me," she cried, raising her hands and plunging the knife deep into his chest.

Father looked momentarily confused, and his hands opened as he dropped Delilah to the floor. She saw him reach for the knife sticking out of his chest, but before he could grasp the handle, his eyes clouded over, and he fell forward, landing on top of the knife.

Chapter 60

Brandon slammed his fist against the steering wheel. It seemed like he'd been climbing the steep mountain road for ages, unable to go faster than five miles per hour. Although the unexpected storm had washed away a lot of the new snow, he still had to contend with the layer of ice left in its wake. It was the fifth time he had skidded off the road after daring to push his speed over twenty miles per hour, and he began to fear that he would never make it in time. The last time his GPS had worked, it told him that he had only seven more miles before he reached the turnoff that led to the farm. That had been more than half an hour ago, and the brush that lined the road remained undisturbed by tread marks.

He wondered if the coordinates he had were all wrong, but he continued on because he didn't know what else to do. There was no way he could go back to the hospital and tell Olivia that she had lost another child to that monster. It would destroy her.

Brandon took a deep breath and pressed down on the accelerator. When the truck lurched from the ditch, he breathed a sigh of relief and forced himself to creep forward.

He had traveled another mile, the light from his high beams bouncing all over the road as he tried to force the truck forward without losing control, when a break in the road appeared to his right without warning. There were no signs marking the rough track as anything more than a trail, except for deep tire tracks sunk into the mud that told him he had found the way to Hurt Mountain Farm.

Brandon turned onto the road, his eyes watchful, his heart racing, his hands clenched around the steering wheel. At the end of the path sat a dilapidated house, seeming to lean against the wind. The dark, empty windows looked out onto the path.

As Brandon stepped out of the truck, he saw the front door was open, but he could see nothing more through the darkness beyond. After slamming his door closed, he walked around to the passenger side. Leaning inside the truck without taking his eyes from the house, he reached into the glove compartment and pulled out first the holster holding his 9mm Glock—he wasn't in the habit of carrying it with him, but his gut had said differently, and he was glad he'd listened—and then the heavy-duty flashlight he stowed there for emergencies.

When he clicked on the power button and a strong beam of light spilled out into the night, he turned and started toward the door, thankful for the heaviness of the weapon in his hand. As he mounted the steps, the sense of déjà vu was so strong that for a minute he felt a bit disoriented.

Just like Ms. Helen's home, this house was as cold inside as out. As fast as he dared, he moved through a small barren kitchen and into a large living area. A massive fireplace took up nearly one whole wall of the room. The fireplace showed no sign of recent use, and Brandon was not surprised to see that there was no electricity.

Two straight-backed chairs sat in front of the fireplace, facing each other. Brandon tried to imagine what life was like for the people who used those stark chairs. A table, made from wooden planks bound together, was pushed against one wall. As he drew closer, he saw a dark stain covering at least half the surface. Blood, he was sure.

Brandon turned around, slowly shining the light over the opposite wall. Then he froze, his hand clenching the flashlight so hard that the light jittered against the wall like a pinball. Whips of various sizes, from a bullwhip to a small riding crop, hung on the wall in descending order of size. An empty space between the largest whip and the horsewhip reminded him of Delilah's wounds.

Brandon felt his grip tighten on his weapon, and he wished Freedman Hurt were standing in front of him. When the time came, he would put him down like a rabid animal, which would be more mercy than he deserved. Brandon forced himself to relax his grip, filling the air with useless curses as he lowered the weapon to his side. He prayed he would be able to find some evidence of Delilah's presence and, if God was with him, some clue as to where he could find her.

Time was running out; that much he knew. Outside, the darkness taunted him. He was aware the night would make the search for Delilah that much harder, but to wait for daylight was unthinkable. Hurt would most likely disappear into the mountains, along with any chances of finding Delilah or sending him back to the hell from which Brandon was convinced he had come. He could not allow that to happen. He wouldn't.

After walking a few steps down a short hallway, he faced two closed doors: one on his right, one directly across the hall. Brandon reached out and turned the doorknob of the door on the right. The door swung open without resistance, revealing a room as barren as the rest of the house, its only furniture two carved, narrow wooden beds. Heavy chains with makeshift steel cuffs hung from each of the four bedposts of both beds. He stepped into the empty room, approaching the beds, dreading what he would find.

A thin wool blanket covered each bed, and there were no pillows. When he pulled back the blankets, he was relieved to find the sheets clean, save for some well-worn stains washed into the fabric long ago. Whatever violence had occurred had not happened here.

Brandon backed from the room, closed the door behind him, and turned to open the second door. Unlike the first, it did not spring open when he turned the knob. Instead, he had to push against it with one shoulder. The bedroom window had been left open, letting in the wind that pushed against the door. As soon as he let go of the door, it slammed shut, closing him inside the room.

The hairs on the back of his neck rose as he noticed the shape of a body laid out on the bed, which was pushed up against the wall under the open window. Barely breathing, he crossed the floor and pulled away the covers and looked down into the face of Allison Moore.

It was impossible to guess how long she had been dead simply by looking at her, but if he had to, he would guess her death had coincided with Delilah's escape. Maybe because of the cold, she looked like she could have been sleeping. According to the file, she would have been around forty years old, but the face he looked down upon could easily have been that of a sixty-year-old woman. Her eyes stared straight ahead and her mouth hung wide open, giving her an appearance of shock, even in death.

A blanket was pulled up to her chin and tucked around her neck like a bib. Brandon pulled the blanket away. Her chest had been hacked open with three gashes that were so deep it looked as if someone had tried to carve her heart out. Another gash ran from one side of her throat to the other, and her stomach, like her chest and throat, had been sliced open.

Allison Moore had been fifteen when she was stolen from her family. The torture she must have endured these past twenty-five years was inconceivable. Staring at the desecrated body of the woman who had once been a beloved child, he thought of the Jessups. How much more pain must they endure? How would he tell them that they had been within months of finding their lost niece?

As he dropped the light toward the floor, his eye fell on a piece of paper lying near his foot. He bent down to pick it up and saw that it wasn't a piece of paper at all, but a picture.

Brandon gasped in shock as he stared down at the picture of Allison Moore looking into the camera, wearing a wedding dress too big for her tiny frame, so old that it had started to turn yellow with age, her eyes pleading for help. Freedman Hurt stood beside her, wearing a heavy-looking, dark suit, a white collar at his neck, as if he were some kind of preacher. One impossibly large hand gripped Allison's arm so tight that even in the picture, the indentations his fingers made were clearly visible on her pale skin.

For a moment, it was Carly's face in the picture. Brandon closed his eyes against the image, swallowing the bile that rose in his throat as he folded the picture and put it in his pocket. Right or wrong, the Jessups would never suffer through the horror of that photo.

Leaning forward, he pulled the blanket back over her body. There was nothing he or anyone else could do to help her now, but he could still find Delilah.

The Teaching Room. The thought blazed through his mind like a meteor. Of course, the Teaching Room. Turning his back on the corpse, he hurried down the narrow hallway and out of the house. As he stepped outside, the still-damp air smacked him across the face, and he sucked it in greedily. As he hurried across the yard to his truck, the door slammed behind him.

As quick as he could, he located the truck's emergency kit. With relief he found another large flashlight. He prayed that the batteries worked. "Thank you," he said as he pushed the button and bright light spilled into the yard.

Quick as he could, he did an inventory of the rest of the kit and was thrilled to find several packs of backup batteries, along with granola bars, water, matches, a Kevlar jacket, a military-issued wool blanket, and the rucksack that had carried him through his entire air force career. He prayed that Hurt was still near, but if he'd already begun his trek into the mountains, Brandon would follow. He'd follow him to the edge of the earth if necessary. Unsure of how long he'd be gone, or even what he would find, Brandon packed all the items into the rucksack and slung it over his back.

Using Delilah's words as his guide, he searched for the path that would lead him to the Teaching Room and, hopefully, to her. It didn't take him long to find the narrow gap that opened between the dense trees.

As he stepped onto the path, he thought he heard the distant sound of a young girl's laughter. His heart clenched with grief, but he pushed forward into the darkness, knowing that Delilah could not spare him the time to allow the tears that lurked so close to the surface to fall. He would have time for that later, years later, in fact, if he left this mountain alive.

Chapter 61

Delilah sat hunched in front of the dying fire, draped in Father's coat. Outside, the wind sounded like a hungry beast as it bashed against the walls of the rickety building. Cold wind swept through the cracks in the walls and under the door. She didn't know how long it had been since Father took his last breath, but she knew it wouldn't be long before the fire died, leaving her unprotected from the cold that seemed so anxious to consume her. Then she supposed she would join the dead who sat vigil with her, staring into the fire, waiting for the last embers to die.

Although the main house wasn't far on a warm, sunny day, she knew she had no chance of making it now. The snow had stopped, but she knew how treacherously low the temperatures could sink in these mountains; it wouldn't take long for the bitter cold to settle into her bones. Even if the cold didn't claim her, how long could she walk? With each step, she could feel the blood seeping from her body. And now, the idea of leaving the shack, even long enough to gather wood, seemed too much, when all she wanted was to lie down and let it be over, once and for all.

Though she could still see Sunny as clear as she ever could when she was alive, she was silent now, sitting beside Delilah, staring into the fire, as if she, too, were waiting. She supposed they all were. Across the room, Jacob stared down at Father's corpse, his head miraculously made whole by her imagination.

"Won't be long now, I suppose," she said, glancing at Sunny.

Sunny shimmered for a moment, fading before her eyes like poor reception on the radio that Father sometimes used to talk to the Family. Sunny and Jacob weren't real, not anymore at least. She knew it, but knowing it did not lessen her need for them. She was afraid, afraid of dying alone without even anyone to bury her in the makeshift grave-yard behind the Teaching Room. She supposed that it wouldn't be long before the animals found her and gorged on her carcass, right along with Father's. Would God punish her for murdering Father by leaving her soul trapped in this room that held so much of her pain?

Delilah stood and walked toward the body. When she tried to imagine life outside these walls, her head filled with empty blackness, her time with Olivia seemingly little more than a dream. Even if God granted her mercy for killing Father, the Family never would. They would find her, and she would pay. But death would bring her the peace she so desperately needed. Behind her, a hidden piece of wood fed the dying flames, giving it a final burst of life, the light illuminating the room.

Delilah looked at the chair that had been kicked into the corner at some point during the struggle. Rope still hung from its arms and legs. *Not a lot, but enough,* she thought. She searched the ceiling for anything that would hold her weight. Her eyes fell on a rusty hook that hung from a beam that ran across the ceiling. Her mind shied away from the memories that the sight of that old hook brought. She looked to where Jacob had stood only a moment ago, but she was alone now.

She walked to the corner and grabbed the chair and dragged it back into the center of the room, directly under the beam. She knew that if she didn't do it quickly, she would lose her nerve.

Outside, a crash like the sound of a large branch falling from the trees startled Delilah. She jumped, tripping over the coat that hung from her body, and fell to the floor, screaming in pain as she landed on her back. The door crashed open, and she twisted her body, trying to get to her feet. Pain ripped through her, making her feel as if she were being sliced in half. How had they found her so soon? she wondered, grateful for the nothingness that enveloped her.

Chapter 62

Brandon stood in the clearing, looking at the old shack, his heart knocking against his chest so hard it was a wonder it didn't burst clean through his rib cage. The shack, made of old wood, topped with an ancient-looking tin roof, was so shoddily put together that a gust of wind made it tremble. One more hit like that would surely turn it back into the pile of rotten sticks it had once been, he thought.

There were no windows, and he saw no light seeping through any of the many cracks. He waited, staring at the shack for any signs of life, but nothing moved. He was too late, he thought, rejecting the idea before it could fully form. A crash came from behind him. He spun around to face the woods and grabbed for his gun, just in time to see a tree limb weighed down with ice come crashing to the earth, dragging smaller branches with it.

"God damn it," he breathed, turning back to face the house. Forcing himself not to rush forward and kick in the door, he took measured steps, shining the light around him, careful that it didn't fall directly on the shack, lest it alert the monster inside.

He felt his heart speed up and his breath quicken as he approached the door, a silent prayer on his lips. A crash, followed by a scream, ripped through the night, and Brandon forgot his vow of caution. Rushing forward, he kicked open the door. In the dim light from the dying fire, he saw a chair lying on its back in the center of the room. Beside the chair, a crumpled form that could have been a mound of rags lay unmoving.

"Delilah?" he called from the open door, where he stood looking into the darkness. Raising the flashlight, he shined it into the room, taking in the ruined, sparse furniture, the dying fire. A few feet from the fireplace, the light fell on a large pair of boots. Slowly he shined the light upward until he was staring into the dead eyes of Freedman Hurt. This was the monster who had held their child captive. How lost and terrified she must have been.

"Say thank you to the nice man, Carly . . ."

The words seemed to hang in the air, and he found himself choking back a sob.

He had failed his Carly, and Delilah, too, he thought as his eyes fell on the butcher knife protruding from Hurt's chest. It should have been him to have ended this nightmare. Delilah had already suffered too much.

"I'm glad I killed him."

The words, so small that Brandon almost believed he had imagined them, brought tears to his eyes, even as his heart soared with relief and gratitude. Turning away from Freedman's body, he raced to what he had mistaken for a bundle of rags. Falling to his knees, he pushed aside a heavy coat and looked down into Delilah's face.

"God Almighty, Delilah," he said as he pulled her to his chest and held her there, being as careful as he could of her injuries, until he felt her trying to wiggle away.

"I'm going to let you go. Can you sit up on your own?" he asked, letting his arms fall away as she nodded.

When he was sure that Delilah could sit without his assistance, he stood up and backed away, giving her space as she looked around the room, as if it were her first time seeing it.

He rested his hand on his weapon as he approached Freedman Hurt's body. "I'm glad you killed him too."

"I'm going to hell. I won't ever see Sunny, Jacob, or none of the others again."

"Others?" Brandon asked, feeling his stomach flip as he turned to face Delilah, buried in Hurt's coat, hugging her knees to her chest and staring back at Brandon.

"All the others Mother said was going to heaven."

"How many others, Delilah?"

"I can't remember now. They were all wrong, so Mother and Father sent them home to the Lord."

"What did they do with them after they sent them home to the Lord?" Brandon asked, needing to hear the answer but praying she didn't know.

"We always had a proper burial for our sisters, as the Lord commanded. Father blessed their bodies and buried them all in the cemetery."

"And the boys?" Brandon asked.

Delilah didn't answer, just shrugged.

"Where is the cemetery?" he said, feeling breathless as he thought of Carly.

"Out back," she said, turning to point at the back wall.

Brandon didn't say anything for a while. His eyes were locked on the flimsy back wall, as if he could see through the rotting wood.

"Is she out there? Is Carly out there?" he asked quietly.

For what seemed like forever, Brandon stood in the middle of the room, the sound of his own blood and his heartbeat pounding in his ears, the wind seeping in from outside brushing across his face, and then Delilah spoke.

"Yes," she said.

Without another word, Brandon turned and walked out the door. Tonight, he would find Carly and bring her home at last.

Chapter 63

Brandon found the makeshift cemetery behind the Teaching Room, just as Delilah had said. A rickety fence made from wood planks of varying sizes separated the meager backyard from the burial ground. The wind that had dogged his every step so far had dissipated, blowing away the clouds that had covered the moon and leaving the earth quiet as the dead who lay beneath his feet.

The light of the moon shone down, revealing crooked rows of wooden crosses. A few of the crosses had names scratched into their surfaces, but most were blank. Brandon counted twelve of the markers before he sank to his knees, shaking his head, his brain refusing to accept what he saw. If every cross represented a dead girl, then over a dozen girls had died at Freedman Hurt's hand.

The last marker was covered in dirt, as if someone had tried to wipe away the name carved into the wood. The part that wasn't hidden by mud was hidden by the shadows. Reluctantly Brandon wiped away the mud and dirt and raised his flashlight to shine on the marker. SARAH, it read in crude letters, but underneath the unfamiliar name, someone, Delilah, he was sure, had carved a picture of the sun. He had found his Carly at last.

Brandon reached out and laid his hands on the ground, sobs shaking his body, the cries ripped from his throat, like an animal driven mad with pain, filling the night air. When the tears were done, he stayed where he was, kneeling in the dirt, his body shuddering as he fought the part of him that wanted to dig her up right then and there and remove her from that evil place. Instead, he wiped the few remaining tears from his face and recited the Lord's Prayer, as he had done with her so many nights before.

Save Delilah. Bring Carly home. He nodded, as if the words, alive only in his brain, had been spoken out loud. Leaning forward, he pressed his lips to the cold hard earth underneath the marker, imagining her face one more time. Struggling to his feet, he turned his back on the makeshift graveyard and started toward the shack where Delilah waited. As he walked, a light snow began to fall again.

Chapter 64

Olivia sat upright in the hospital bed, trying her best to focus on the words coming from Lieutenant Webber's mouth. Her world had collapsed into itself, and other than the unrelenting panic that crushed her in its grip, she couldn't feel anything anymore. Not long after Brandon had left, eons ago, it seemed, FBI agents had descended in a black-suited flock, their cold faces and empty voices seeming to suck the very air from the room. As best as she could, she had explained about Hurt and the farm.

"I told them everything I knew," Olivia said, cutting off Lieutenant Webber in midsentence.

"I'm sorry?" he said, his face crinkling into a baffled frown.

"The FBI, I told them about Hurt."

Lieutenant Webber sighed and sank into the chair left empty by Arlene, who had finally been convinced to go get food. "It's good that you told them."

"Is Brandon in trouble? I haven't heard from him since he left. He hasn't called, and his phone is off. Do you think he's all right?"

"I'm sure he is, but it's not him I'm worried about."

"He's going to kill him, you know. He's going to kill him for Carly."

"I don't know that," he said firmly, looking Olivia in the eye as he spoke.

"Of course," Olivia agreed, nodding.

"I didn't come here in an official capacity. I'm not here to question you about anything. I'm here because Brandon is a damn good man. It makes me sick that you have to suffer through this again. I saw the file on Freedman Hurt."

"Brandon's alone out there," Olivia said.

"I wish Brandon hadn't gone, but we both know he's fully capable of taking care of himself. He knows you're waiting for him. He'll be back. And as soon as we're able, our guys will be right behind him. Trust me, Olivia, we're going to get him and end this once and for all."

"Thank you, Lieutenant."

"No thanks necessary. I just wanted to drop by to let you know we're here. If you need anything, don't hesitate to call."

Olivia nodded, reaching out her hand to the lieutenant as he rose from the chair.

"Don't worry, Doc. He's going to be okay. You'll see. Try and get some rest. Oh, I took care of a little housekeeping for you. You won't have to worry about them so-called reporters, at least for a little while, but you know they're like roaches. You think you got rid of them, and they come right on back."

Olivia looked up as Arlene walked into the room.

"Well, well, well, so this is what has the nurses all aflutter," she said, looking Lieutenant Webber up and down. Olivia was surprised to see him blush at Arlene's insinuating grin.

"Arlene, behave—this is Brandon's friend Lieutenant Webber. He just stopped by to check on me."

"Well, who knew the state had such a fine man running things over there. Lieutenant, if you're single, I have at least a dozen ladies that would love to change that for you."

"As tempting as that sounds, I'm sure my Agnes would have something to say about that," he said, tapping the gold band on his ring finger. "Twenty-five years and counting."

"If you don't tell, I surely won't," Arlene said.

"Arlene!" Olivia said as Lieutenant Webber and Arlene both started to laugh.

"Honestly, what is going on in here? I could hear you all the way down the hall."

Instantly the room grew silent as they turned to where Minnie stood in the doorway, her eyes swinging from person to person.

"Mom, what are you doing here?" Olivia said as Minnie reached the bed and began fussing with the covers.

"Well, I'm going to leave you now, Olivia," the lieutenant said. "Arlene, nice to meet you. Ma'am," he said, nodding at Minnie as he walked from the room.

"Oh, Mom, please."

"You would think he had more important things to do at a time like this," Minnie said.

"Mom, please just stop it. Lieutenant Webber is doing everything he can. He was only trying to make me feel better. There's no crime in that, is there?" Olivia said, all lightness from a few moments ago crushed under the weight of Minnie's disapproval.

"When I heard what happened on the news, I thought my daughter needed me, but I can see I was wrong. I suppose if you needed me, you would have called yourself. I'll go."

"Mom, I'm sorry, I really am. I was going to call you. I just didn't want you to worry. Please sit down. I'm glad you're here."

"Ms. Minnie, I'm sorry. I was just trying to lighten the mood," Arlene said. "I've been here for a while. I think it's time for me to go check in at home."

"Fine," Minnie said, keeping her back turned to them as she took off her coat.

"I'm going to give you some time alone, but I'll be back before you kill each other," Arlene whispered as she bent down to kiss Olivia on the cheek.

"Thanks," Olivia said, squeezing her hand.

"Goodbye, Ms. Minnie," Arlene said before she walked out of the room.

"Mom, I'm tired. I think I'll take a nap," Olivia said after Arlene had gone, leaving her alone with her mother.

"Of course, dear, you need your rest. You look terrible. Have you heard anything from Brandon? I'm so worried. I'm not one to talk out of turn, but I knew it wasn't a good idea to bring this girl into your home, and now look at you—you could have been killed, and Brandon . . . after all you've been through . . ."

"I'm okay, Mom."

"He's going to be fine, you know that, right? God will hold Brandon safe in the palm of his hand. He'll come back to you just fine, don't you worry," Minnie said as she sat next to Olivia on the hospital bed, stroking her hair as if Olivia were still a little girl.

"And Delilah?" Olivia asked.

"The Lord loves all his children; you know that, Olivia."

"Mom, I'm so scared," Olivia said. Unable to hold back the tears any longer, she collapsed in her mother's arms and cried like she hadn't since she was a small child.

"There now, get some rest," Minnie said, rising from the bed after Olivia had finally cried herself out.

"Mom, I'm sorry about Ms. Helen and Mr. Otis. I know they meant a lot to you."

"What does any of this have to do with Helen or Otis?"

"Well, it's just that . . . well, I know . . . I'm sorry," Olivia spluttered as she looked into her mother's confused face.

"Olivia, please, you're not making any sense."

"Mom, I thought you said you heard about what happened on the news?"

"We did," her father said, stepping into the room from the hallway. "And as soon as your mother heard about the girl going missing, she insisted we get here right away."

"Yes, I knew you would be frantic, but your father couldn't be bothered to listen to the news. He turned it off—said it was distracting him from driving. Lord knows the man can barely drive on a good day, so we had to drive all the way down here in near silence."

"We made it here safely, didn't we, Minerva?"

Olivia turned her head toward the voice. For one second, her joy at seeing her father again obliterated everything else. "Daddy," she said, feeling like a little girl as she sat up and reached out for him. He seemed too pale, and new wrinkles covered his face. But although his blond hair had turned all white, his eyes were still the brilliant blue of a flawless summer sky.

"Olivia, are you okay?" he asked as he folded her into his arms. "Minerva, why don't you go get Olivia some clean water instead of fidgeting about?"

"Why don't you be honest for once, Leland, and just ask me to go," Minnie said. She snatched the pitcher from the table and stomped out of the room.

"Ah, Minnie, she's nothing if not dramatic," her father said, lowering himself into the chair by her bed.

"You didn't tell her about Ms. Helen or Otis, did you?" Olivia asked.

"No, I just couldn't."

"We have to tell her before someone else does or she sees it on TV."

"I know, I just thought it would be easier if you were here."

Olivia's father reached out and took her hand in his, neither of them speaking as they fell into their own thoughts.

"Leland." Minnie stood in the doorway, her face gray, her eyes wide, her small frame visibly shaking. Sheldon Myers stood beside her, his eyes wary as they moved between Olivia and her father.

"Leland, Mr. Myers just told me the most awful thing," Minnie said, her voice just above a whisper as she took a few wobbly steps into the room.

She's going to fall, Olivia thought as her mom took another shaky step forward, reaching an arm out to her husband, just as she pitched forward.

Chapter 65

By the time Brandon returned to the yard, he felt as if he had aged fifty years. He had always believed that finding Carly would bring him closure, but seeing that sad little grave that was no more than a dump site brought him nothing but more pain, if that was possible.

As much as he wanted to quit this evil place and rush back to Olivia and just hold her, he knew stumbling through these unfamiliar woods filled with God knew what (or whom), with an injured, traumatized Delilah, would be foolish beyond measure. He had lost Carly forever. He wouldn't risk Delilah.

At first light, he would make his way back to the truck and find help for Delilah, but he would not allow whatever small part of Carly was left in that desolate hole to spend one more night on this cursed mountain. When he returned to Olivia's side, he would bring home their daughter once and for all.

A ragged sigh tore through his chest, threatening to turn into a sob, but he forced himself to steady his breathing. There was still work to be done this night.

Slowly he approached the Teaching Room, stopping to listen at the door before he pushed it open. The room was just as he had left it, except the fire had burned down to nearly nothing. Hurt's body still lay on the floor, staring sightlessly into the air. Delilah sat unmoving, seemingly mesmerized, by the dying fire.

"Delilah," Brandon called, but she did not move.

Brandon turned away and stepped outside to get wood. When he returned, he tossed a new log on the fire, sending a shower of sparks into the air. A few of the sparks flew out of the fireplace, landing near Delilah, but she still did not move.

Brandon lowered himself to the floor beside her and stared into the fire while he waited for her to acknowledge his presence. For a long while they sat, two human statues throwing their thoughts into the greedy flames.

Outside, a strange cry echoed through the woods. Nothing more than a night bird, Brandon thought, but it still raised his hackles. Delilah must have felt the same because her head whipped around, as if she expected the bird to come crashing through the door.

"They're close now," she said.

"Who, Delilah? Who's close?" Brandon asked, fearing the answer he knew was coming.

Brandon looked into Delilah's vacant face, fear and anger making him want to snatch her and shake her back to reality, but he knew to do so would only make her retreat further into the world that offered her the protection she needed.

"Delilah," he said softly, "you have to listen to me. We don't have to die here. We can survive this, but I need your help, please."

Delilah continued to stare through him, and he wondered if she was so far gone that she could no longer see him.

"They are almost here," she said.

The Family. Brandon knew she was right. He could feel them in his bones, same as her, like the coming of a storm.

"Delilah, please, if not for you and me, then for Sunny, and even more than that for Olivia, who loves you as if you were her own. If we die here, we condemn her to death too. You know what I'm saying is true."

Delilah did not speak, but he saw life seep into her eyes as she continued to look at him.

"Remember how brave you were for Sunny, how you helped each other, how you loved each other. She needs you again now, to save yourself and her mother too."

Tears slid from Delilah's eyes, and never had Brandon been so happy to see anyone cry. He gathered her close, careful to avoid the wounds on her back, as her tears fell on his shirt. After a few moments he leaned her away from his body so that he could look into her eyes. She looked back at him, and he was sure that the fear he saw on her face was an echo of his own.

"I don't know how," she said.

"We'll find a way," Brandon said.

Delilah nodded, looking up at him, waiting for him to tell her what to do.

Chapter 66

"Tell me about the Family," Brandon said.

"The Family, they just are," she said, shrugging.

"How many are there? Where do they live?" he asked, his sense of desperation growing with every word.

"They live in the mountains, serving the whims of the Lord. They are as many as he provides. They are his sword. They will mete out his punishment as God wills."

"Jacob," he said. "Do you know where he would go when he wasn't here?" Brandon was desperate for any idea that would keep them from stumbling blindly through the woods. He knew that if they were forced to run, they wouldn't stand a chance out in the open.

"The secret place. We made it together—me, Sunny, and Jacob."

"How far is it from here?"

"Just through the graveyard and a small piece of the woods."

"If we make it there, would it be safe until morning?"

"Yes, but they own the woods. We could not escape them."

"Well, we'll just have to improvise," he said, looking around the meager cabin. There wasn't much to work with. He knew their only hope would be a distraction that would allow them to sneak away unnoticed.

Moving quickly, he opened his rucksack and removed the several pairs of socks he had brought and put them on Delilah's feet. Then he approached the body of Freedman Hurt and yanked the shoes from his corpse. They were too big for her to wear as they were, so he cut off the sole of one huge shoe and cut it in half before tying each piece to the bottom of Delilah's feet. If she had to walk on her own, at least her feet would be protected.

He took another piece of rope and tied the coat close to her body. Under different circumstances, he might have thought she looked cute or funny.

Once he was sure she was as ready as either of them could be, he approached the back wall. Here he stopped to offer his own prayer that the men who hunted them in the night would focus their attention on the front of the shack. If they were not at least that lucky, then all hope would be lost. He did not have a backup plan.

Careful to make as little noise as possible, he worked on forcing a board loose from the back wall until he was able to squeeze through it to get outside. Once he was outside, he stopped and waited—for a bullet, for someone to hurl themselves at him from the darkness, or for even a bow and arrow; he didn't know what—but nothing came. He listened for any more of the calls, but the night was silent for now.

Grateful, Brandon squeezed back inside and helped Delilah through the crack.

"Delilah, I want you to go to the edge of the trees and wait for just a little while. Don't go so far that you can't clearly see. If I don't come for you in just a little while, I want you to get to the secret place the best you can and stay there until morning. As soon as you see the first bit of light, get back to the main house. I expect that you'll have all the help you need waiting for you, but if you get there and you're alone, then head down to the road and stay hidden. Don't show yourself until you see a police car. You understand?"

Delilah looked up at him like she wanted to ask a question, but instead she nodded.

"It's going to be okay, you'll see," he said. He watched as she disappeared across the yard and into the trees before turning back to the room. He was running out of time. He was as sure of that as if someone had screamed the words out loud. His blood quickened in his veins, and his heart raced in his chest.

As if to confirm his intuition, a loud hoot sounded like it had come from right outside the front door. Rushing across the floor, he grabbed hold of Freedman Hurt's ankle and pulled. Even using all his strength, it seemed as if the dead body would not move. Just as he felt the strength draining from his arms, the body slid. Adrenaline rushed through him at the small gain, and he redoubled his efforts. Outside, the solitary hoot was joined by first one, then another, then another, cry.

Leaving the body of Freedman Hurt blocking the front door, Brandon rushed across the room toward the fireplace, grabbing a discarded rag as he went. Quickly, he wrapped the rag around the end of one of the sticks he had picked up to feed the fire and thrust it into the flame. Once the flame caught, he raced across the room, dropping the fire first onto Hurt's body, then onto the bed, leaving a trail of flame in front of him as he backed toward the crack in the wall.

He imagined he heard a thump from outside, but he had no more time to hesitate. As the room filled with smoke and he began to cough, he squeezed through the crack in the back wall, carrying his rucksack, and ran in a crouch toward the tree line. He nearly tripped over Delilah, who was crouched low, staring out of the trees at the burning cabin. Brandon watched, barely breathing, as forms stepped from the woods to surround the cabin. At first the air was silent, save for the crackling of the hungry fire consuming the wood, but then the sound of singing floated through the air, raising the flesh all over Brandon's body.

"Let's get out of here," he said, turning away from the fire and lifting Delilah in his arms.

Delilah pointed out the directions, sometimes giving him instructions in a low whisper when he couldn't see where she wanted him to go. A short time later, she asked him to put her down, and she scurried into what looked like a wall of brush and trees. She'd disappeared from his sight just long enough for him to start to worry before she popped back out onto the path, motioning him to follow.

As he stepped through the brush behind Delilah, the ground seemed to give way, and he found himself sliding down an embankment. When he stopped, he was lying in front of the mouth of a cave. A stream ran beside the cave, and tall trees surrounded it on all sides. Brandon lay on his back and looked back up the incline. He was surprised to see that the entrance was no longer visible.

"Come on," Delilah said, motioning him forward before disappearing into the cave.

As quick as he could, he got up and lurched into the cave. Inside were three handmade cots on the floor. Someone, or maybe all of them, had gathered old rags and pillows and stuffed them between a pair of sheets and sewn them together. He couldn't help but wonder how long it had taken. Mismatched candles in an assortment of jars were all over, and canned goods of different varieties were stacked against another wall. A few pots and pans, a stack of firewood, and a pile of blankets completed the supplies in the cave.

"Who did this?" Brandon asked.

"Jacob," Delilah said.

"Why? How?"

"Some of it me and Sunny stole from the main house, but mostly Jacob brought it here."

"Where did he get it from?"

"Because he was a boy, Father said he had to be trained up in the ways to run his own family one day, so he took him with him during the Gathering and to visit the Family, even off the mountain sometimes for work. That's why Sunny wouldn't believe that you and Olivia were dead. Jacob would tell her that he had seen you and that you were alive."

"Why didn't he tell us, or go to the police?" Brandon asked.

"'Cause Father would know, and then he would kill you all," Delilah said, as if it made all the sense in the world.

All of a sudden Brandon was more tired than he had ever been in his life. He felt the world closing in. All he wanted was to close his eyes, but he knew sleep would have to wait. After starting a fire in the pit that Jacob had dug, Brandon moved two of the cots close, but instead of sitting on another cot, Delilah sat down next to him.

"How did you get away?" he asked. Beside him, Delilah's tiny body trembled. Brandon wrapped one of the wool blankets around her. When the tremors stopped, she began to talk.

"It was Mother who helped us get away, because of Jacob, I'm sure."

"Why?" Brandon asked.

"I don't know," Delilah said, shrugging. "But after Sunny was gone, Jacob was like a wild animal. He never came to the main house anymore when Father was there. He wouldn't even go with him during the Gathering. He told Mother that he was going to kill him. Mother got real scared. I think she believed that he would. That's when Mother told us it was time for us to leave.

"She started sneaking money to Jacob to get what he needed to fix the car. Once he got it to working, anytime Father was away, she would teach us how to drive. Jacob learned better than me. I just couldn't get it, but Mother, she said I had to. She wouldn't let me quit until I could drive straight and back up. Maybe we wouldn't have got caught if I hadn't been so slow to learn, but we did."

"What's the Gathering?" Brandon asked, sure he didn't really want to know but feeling like he had no choice but to hear it all.

"Every year when spring comes, Father would join together the Families from all over the mountain and go out into the world to bring back new sisters to strengthen the Family. Sometimes they would be just babies, but mostly they would be little kids like Sunny. If they pleased Father, then he would marry them to a good shepherd, and they would go away and make their own family. But if they were disobedient, then Father would send them home to Jesus, once they were bred."

"Jesus," Brandon said, the magnitude of what her words meant sending him into shock all over again.

A loud pop from the fire made him jump, but Delilah didn't move; she just kept staring into the flames. Brandon looked toward the mouth of the cave, but there was nothing but blackness and the wind rustling through the branches that he'd used to cover the entrance.

"How did you get caught?" he asked, turning his attention back to Delilah.

"We were supposed to go before the snows came, but we weren't ready, and then my blood came. Mother tried to hide it from Father, but he brought the healer, and she said it was time for me to be a wife."

Brandon fought to stay seated beside Delilah even as his stomach burned with rage and disgust.

"The healer said my womb was blessed by the Lord. She said the Lord was pleased, and I would catch quick with child."

Brandon's teeth were clenched so tight that he felt pain shoot from his jaw to his head. He thought about Hurt and prayed that there really was a hell. "How did you get away, Delilah?"

"When Father went into the mountains to visit the Family, Mother decided it was time. We begged her to leave with us, but she wouldn't. She said there wasn't nothing left for her in this world. Jacob went to the Teaching Room alone. He was supposed to load the car. Mother kept stomping around the house, yelling at me about how long Jacob was taking to come back. She was scared. So was I. We both felt something was wrong."

Delilah jumped up from beside Brandon and began pacing in front of the fire. Brandon could see blood starting to seep through the rough bandages on her back that he'd fashioned from the sheets he'd found in the cave. He opened his mouth to call her back, but then she stopped and turned to face him. Her eyes were distant and cloudy, and he knew she was no longer there.

"Delilah, come sit down. You're shaking," he said. He got up and put his arm around her shoulders, then gently guided her back to her place in front of the fire. "You don't have to say anything more. You're safe, you're free, and that's all that matters."

"I was going to go find Jacob, but when I opened the door—"

"That's enough," Brandon said, his voice rougher than he intended, but she continued to talk, as if she hadn't heard him.

"Father, he was just standing there, like he had been waiting for me. He was holding the sledgehammer, the one he used to stun the hogs before he slit their throats. I thought Father was going to hit Mother with the sledgehammer, but he didn't. He grabbed the big knife from the table. Then the screaming started. I ran. I ran away in the woods, and I hid. I thought Jacob would come find me, like he always did. He never came, but Father did. He was covered in blood.

"He took me to the Teaching Room. I was crying," she said, reaching up to touch her dry cheeks as if she expected to still feel the tears there. "He told me not to be afraid, and then he started to sing. 'Yes, Jesus loves me; yes, Jesus loves me; yes, Jesus loves me, for the Bible tells me so.'"

The sound of her voice, high and sweet, sounding for the first time like the child she was, shook Brandon to his core. Gooseflesh ran up his arms and down his back. Again, his head snapped toward the mouth of the cave. Had something moved?

"When we got to the Teaching Room, I knelt at his feet and begged the Lord's forgiveness for being disobedient. When I was done, he told me that the Lord had wiped my soul clean, but he still needed to mete out punishment, as the Lord wanted."

Outside, another cry echoed through the night, but this time Brandon and Delilah barely noticed. Their world had shrunk to the tiny circle around the fire, where only the two of them existed.

"I miss them," Delilah said, leaning her head against Brandon's arm.

"It sounds like Jacob loved you very much," Brandon said. "He looked out for you, like all big brothers should."

"He could have gotten away, but he came back for me. When I woke up in the Teaching Room, I was tied to a chair. Father was asleep. I hurt all over, and all I wanted to do was die, but then Jacob was there, standing in front of me. He cut me free and told me to run, so I did. I got to the car. It even started on the first try, but I couldn't go, not without Jacob. But he didn't come with me. I think he went back to kill Father, because he knew that Father would never stop looking for us.

"Then I saw him—he was running, but not really running, more like falling toward me. There was something wrong with his head. At first, I couldn't tell what, but when he got close, I saw. It was gone. Half his head was just gone. I thought sure Father would be coming right behind him, but he never did, but I always knew he would find me."

"It's over now," Brandon said as another bird's call echoed through the night.

Delilah didn't say anything else, and Brandon was glad.

"You need to get some sleep. Don't worry, I'll sit watch. Nothing will ever hurt you again," he said, praying, as the words left his mouth, that he was telling the truth.

Chapter 67

Olivia watched as her father jumped from the chair and raced toward her mother, by some miracle catching her in his arms before her body hit the floor.

"I . . . Dr. Blake . . . I didn't know . . . I thought you must have told her already. I'm so sorry," Sheldon stammered from the door.

"Get out," Olivia said.

"Dr. Blake, please. I know you're upset, but I was just trying to help your mother with the chair, and we started talking."

"What's going on here?"

Olivia felt sick as she looked up to see Dr. Iso standing in the doorway, looking in at the scene.

"Dr. Blake?" he said.

"Doctor, thank God you're here. This woman needs help," Sheldon said, rushing to her father's side.

"What happened?" Dr. Iso asked, pushing past Sheldon to where her mother sat in a chair, her eyes wide and unfocused, staring straight ahead, blowing tiny puffs of air through her ashen lips as if she were no longer capable of making words.

"I think she must be in shock. Her friends . . . ," her father said, his own voice failing as he tried to say the words out loud.

"Sir, you don't look so good yourself. Please, take a seat and try to calm down," Dr. Iso said, placing his hand on her father's shoulder and pushing him back into the chair.

"You're Sheldon Myers? You almost destroyed my daughter with your filthy lies. How dare you show your face anywhere around here?" her father said, leaning so far forward that Olivia was afraid he was going to leap from the chair and attack Sheldon.

"Sir, you don't understand."

"Oh, I understand. You're a snake, a lying, vicious snake. No one here is confused about that."

"I'm only here to offer my assistance to Dr. Blake—that is all. I have no ulterior motives."

"Get out of here, and don't ever come back," her father said. "We don't need your kind of help. If I see you around here again, I'll be calling the police to report you for harassment, right after I talk to every one of your competitors and tell them what kind of garbage they work with. You're not the only one who knows how to play dirty, believe that." He pushed himself up from the chair and walked toward Sheldon. No one tried to stop him this time, not even Dr. Iso, who had turned his attention to Minnie as Sheldon backed away from her father before turning and hurrying from the room.

"Mr. Blake, we need to see about Mrs. Blake," Dr. Iso said, gesturing to where her mother sat slumped in the chair.

"Minnie," her father called, rushing to kneel at her side as Dr. Iso pushed the button on Olivia's bed to call for help.

A few moments later, a doctor and a nurse hurried into the room with a wheelchair and wheeled her mother away, her father following behind them. Olivia tried to get up from the bed, but Dr. Iso laid his hand on her shoulder.

"Dr. Iso, please, I have to see about my mom."

"She's going to be fine. Let them take care of her. You can do your part by letting us take care of you."

"It's okay. I can assure you; I'm fully recovered."

"Please, rest just a bit longer. I'm sure when your husband returns, he'll want to see that you are all better." Dr. Iso smiled down at her, patting her hand. "Have you heard any news?"

"No, sir, not since he left," Olivia said, not bothering to correct Dr. Iso. Brandon *was* her husband—he always had been. She only hoped they got a chance to live as man and wife again.

"I understand the FBI and the state police have identified the madman responsible for all of this carnage, is that correct?"

"Yes, sir. Brandon went after him alone to try to save Delilah," Olivia said, her voice quivering with new tears.

"He's going to be just fine. He has everything in the world to come home to," he said, patting her hand again.

"I'm sure you're right. My mother . . ."

"You lie back and get some rest, and I'll go check on your mother."

"Thank you, Dr. Iso," she said as he turned to walk out of the room.

Olivia lay back and closed her eyes, savoring the quiet as she started to drift to sleep.

"Excuse me." The voice sounded far away, but there was an urgency to the whisper that Olivia couldn't ignore.

Slowly Olivia forced her eyelids open and found herself looking into the face of an older black woman who looked like everybody's idea of an old-school country grandma. That idea was cemented when she opened her mouth and started to speak.

"I'm sorry to wake you—my name is Sadie Jessup. My husband and me, we came all the way here from Selma, Alabama."

Olivia stared at Sadie Jessup but found she couldn't speak.

"Are you okay?" the woman asked, concern clouding her eyes as she moved closer to Olivia.

"Why are you here?" Olivia managed to say, even though her heart already knew.

"Well, it's like we told that young man, we saw the story on the news. That girl they found, she our kin. I don't need no blood test to tell me nothing my spirit already knows. Lord knows how that's even possible after all this time, but it is. I recognized her; how could I not? She looks just like our Allison. We had to come."

"What young man?" Olivia asked, trying her best to absorb the woman's words.

"Brandon Hall," she said, reading from a card that she pulled from her pocket. "It's been a long few days, and we're a long way away from home. With all the excitement going on, Mr. Jessup forgot to take his blood pressure medicine. He couldn't sleep, what with his head hurting him so. He didn't want to come here, but I wasn't going to let up till he agreed."

"I'm sorry he doesn't feel well," Olivia said, wishing she could close her eyes and the woman would be gone, just a part of her exhausted imagination.

"I heard the nurses talking," Mrs. Jessup said. "Mr. Hall is your man? He was very nice to me and Mr. Jessup."

Olivia felt like she should say something to this woman who had obviously been suffering for so long, but all she could think of was that the woman was going to take Delilah away. The pain of that thought kept her lips sealed even as she screamed inside.

"I'm sorry for coming here like this, but when I heard that she was missing, I couldn't stay away. Losing Allison nearly destroyed our family. It's been so long. You'd think we would have gotten over it by now. But it seem like it won't never go away, not really. We didn't dare say the words out loud, but I know when I saw the story about Allison on the news, I hoped it would finally be over, that we'd finally get to bring her home. One way or another.

"Henry—that's my husband—he never said nothing, either, but I know he was thinking the same thing. I don't reckon there's any real chance Allison is still alive, but that girl they found, well, the Lord works in mysterious ways." Mrs. Jessup shrugged as the words died away, leaving the room quiet as Olivia struggled with finding anything to say.

"I'm sorry to bother you—I'll go now," Mrs. Jessup said as Olivia continued to lie there, staring ahead at nothing.

"Mrs. Jessup, you know she's been through a lot," Olivia finally managed to say as Mrs. Jessup reached the doorway and turned to look back at her. "It could take her a long time to get used to being part of a family again. It'll be strange for her."

"I reckon it'll be hard for us all, but we're family. We'll do whatever it takes," Mrs. Jessup said, tears shining in her eyes.

"As soon as Brandon returns, I'll make sure to get word to you," Olivia said.

"Thank you," Mrs. Jessup said before turning to walk from the room.

Olivia lay back on the bed and tried to fall asleep, but it was impossible; every time she closed her eyes, alternating images of Brandon and Delilah crowded her head.

"Who do you want to kill?" Arlene said.

"What do you mean?" Olivia asked, turning her head to where her friend stood in the doorway.

"Well, I've been standing here watching you knead that poor pillow to death. If it had feelings, it could apply for asylum."

"I just had the most bizarre experience."

"More bizarre than finding two dead bodies and barely escaping death at the hands of a homicidal maniac? Do tell."

"I just met Delilah's great-aunt, her real honest-to-goodness family."

"What the hell, girl? How is that even possible?"

"She saw the story Brandon put on the news about Delilah, and she and Delilah's great-uncle flew here from Selma, Alabama, of all places."

"Oh my God. How do you know she was telling the truth?"

"I looked into her eyes."

"Oh wow, so Delilah has a family? I'm blown away."

"I'm in shock. I don't know how to feel. I just want them to come home," Olivia said, fighting back fresh tears.

"Oh, honey, they will. Brandon will keep them safe. Just hang in there," she said, leaning over to kiss Olivia on the forehead.

"I hope you're right," Olivia said.

"I am. Olivia?"

"Uh-oh, I don't even remember the last time you called me by my whole name. What's up?"

"You know I love you, right?"

"As I love you, Arlene. Spit it out, please."

"You've been drinking again."

"I . . . yeah, I have," Olivia said, turning her face away from Arlene's sad eyes.

"I think it's time for you to address it."

"What do you mean?"

"You know what I mean. You promised me and, more importantly, yourself that you would go to a meeting if it started again. I think it's time," Arlene said, taking hold of Olivia's hand.

"Yeah," Olivia said, turning to face her friend, not bothering to hide the tears gathering in her eyes.

Chapter 68

Olivia's eyes sprang open. Her heart was racing in her chest as if she'd just finished a marathon. She sat up in the bed and looked around the semidark room. Arlene was curled up in one of the sleeper chairs provided for overnight guests. There was no sign of her father, which didn't surprise her, and no sign of Brandon, at least no physical sign of him, but she felt him. Her heart sensed him so close to her that it seemed as if she could reach out and touch him.

Carly appeared beside Olivia's bed in the time it took her to blink, but Olivia was not afraid. The vision did not fill her with sadness, or regret. The light around the figure was as warm as the sun, turning her curls into a ring of golden flame.

"Thank you," Olivia said, reaching out but not touching the girl.

The figure seemed to smile down at her.

"I will take good care of Delilah, no matter where she goes. I will always be there."

The vision nodded once before reaching out to touch Olivia's brow.

"I love you," Olivia said as the world turned golden around her, and she found herself drifting, floating away on a cloud of contentment. In that moment before she drifted slowly back to herself, she saw herself and Brandon with a beautiful little girl, her head covered in golden ringlets, surrounded by love.

✳

At some point in the night, Olivia briefly woke up and saw Arlene standing over her.

"You know what?" her friend said. "I haven't seen a smile like that on your face in years."

Chapter 69

Brandon walked as slowly as he could, but even so, he still had to stop every few steps in order to make sure that Delilah would not be pulled along too fast. Adrenaline had carried them to the cave, but he knew the walk back would be extraordinarily painful for her. He wasn't sure if she could make it. The wounds on her back made it impossible for him to carry her without causing her unbearable pain.

He had found a stash of old clothes and shoes as well as a potato sack filled with cans of sardines, packets of hard white crackers, bags of nuts, and apples that had begun to go soft but were still good enough for them to eat. He'd even found more old sheets, which he used to rebandage Delilah's wounds. When he'd found the jugs of water, he dropped to his knees and said a silent thank-you to the brave boy who had tried to think of everything and ended up giving his life for the people he loved.

By the time they stepped out of the cave, light had barely begun to fill the sky. At first Brandon walked behind Delilah, allowing her to lead the way and set the pace, but before long he saw how her steps faltered and how much each one cost her, so he moved beside her and held her hand.

As the woods came alive around them, Brandon couldn't help but wonder what lay behind each crackling leaf or creaking tree branch. When two raucous squirrels popped out of a tree, Delilah screamed and nearly toppled over with fear.

Brandon had just started to worry that Delilah couldn't make it any farther when he realized that he could see through the trees and knew they had at least come to the end of the woods. When they stepped out of the clearing, it took him a moment to understand what he was seeing.

Police from what looked like every agency in Colorado swarmed around the sad little cemetery and the still-smoldering grounds where the Teaching Room had stood.

Brandon felt a hitch in his chest and thought he might break down into sobs as he stared at the scene. He felt the tiny squeeze of his hand, looked down into Delilah's tear-filled eyes, and forced a smile to his lips.

"See, I told you everything would be all right," he said, taking a deep breath of the cold mountain air. "Are you ready to go home, Delilah?"

"To Olivia?" she asked, the hope in her eyes breaking his heart.

"To Olivia and so much more," he said, thinking about the Jessups and what their presence meant—not only to Delilah but to Olivia and himself too.

Not so long ago, the Jessups' arrival was everything he'd believed he wanted, but now, as he looked down into Delilah's face, so much like his lost Carly's, he felt a bitter sadness at the thought of losing her and what it would mean to their lives.

Delilah took a step forward, holding tightly to his hand as they moved toward the officers.

"Home," she said, smiling up at Brandon.

"Home," he echoed. They walked out of the woods, and one of the officers noticed them and shouted, waving his arms as he ran toward them. As he grew closer, Brandon smiled, recognizing Officer Hernandez.

Epilogue

Five years later, Olivia walked around the duck pond that lay in the majestic shadow of the Cleveland Museum of Art. It was a favorite spot for her to spend time with her daughter Isabell whenever she could squeeze in a lunch away from the hospital. On such a beautiful spring day, it was hard to even believe the events in Colorado had ever happened.

After the night at Hurt Mountain Farm, Olivia and Brandon had chosen to leave Colorado behind. With the glowing recommendation written by Dr. Iso, Olivia hadn't had any trouble securing a position in Cleveland's premier children's hospital. Lieutenant Webber's recommendation, and a little help from Mike, had landed Brandon a job in the Cleveland Police Department.

As Olivia pushed their daughter Isabell's empty stroller around the pond, she watched Delilah and Izzy roll around in the grass, Delilah's wild giggles lifting her heart with a joy she couldn't have even imagined not so long ago. Even her mother had found a new chance at happiness with her new friend Dr. Shubert. A retired professor, he somehow always seemed to find himself in the park just in time to bump into her mother.

After all the horror, Olivia, her mother, and her father had worked diligently to put the anger and bitterness that had colored their relationship behind them. And when her parents' divorce became final,

Olivia had reached out, inviting her mother to come live with them in Cleveland.

Minnie had declined the invitation to live with them, choosing instead to rent a one-bedroom apartment near Brandon and Olivia in Cleveland's trendy Shaker Square area, where she spent her time with her new friends at Dewey's Coffee, or catching the train downtown to see a show, or strolling along Lake Erie.

Her father had officially come out. No one had been surprised when he and Brian had married as soon as it became legal in Colorado.

Delilah, too, was thriving. According to the Jessups, Delilah Jessup, her official new name, still struggled to understand the new world she found herself a part of, but she continued to work hard with a therapist on a regular basis and was busy preparing for college in the fall, where she intended to study to become a child psychiatrist. On school breaks and some holidays, she came to Cleveland to spend time with her second family, as she called them.

Hurt Mountain Farm had burned to the ground that night, another fire mysteriously taking the main house at the same time the Teaching Room burned. Every law enforcement branch in Colorado had descended on the mountain. Though they'd searched for weeks, no other person was ever found. All twelve graves held the remains of a girl or woman stolen from her family, but no graves for the many babies born on Hurt Mountain were ever found. When Brandon and Olivia were finally able to lay Carly to rest, it felt like a fresh start instead of an ending.

The Jessups and the Halls had built a friendship that they each cherished, leaning on each other as they helped Delilah heal from the years of trauma she had suffered. Every year at Christmas, they came together and thanked God for all their blessings and remembered those they had lost.

Acknowledgments

Ever since I was a little girl, I have always loved to read—anything and everything I can get my hands on. It took me thirty years to try my hand at writing my own story. For years after that first attempt, I wrote alone, cheered on by a small group of family and friends—my first fans, including Charmaine Molette, Kevin Smith, Narkita Banks, Janice and Kenneth (Buddy) Crook, and Chana Johnson. They were my guinea pig group, and it was their demand for more pages, sometimes daily, that drove me to complete my first novel. To them I will always be grateful. Because of them, a dream was born.

I owe so many people a debt of gratitude, starting with my writers' group, the Literary Llamas (Lisa Ferranti, Melissa Hintz, and Mary Rynes), who took me out of my lonely room, gave me a writing community, and taught me the beauty of editing. Without their constant support—their unwavering willingness to read, then reread, and reread again, always giving me the good, the bad, and the downright ugly and gently pushing me forward every time I felt discouraged—this dream would have remained just that, a dream.

I also want to thank the amazingly talented Kellye Garrett, who took time out of her busy life to support me in every way she could. I can't thank you enough. Thanks to my agent, Paula Munier, for agreeing to take me on as a client—truly a dream fulfilled. And of course, thank you to my editors, Chantelle Aimée Osman and Manu Velasco, for showing me all the ways to make this book better. I literally could not have done it without you.

About the Author

Photo © Mary Rynes

Angela Crook is a novelist and mother who loves writing dark thrillers that often explore the inner workings of family relationships. She grew up splitting her time between Cleveland, Ohio, and Selma, Alabama, where she used her love of reading to escape the scorching heat. As soon as she was able, she escaped to the United States Air Force, where she spent ten years traveling the world. She currently lives in Cleveland with her two sons and three very frisky kitties. There, with the support of her writers' group, the Literary Llamas, she is always working on her next great story.